A
SECRET
at
TANSY
FALLS

BOOKS BY CATE WOODS

CATE WOODS

A SECRET at TANSY FALLS

bookouture

Published by Bookouture in 2022

An imprint of Storyfire Ltd.
Carmelite House
50 Victoria Embankment
London EC4Y 0DZ

www.bookouture.com

ISBN: 978-1-80019-065-8
eBook ISBN: 978-1-80019-064-1

This book is a work of fiction. Names, characters, businesses, organizations, places and events other than those clearly in the public domain, are either the product of the author's imagination or are used fictitiously. Any resemblance to actual persons, living or dead, events or locales is entirely coincidental.

ONE

It was just before 6:30 a.m. on a Friday in late June when Connie Austen stepped out of her house into the early morning sunshine and wondered if she was being unreasonable to have expected her husband to have remembered that today was her birthday. After all, they had been married for twenty-two years: that was twenty-two times Nate had bought her a gift, serenaded her with Stevie Wonder's "Happy Birthday" (all three verses) and made her feel loved and special. One small slip-up was forgivable, she told herself. Inevitable, perhaps.

Having said that, Connie hadn't been feeling quite so fair-minded a few moments earlier when she had left Nate asleep in their bed. She had hovered in the doorway, fists jammed at her hips, eyeballing the lump under the sheets. He'd even had the nerve to be snoring, just to underline the fact that he was still cozy in bed while she was off to work. *On her birthday*.

Now, though, as she stood on their dirt driveway, taking in the spread of trees, hills and meadows laid out in front of her, her spirits started to lift. Other than a small yellow house across the field that belonged to their elderly neighbor, Frank Whitman, the landscape was a symphony of green: cascades of birch leaves draped like feather boas, plumes of fiddlehead ferns, dark spears of conifers and such a vast expanse of grass it was as if the whole world was made out of the stuff. In the early years of her career, she had traveled the world but she'd never been anywhere that made her soul sing in quite the same way as this place: Tansy Falls, a little patch of paradise in the hills of northern Vermont.

Connie looked down the slope dotted with daisies and blue chicory that led toward their lake, catching the iridescent flash of dragonflies between the cattails in the shallows. At the far side, an ancient Eastern cottonwood tree stood by the water's edge. It had been the lake that had sold this place to them when she and Nate had first seen it, back when their son, Ethan—now a college student—was still a baby. They couldn't afford it, and the house itself, which had been the farmhouse of an old cider farm, was in a state that at best could be described as shabby (though most people would have used the words "complete wreck"). But waking up every morning to this view had made all the sacrifices it had taken to restore the house worthwhile. Now Connie could never imagine leaving The Old Cider Farmhouse, as they had christened their home in honor of its origins. The original orchards had been dug over long before the Austens arrived, but here and there the odd apple tree survived, and in the fall Connie's kitchen was filled with the scent of freshly baked apple crisp, apple pie and—her specialty —puffed apple pancakes.

Soothed by the velvety air and murmur of insects, the morning's irritations began to fade away. It had been a tough couple of years for them both, and Nate had a lot on his mind; something was bound to give—and if it was remembering her forty-blah-blah birthday, then so be it.

Connie got in the car and flipped down the sun visor against the early morning glare, catching a glimpse of herself in the mirror. She turned her head to either side, checking for changes now that she was another year older. Her light brown hair was in decent shape, as thick as it had been in her twenties, her cheekbones were well-defined and there was still a sparkle in the dark blue eyes that a long-forgotten boyfriend had described as unforgettable. It was a shame, then, that the rest of her looked so darn miserable. Since hitting her forties her lower face had begun to sag, and her resting expression now resembled that of a particularly stern and humorless high school principal. She remembered Ethan complaining not so long ago: "Why d'you always look so pissed at me, Mom?" And she'd replied, laughing, "It's not me, honey, it's just my face!"

At the memory, Connie smiled. Gosh, that made her look so much better! Well, she'd just have to smile as much as she could. It was a heck of a lot cheaper than a facelift, that was for sure.

Connie spun the car in a circle and as she glided back past their house her eyes were drawn to the French doors that led to the basement. *A stranger will be living down there soon.* The thought still made her uneasy—which was odd, as getting a lodger had been her idea in the first place, a way out of their financial struggles. She couldn't imagine what it would be like having someone else sharing her and Nate's home: cooking food in their kitchen, showering in their bathroom, stalking their hallways at night with an axe...

With a snort of laughter, Connie turned onto the road that led into town, cranking up the volume on the stereo to blast away any lingering phantoms.

Ten minutes later she pulled up on Main Street outside a redbrick building trimmed with pine-green shutters that was as familiar to her as her own home—although unlike her home, was listed on the National Register of Historic Places. The ornate gold-lettered sign above the entrance read WELCOME TO THE COVERED BRIDGE INN, and underneath, in smaller, block script, SHARING WHITE CHRISTMASES SINCE 1878. Right now it was impossible to imagine the snow and cold that gripped Tansy Falls for over half the year, but, no matter the season, the Covered Bridge Inn always looked like Christmas in building form. Today, the rocking chairs along the deck were ready for guests to relax before hiking in the hills or swimming up at Smugglers Leap waterfall, but in a few months' time they would be draped with fake-fur throws waiting to be snuggled in to watch the snow fall with a mug of spiced cider.

It was quiet in reception—the morning's breakfast service had only just begun—so Connie headed straight to her office just off the lobby. She was leafing through some paperwork when the door swung open and a chocolate-brown Labrador waddled in as quickly as his advanced years would allow. Tucked in his collar was an envelope and a posy of ox-eye daisies, which, like the dog, was already wilting in the morning's heat.

"Hey, Boomer," she said, bending down to greet him. "What have you got there?"

She was just retrieving the envelope from his collar when she heard footsteps and looked up to see her boss, Piper, holding out a cake lit with candles.

"Happy birthday, Connie!"

"Oh, Piper, you shouldn't have..."

"Of course I should! Gotta keep the best hotel manager in the business happy. This place couldn't function without you, honey." Piper placed the cake on Connie's desk. It was covered with pale lemon buttercream, as smooth as perfectly plastered walls. Piper ran the Covered Bridge Inn with her husband, Spencer, in whose family it had been for over two hundred years, but she also happened to be a professionally trained pastry chef.

"This is from me and Spencer—and from this little dude too," said Piper, patting the bulge beneath her dress. "Boomer wanted to do his own thing this year, though I had to help him with the card." She dropped her voice. "He's still having a little trouble holding the pen."

Connie swept Piper into a hug as best she could around her seven-month-old baby bump. "Thank you, sweetie. You guys are the best."

The two women beamed at each other with real affection. Despite the two-decade age difference, they had become close friends in the years they had worked together, sharing a love of hiking in the hills nearby, and Piper had been a real support to Connie when her mom had died a few years back.

"Well, come on then, blow out the candles," urged Piper. "And don't forget to make a wish!"

Connie did as she was told, although she ignored the bit about making wishes. She'd given up on that around the same time she'd stopped believing in happy-ever-afters.

Piper leaned on the edge of the desk with a heavy exhale. She was usually tireless, starting work in the kitchen well before dawn, but pregnancy was starting to slow her down.

"So what are you doing to celebrate?" she asked.

"Not much—it isn't a big one. Forty-nine." Wow, that sounded old—and to Piper, who was still in her twenties, it must seem prehistoric. "Well, *a* big one, but not *the* big one, if you get what I mean."

"Listen, another year on earth is always reason to celebrate. Hopefully Nate has something special planned for you?"

Connie was still smiling, but it suddenly felt an effort. "Hopefully, yes."

"Well, you sure look good for forty-nine, Connie. I better take Boomer around the block before it gets too hot—for both of us." She nodded to the cake. "Enjoy your breakfast, birthday girl."

Connie had fetched herself a coffee from the kitchen and had settled back at her desk with a slice of cake when her phone vibrated with a message. It was from her father, Kurt.

Happy birthday, sweet Conifer! Come over for lunch tomorrow—I have news. Pa.

Connie frowned at the sight of her real name, a throwback to her parents' hippie phase. She wondered what his news might be: knowing her father, he had probably signed up for a triathlon and was on the hunt for sponsors. He'd always been young for his age, but since hitting his seventies Kurt seemed hellbent on transforming into the Rock.

As always, Connie's morning passed in a blur of activity: checking guests in and out, planning the staff schedule, overseeing the groundskeepers to ensure they were in the running for this year's Prettiest New England Inn contest: all the little jobs that kept the Covered Bridge machine well-oiled and running smoothly. As well as her usual tasks, today Connie was sifting through a mountain of résumés for the position of events manager. It had been a role that she, Piper and Spencer had been juggling between them up until now, but demand for weddings at the inn had recently rocketed and they needed someone to oversee the job full-time. A new five-star resort was opening up nearby, and the Covered Bridge needed to be on its A-game to compete.

She had all but forgotten about her birthday until late morning when she returned to her office to find the most magnificent flowers on her desk: a cartwheel-sized bunch of gardenias, roses and peonies in shades of white, cream and putty, wrapped in a swathe of raffia. Nate had remembered after all! She felt such a rush of happiness it made her realize how upset she'd really been about him forgetting her birthday, despite her brave face.

She tore open the envelope attached to the bouquet with a pearl-headed pin, and read the card inside.

Wishing you a wonderful birthday.
With all our love, Everly, Charles, Suki and Harper.

Connie fought down her disappointment. Of course—they were from Everly. Only her high-flying, Manhattan-dwelling, corporate-ass-kicking sister would send flowers that looked like they were meant for Mariah Carey's dressing room. Everly was the youngest of the two sisters, but years were the only thing she had less of. Connie imagined that her sister's idea of "a wonderful birthday" would be an afternoon at a Fifth Avenue spa followed by a gourmet dinner at which she was presented with several carats of something sparkly. Not quite the day Connie had lined up. She could only imagine what Everly would do if her husband, Charles, had forgotten her birthday; she'd probably be straight on the phone to her lawyer demanding a divorce.

After a moment's thought, Connie took out her phone and sent a message to Nate.

Hey, honey. I'm going to meet up with Lana after work if that's OK?

Her best friend had messaged to ask if she was free tonight, and Connie wanted to do at least *something* to mark the occasion.

A moment later Nate replied.

Sure thing. I'm going to fix that loose handle on the kitchen cabinet today—finally. Have fun tonight. I won't wait up!

Frowning, Connie tapped out a response.

Please do. It's my birthday and I'd really like to celebrate with you later.

Her thumb hovered above the send button. Was it really worth making a fuss? It would just make Nate feel bad for forgetting, and it wasn't that important—not really. Connie was proud to be a glass-half-full person, and really it was just another day when it came down to it. At her age it was unrealistic to expect a big performance. Birthdays were for kids, not nearly fifty-year-olds. She held down the delete button on the message until it vanished, then wrote:

OK, I'll see you tomorrow.

TWO

The Lana Frost Gallery was located a little way out of town at the point where the valley floor began to rise up toward the slopes of Mount Maverick. The mountain was the reason most visitors came to Tansy Falls: for skiing and snowboarding in the winter, leaf-peeping in the fall and hiking in the summer. And those visitors were the reason that Connie's best friend, Lana, was able to make a success out of a fine art gallery in a sleepy spot like Tansy Falls.

The gallery was not universally liked among the locals, however. Lana had preserved the industrial look of the original building, a former animal-feed warehouse on the mountain road that had been earmarked for demolishment, and when the plans for the gallery were revealed there had been a blizzard of complaints at the annual town meeting.

"Acceptable in downtown Brooklyn, not in Tansy Falls," one resident had sniffed.

"I can't imagine what sort of 'art' will be on show in an eyesore like this," fumed another.

Still, they couldn't argue with the fact that the gallery had become one of the most popular visitor attractions since it opened six years ago. There were other galleries in town, but whereas the other places showcased local craftspeople, the Lana Frost Gallery attracted big-name artists from all over the country.

Connie welcomed the blast of turbo-chilled air as she opened the gallery's glass doors and ducked inside, relieved to be out of the late afternoon heat. It was past closing time, but Lana was deep in conversation with a well-dressed couple by one of the spotlit display panels. They were standing in front of a vast painting that looked, to Connie, like a giant lemon with green mold growing all over it. Despite Lana's best efforts to educate her, Connie still preferred her art to be, well, nice to look at.

Noticing her by the door, Lana flicked her eyes toward the L-shaped couch where she schmoozed clients over coffee (or something stronger if there was the prospect of a big deal) and Connie took a seat. From here, she had the perfect vantage point to watch her friend at work—and judging by her body language, she was going in strong for a sale. Lana's husband, Tom, had a point when he joked she could sell medium-rare ribeye to vegans.

Like the gallery itself, Lana looked as if she belonged in New York. She had a blond bob with blunt bangs, favored clashing prints and asymmetrical hemlines and wore red lipstick even when taking a bath. In a town known for dairy farming rather than fashion, Lana Frost stood out—which was just the way she wanted it. The couple she was talking to was of a type Connie knew well from the Covered Bridge Inn: city-dwellers, here for a weekend break, with plenty of money to spend on little luxuries like art. The one person Connie couldn't place, however, was the man standing alongside Lana and the couple, who was in his early thirties and eye-catchingly handsome. As Connie's eyes lingered on him, he turned and looked her straight in the eye. Blushing, she turned away, embarrassed to have been caught staring.

A few minutes later, Lana steered the couple toward the exit, pressing her business card into their hands, then once she'd locked the door behind them she swept over to Connie.

"Happy birthday, sweet cheeks!" She gave her a kiss. "Sorry about that. They couldn't make up their minds."

"Did they buy it?"

"They're 'gonna think about it.'" Lana made air quotes with her fingers, rolling her eyes. "I mean, honestly, what is there to think about?"

"Yeah, who wouldn't want a painting of a giant moldy lemon?"

The dark-haired man, who was still hovering nearby looking at his phone, stifled a snigger.

Lana waved him over. "Connie, I'd like you to meet Theo Welles, an extremely successful and talented artist. And Theo, this is Connie Wilson, my best friend and, I'm afraid, a total philistine."

"Ah." Connie smiled sheepishly. "So I'm guessing it was you who painted the..."

"The giant moldy lemon? Yes, that's one of mine." At least he seemed to find it funny. "It's a pleasure to meet you, Connie. And please, don't worry, I welcome all interpretations of my work."

He was looking at her appraisingly, as if she herself was a painting on display, and Connie fidgeted under his gaze. It felt like a long while since a stranger had looked at her like that and she wasn't sure how to handle it. It was almost a relief when his phone started to ring.

"Sorry, I must take this..." With another quick smile, he disappeared into the back office.

"Gorgeous, isn't he?" murmured Lana, watching him go. "He lives with an older Frenchwoman in Connecticut. She's stunning, but when I met her I assumed she was his mom. I was *this close* to asking if she was still with Theo's father." She shuddered theatrically. "Anyway—we must celebrate!" Lana reached into her desk drawer and brought out a small box tied with a bow. "This is for you, from Tom and me. And while you open that, I'll open this..."

While Connie unwrapped the box, which contained her favorite perfume, Lana eased the top off a champagne bottle and poured two glassfuls.

"Here's to you, honey." Lana raised her glass. "Happy birthday."

"Cheers." The bubbles instantly put Connie in a celebratory mood, and she relaxed back into the cushions of the couch with a happy sigh.

"So what did Nate get you?"

"Nate forgot." Connie shrugged. "It's fine, he's got a lot on his mind right now."

"Don't make excuses for him, Connie. That's really not okay."

"Oh, it's not such a big deal."

"It *is* a big deal. He's your husband. You need talk to him about it."

"What's the point? It's not going to achieve anything. Since he lost his job... well, like I've said to you before, things between us have drifted a little."

"All the more reason to try to get them back on track! You two were always such a fantastic team—and you could tell how much Nate loved you. Not like Tom." Lana's husband worked in finance, and when he wasn't in the office he was on the golf course— although this arrangement seemed to suit both of them. "I'm sure you can fix this, Conn."

"Maybe, but... The thing is, I sort of get the impression he's... lost interest in me. In *us*."

"You mean in the bedroom?"

"Well, yes, but we've been married for over twenty years, so we weren't exactly ripping each other's clothes off every night *before* things got bad. But we were always there for each other, you know? Nate was my partner—my best friend. My rock. Now, though, it's like we're two people who just happen to be living in the same house. I can't remember the last time we had a proper conversation. And I miss doing things with him. I miss doing *nothing* with him."

"Then talk to him. It's either that or sit back and watch your marriage fall apart."

"But what would I say? It's not as if there's anything seriously wrong. He's not being nasty, or unreasonable in any way. I don't know, perhaps this happens in a lot of long marriages. Maybe I'm expecting too much."

Lana chewed her lip, the internal gears working. "Are you quite sure there's not something else going on?"

"What do you mean?"

"Well, knowing Nate, I can't imagine this is the case, but do you think there's a chance he might be having an affair?"

"*What?* Of course not!"

"Okay, I'm just checking." Lana held up her hands. "But he wouldn't be the first guy to look elsewhere after his confidence had been knocked at work."

"Nate would never cheat on me. No way."

Her voice was unwavering, but inside Connie felt as if she'd been punched in the stomach. While she knew something wasn't right with their marriage, this particular explanation hadn't even occurred to her. The idea that her husband—*her Nate*—might be interested in another woman... it was unthinkable. Like a horror movie.

"Don't worry, it doesn't seem likely to me either," said Lana, giving Connie's arm a squeeze.

Still, Lana's suggestion had planted a seed, and no doubt it would be the first thing that popped into Connie's head at 4 a.m. tomorrow, which was the worst time to be worrying about anything.

"I hope I'm not interrupting?"

With a start, Connie turned to find Theo Welles. She had all but forgotten he was still there, and her cheeks burned at the thought of what he might have overheard.

Lana picked up the bottle. "Would you like a glass, Theo?"

"If that's okay with Connie?"

She waved her assent, her mind still gripped by the conversation she'd just had with Lana. Although she was sure Nate wasn't having an affair, would she actually know if he was? They were virtually living separate lives these days, after all. She had a flashback to first thing that morning, when she'd woken up next to him in bed and had turned over to look at him, taking in his full lips and lashes fanned against his tanned cheek. His face was as familiar to Connie as her own—and, like her own, was marked with faint lines that hadn't been there a few years ago—but she could see he was still a very handsome man. No doubt other women could see that too.

"So how's your birthday been so far?" Theo took a seat next to her on the couch, forcing her back into the present.

"Well, I've been given cake, champagne and some perfume, so I'd say pretty wonderful all in all."

"Except that Connie's husband forgot," added Lana.

"Lana!"

"Oh, shush, it's fine. Theo won't tell anyone."

But Connie felt she should defend Nate. "He's been through a tough time recently. He was the editor of a travel magazine—*Roam* —but was made redundant eighteen months ago. He's a freelance writer now."

Lana arched an eyebrow. "Is *that* what he calls it?"

"He's trying, okay? There's not much work around right now. Publications are either closing down or cutting staff. It's not an easy time to be a journalist."

"And what do you do, Connie?" asked Theo.

"I'm the manager of a hotel in town. The Covered Bridge Inn."

"The place that looks like it belongs to Anne of Green Gables," added Lana.

"Yes, I've seen it," said Theo.

"It's actually the best hotel in Tansy Falls," Lana went on. "All thanks to Connie's brilliance, of course."

"I'll have to stay with you when I'm next in town," said Theo, fixing her with the sort of smile that seemed to imply he would like to be staying in her bed, ideally with her still in it.

Connie narrowed her eyes, confused. Surely Theo wasn't flirting with her? She smiled to herself at the ridiculousness of this notion. Perhaps when she was younger, but in her experience women of her age were pretty much invisible. Clearly, he was just being polite.

Yet when she glanced back in his direction, Theo was still looking at her in a strangely intense way. Deep inside, Connie felt a quiver of excitement.

THREE

Just then there was a tap at the glass doors; a man in a motorcycle helmet was standing outside with two paper bags.

Lara jumped up. "Egg rolls and kung pao chicken for the birthday girl!"

They ate the food straight out of the cartons, washing it down with more champagne. Theo didn't appear to be in any rush to leave, and though Connie had hoped to continue the conversation with Lana about her problems with Nate, it was actually quite nice to put her marriage woes aside for the evening and have one of those tipsy, rambling chats where you laugh a lot and nothing much seems to matter beyond having fun.

After they'd emptied the cartons, Lana doled out the fortune cookies. She broke hers open and read the fortune inside. "The early bird gets the worm, but the second mouse gets the cheese." She wrinkled her nose. "What does that even mean? What's yours say, Theo?"

"You will meet a gorgeous and fascinating woman who doesn't appreciate abstract art."

Connie nearly snorted champagne out of her nose. Okay, he was *definitely* flirting with her. Enveloped in a veil of pleasant fuzziness, it no longer seemed like such an outrageous idea.

"What about yours, Conn?" asked Lana.

"Change is happening in your life, so go with the flow." She paused. "Well, that's obviously referring to the menopause."

The other two laughed. *That should put Theo off*, thought Connie. Nothing like raising the specter of hot flashes and total-body sagging to kill any flirtation stone-dead.

Lana swigged down the rest of her champagne, stretched like a cat and got up. "Back in a sec, guys."

Then she headed off toward the bathroom, leaving Connie and Theo alone.

Now it was just the two of them, Connie sensed a sudden change in atmosphere. The lighthearted silliness of a moment earlier was replaced with something altogether more intense. Theo put down his glass and stretched his arm along the back of the sofa behind her; not touching her, though the meaning behind the gesture was clear. Connie shuffled forward until she was perching right on the edge of the couch.

"I should probably be getting home soon," she said.

Theo was gazing at her, head tipped to one side. "You have the most incredible bone structure. Like a young Meryl Streep."

Connie snorted. "A middle-aged Meryl Streep, more like."

"Would you come for a drink with me sometime?"

"Why?"

"Because I'd like to get to know you better."

"As in—a date?"

Theo smiled. "Of course."

His tone implied this was the most natural thing in the world, but to Connie the conversation felt as unreal as if she was playing a role in a movie. That was surely the only rational explanation for why he appeared to be hitting on her.

"Thank you, but no," she said.

"Why not?"

"Well, firstly, I'm almost old enough to be your mother…"

Theo rolled his eyes. "Jeez, it's such a bourgeois notion, this idea that men must only find younger women attractive. Did you know that throughout history women were believed to be at the height of their seductive powers in middle age? Henri II of France, for instance, was obsessed with his mistress who was over twenty years his senior."

"Thank you for the history lesson, but I was under the impression you were living with someone," said Connie, focusing hard on the words coming out of her mouth. She wished her head were a little clearer so she could handle this bizarre situation better.

"Estelle and I have an open relationship," said Theo. "I'd highly recommend it."

"You're very sweet, but no, thank you. I'm married—and our relationship is very much closed."

"And are you enjoying being married?"

"I love my husband," she replied firmly.

"You didn't answer me."

"And *you* are very nosy," she said, attempting to lighten the atmosphere. A bit of flirting was fine, but this was altogether too intense.

Thankfully at that moment Lana hopped over the back of the couch. She glanced between the pair of them, frowning.

"Theo, have you been behaving yourself?"

"Of course! I've been a complete gentleman. Haven't I, Connie?"

He turned to look directly at her, so that Lana didn't see him wink.

A little later that evening, Connie walked home under a golden moon, the air as soft as cashmere on her bare arms. It was less than a mile from Lana's gallery to her house and after all that champagne she was in no fit state to drive. The night was still, the only sound her footfalls in the roadside dirt and the cry of a whippoorwill. Theo had lobbied hard to escort her home—"to protect you from coyotes"—but she'd declined the offer, laughing. It was far more likely that she'd need protection from Theo.

When they'd said goodbye he had kissed her slowly on both cheeks, the touch of his lips sending color rushing to her face, and had pressed his business card into her hands, which she'd immediately stuffed into her pocket. She pulled the card out, examining it in the moonlight, and it was only now she discovered that Theo had written something on the back.

"À la prochaine." *Until next time.* (Connie used to work in Paris, so her French wasn't bad.) And he'd signed it "Henri II."

She smiled, tucking it back in her pocket. The guy was persistent, she'd give him that.

Within fifteen minutes she was home. She let herself into the house, dropped her keys in their usual spot by the door, put her phone on charge and switched off the kitchen lights. Against the familiarity of her nighttime routine, the events of the evening seemed even more surreal. It was such a novelty to be flirted with, to feel pretty and noticed, as opposed than her usual wallpaper-like state of invisibility. It stirred up long-forgotten feelings that Connie had assumed she would never experience again.

When she reached the bedroom, she paused in the doorway. Nate was asleep; if he hadn't replied to her text earlier, she could well have imagined he hadn't moved all day. She stared at him now, jutting her chin, a little indignant and more than a little bit drunk.

I'm still an attractive woman, Nate Austen. Even if you can't see it.

She would never in a million years take Theo Welles up on his offer, but she felt he had woken something inside her, a part of her that she thought was long dead, and that knowledge had lit a dangerous spark. At that moment, Connie felt as if she had been handed a burning match and she could choose to either snuff it out or throw it into a pool of gasoline. Staring at her sleeping husband, she suddenly felt unsure which would be the right choice.

FOUR

When Connie woke the next morning she found herself alone in bed. A breeze stirred the bedroom drapes, letting in glimpses of daylight that seemed far more dazzling than it usually was at 6 a.m., which was the time she woke each morning with a regularity that rendered an alarm unnecessary. She struggled to sitting, a dull ache throbbing at her temples, and glanced at the clock. Eight thirty already! She must have drunk more than she thought last night to have slept through Nate getting out of bed.

Rubbing some life into her face, which seemed to have the texture of unleavened dough, Connie got out of bed and flung open the drapes, wincing at the sudden brightness. She loved the view from her bedroom window, which was an ever-changing kaleidoscope: from the fiery blaze of fall foliage to the white expanse of winter—and now summer, when the blue of the sky and the green of the earth were so intense it was as if nature was using an Instagram filter. This morning, though, Connie wasn't in a state to cope with so much color.

At this time of the morning Nate would be on a run or playing golf, and Connie was scanning the distant ribbon of Cider Farm Road to see whether she could spot him when a screeching honk echoed around the valley. "Morning, Jocelyn," she muttered, looking over to the paddock behind their neighbor Frank Whitman's house, where the most enormous donkey was kicking up an almighty fuss. "She's an American Mammoth Jackstock," Frank had told her when the beast first arrived. "Ain't she a beauty?" And Connie had nodded politely, while Jocelyn had furiously swiveled her ears and bared her teeth at her. Frank always had an eclectic selection of rescue animals staying with him, and Jocelyn was his latest—and loudest—arrival. She was even worse than the insomniac rooster he'd taken in a couple of years back until, to everyone's relief, a local bobcat had taken matters into its own paws.

On the way to the bathroom, Connie passed her son Ethan's bedroom and glanced inside. For the past eighteen years the floor, the bed and every available surface had been covered with stuff. This morning, though, it looked like a room in a show home. A quilt was tightened over the bed and sports trophies and framed photos were neatly lined up on the bookshelf. It was funny, but right now Connie would have preferred the mess. Ethan had just finished his first year of a bachelor's degree at the University of Pennsylvania, with a view to going on to law school, and was staying with a friend whose family lived in Philadelphia over the summer, working in an Amazon fulfilment center with some buddies from his course. Connie missed her only child every day, but she knew he was happy—she could tell by the excitement in his voice whenever he called—and that made her happy too.

It was strange and a little scary, thought Connie, closing the bathroom door behind her, how your sense of wellbeing was so dependent on that of your child. Her own parents had always been more into each other than they were their children, which was fine, but it had made Connie fiercely the other way. Ethan had been her whole world; he still was.

In the shower, Connie squeezed out a dollop of the expensive body wash she had treated herself to because it smelled so deliciously of pomegranates, a scent that fueled her dreams of Granada, where the fruit grew wild on trees around the Moorish walled city. It was a place she had longed to visit since a fleeting trip to Spain in her twenties, and not so long ago she had hoped that she and Nate might go there to celebrate her fiftieth birthday, imagining romantic strolls around the narrow streets and sharing tapas under the stars. She couldn't see it happening now, though. She couldn't even remember the last time Nate had taken her out to dinner—let alone planned a special vacation.

Sensing herself spiraling into sadness, Connie gave herself a stern talking-to: moping was hardly going to make Nate fall in love with her again, was it? No, she would just soldier on and hope her husband got over whatever was troubling him. Instead, she found herself thinking back to last night, and the way Theo Welles had looked at her. *Still got it, honey*, she thought with a smile, smoothing the foam over her skin.

Connie was back in the bedroom getting dressed when she heard the front door open, then footsteps on the stairs and the door opened to reveal Nate. Sitting on the edge of the bed in her underwear, she turned to greet him, automatically clutching her T-shirt to cover her body.

"Morning, Conn." He clocked the fact she was half-dressed. "Oh—I'm sorry, I'll just give you a minute."

As the door closed behind him, she let out her breath in a great whoosh, her sadness surfacing again. Not so long ago she'd have happily paraded around the bedroom naked in front of Nate without a second thought. She longed for their old, easy intimacy, but had no idea how to get it back.

A few minutes later, Connie went downstairs and found Nate in the kitchen. He was holding a stack of mail, among which were some telltale brightly colored envelopes.

"I can't believe I forgot." He was shaking his head in disbelief. "It was yesterday, right?"

Connie forced a smile. "It doesn't matter, Nate."

"It *does* matter! I'm so sorry, Connie, I feel terrible."

"It's understandable. You've had a lot on your mind."

"I haven't. I literally have *zero* excuse. All I'm doing these days is... is fixing darn cabinet handles."

In a sudden move, he dropped the mail on the counter and came over to where Connie was standing, reaching for her hands. She responded instinctively to his touch, her body softening toward him—but the spark of tenderness vanished as quickly as it had appeared, smothered by the awkwardness that hung around them like a bad smell. Nate must have sensed it too, as he let her hands fall and took a step away from her.

"I'm sorry. About this—about everything."

"I told you, it's not important. It's just another birthday. Please, let's just forget about it." She walked past him toward the coffee machine. "I have!"

Connie hoped that would be the end of it, but as she filled the pot she could sense him still standing there, watching her. What on earth had happened to them? Once upon a time they were the couple who finished each other's sentences and always chose the same dishes when they ate out. Now they were like fairground bumper cars, weaving wildly around with just the occasional uncomfortable crash.

"We should talk," said Nate.

"It's fine! Let's just move on, shall we? It's only a birthday—and not a very important one at that."

"It's not about your birthday. There are things I need to say to you. Things I should have said before now."

Connie froze, remembering what Lana had said last night. Was this the moment Nate would tell her he'd been having an affair? That he was leaving her for another woman?

"Please, Connie," he said, his eyes beseeching.

"Another time, okay? It's a beautiful day and I've got so much to do this morning." The words came out in a rush. "Would you like a coffee?"

He hesitated, clearly intending to argue, but then gave a nod of defeat.

"One coffee coming up!" Connie buzzed manically about the kitchen. "I meant to ask, have there been any more replies to our ad?"

"We had a new one this morning." Nate reached for his phone. "Here we go—a James Ortiz. He lives in Manhattan but he's looking for a room in Tansy Falls from the start of July. He's an interior designer, working up at the new lodge."

"Sounds promising," said Connie. "Are you happy to get in touch with him?"

"Sure, I'll speak to him early next week."

The conversation dried up. Connie put some bread in the toaster and washed the coffee pot. Nate unloaded the dishwasher, then took the recycling bag outside. They moved around the kitchen as if performing a well-choreographed dance routine, but whereas once they wouldn't have passed each other without a touch or a smile, now they might as well have been robots on a production line.

Chores completed, Nate hovered by the door. "I better go and have a shower."

"Sure. I'm going to see Kurt in a little while."

"Are you sure you're okay with this, Conn? Getting a lodger, I mean."

"We don't really have much choice, do we?"

This came out before she could stop herself, and she cursed her insensitivity. It wasn't Nate's fault he'd been made redundant.

"I mean, we've got all this extra space now that Ethan's gone to college," she said. "We don't even use the basement these days, so it makes perfect sense to make some money out of it."

"Just until I find another job," said Nate.

"Absolutely."

He nodded, his lips forming a smile that didn't reach his eyes. Connie thought back to how he used to be before he was made redundant: confident and carefree, always so sure of himself and never less than totally reliable. Now—and she hated herself for thinking this—he seemed diminished, smaller somehow.

As he turned to leave, he glanced back. "I meant to ask, did you have a good time last night?"

"Yeah. We had drinks at the gallery and got take-out. An artist friend of Lana's was there too. Theo Welles—young guy, really friendly. We stayed up pretty late talking and drinking champagne."

Connie was laboring the point and was ashamed of the reason why: she wanted Nate to be jealous, to see some evidence that he still found her attractive. But he just smiled briefly—"That's great" —and left the room.

Watching him head upstairs, Connie thought back to last night, apprizing the memory of Theo's attention like a precious jewel. Inside, she felt a prickle of irritation. She was doing her best to keep this marriage alive. Why on earth couldn't Nate?

FIVE

Connie's father, Kurt, still lived in the house that she had grown up in. She had been born there too, as her mother had never tired of telling her, in an old tin bath beneath the lilac tree in the yard, its white flowers floating down like snowflakes as she took her first breath in the world. Her mom had worn a crown of honeysuckle, while her "birthing companions" had held hands around the bath and sung ancient songs to welcome the baby into the world. Clothes had apparently been optional for everyone. The whole thing had been documented on her dad's camera, right down to the ceremonial burying of the umbilical cord under a juniper bush, and the photos were passed round every birthday—even on one particularly memorable occasion when the teenage Connie had some friends for a sleepover. It was perhaps unsurprising that when the time came for her to give birth to Ethan, she had opted for a hospital bed, a team of obstetric doctors and all the drugs.

The house had originally been a single-story log cabin, but over the years her parents had developed and extended it, and now the folksy frontage gave way to a sprawling glass and aluminum structure that housed a gym, sauna, chef's kitchen with pizza oven and cinema room. It had even been featured in an architectural magazine a few years back. Connie could still remember the article's ridiculous opening line:

"With his leonine mane of hair and piercing gaze, Kurt Wilson may look like king of the beasts, but the renowned therapist enjoys a humble life in the Vermont mountains."

Ha! Her father had never had a humble day in his whole life.

Kurt's parents had lived in a magnificent colonial mansion in western Massachusetts. Kurt, their only child, had been expected to take over the family business, which manufactured outdoor footwear, but after turning twenty-one he had rebelled and fled to the hippie promised land of Vermont, taking his very generous trust fund along with him. He had met Connie's mom, Beth, at an antiwar rally in San Francisco the following year and they had married six months later. In the wedding photos they were both beautiful, long-haired and barefoot.

With no need to worry about anything so bourgeois as getting a job, Kurt and Beth had enjoyed a life of pleasure in the mountains —hiking in the summer, skiing in the winter, worshipping each other's inner god/goddess all year round—and neither of them was willing to let the arrival of their two daughters, Conifer and Evergreen, interrupt that. They believed in "free-range parenting," which basically involved letting their kids run as wild as bear cubs. Inconveniently, though, human children also needed feeding, bathing and putting to bed at a regular hour, and in the absence of much parental involvement Connie had taken on these responsibilities for both her and Everly. (It was telling that neither sister now used her real name, leaving it behind along with the chaos of their early years). As a result, Connie had become self-sufficient at a very young age: whatever life threw at her, she dealt with it without complaint.

By the time she was in her late teens, both her parents had begun to work—her mom as a high school drama teacher and dad as a therapist—but while Beth grew into a more conventional parental figure, Kurt did not. Despite spending his working life analyzing other people, he remained blissfully ignorant to his own shortcomings. Connie was no expert in human psychology (ironically, that was Kurt's role) but she often wondered if her father was actually a very charming and entertaining narcissist. After Nate had been made redundant and the bills started piling up, Connie had swallowed her pride and had gone to ask Kurt for a loan to help tide them over. Without a moment's consideration, he had turned her down. Connie had tried to explain that it would only be a short-term loan, but he was unyielding. It was the principle, he had said. Adults should not be supported financially by their parents—which was a little ironic, as his entire fortune had been inherited. Still, Connie knew that he loved her in his own, Kurt-like way, even if he wasn't exactly doting.

She rang the doorbell and moments later the heavy pine door opened to reveal her smiling father. He was wearing a gray T-shirt and battered khakis, the legs rolled up just above his ankles, and a leather thong around his neck, from which hung a charm from Beth's favorite bracelet. With his shoulder-length hair and hipster beard, threaded fetchingly with silver, he looked like a walking J. Crew ad.

"Happy birthday, pumpkin!" Kurt gathered her in for a hug. "I can't believe I'm old enough to have a nearly fifty-year-old daughter."

"Gee, thanks, Pa."

He pulled back and gazed at her. "You look so much like your mom," he murmured.

For all his flaws, it was impossible to fault Kurt's devotion to his wife. When Beth had died five years ago he'd been a broken man, closing his therapy practice because he reasoned he wouldn't be able to help other people "when I'm in so much pain myself."

Connie followed him through the house to the den, where he had laid out turmeric lattes and vegan cookies. This was where he used to see his patients, and even now, sitting on the couch (next to which still sat a box of Kleenex) Connie felt as if she was here to have psychoanalysis.

"It's great to see you, honey," said Kurt, settling into his leather armchair.

"You too. How are you, Pa?"

"I'm good—real good, actually. How's Nate doing?"

"He's okay."

"Has he found any work?"

"No, not yet."

Kurt nodded thoughtfully. "That must be really tough for him."

Irritation flared up inside Connie like a raw patch of eczema.

Tough for him? What about me? *My husband just sits home all day tinkering with bits of wood, going on endless runs and possibly having an affair.* I'm *the one holding it all together.*

She would never say any of this to her father though, so instead just shrugged.

"I mean for a man, losing his job—that's his status," Kurt went on. "Especially for someone like Nate, who was editor of such a prestigious travel magazine, and was effectively pushed out because of his age. That can be—well, devastating. I wonder how he's dealing with it."

It sounded like a rhetorical question, but judging by his body language he was expecting an answer. Connie wasn't going to take the bait, though. There was a fine line between soul-searching and navel-gazing, she had always thought, and her father persistently trampled all over it.

"I'm sure he'll get an assignment soon," she said. "He's sending feature ideas to newspapers and magazines. Something will come up."

Kurt just nodded, in that way Connie knew was designed to encourage his patients to open up.

Connie took a sip of her turmeric latte and longed for caffeine. "You said you had some news, Pa?"

At this, Kurt's eyes lit up. "Honey, I've met someone. A woman."

"Oh! Oh—wow. I mean... that's fantastic."

"She's really special." He looked like a smitten teenager. "This isn't weird for you, I hope? You know how much your mom meant to me."

"Of course! And it's been five years since she died. I hoped you'd meet someone else. No, I'm really pleased for you. Tell me about her."

"Well, her name's Skye Peters and we met at the organic grocery store in Thompsonville. She's recently moved nearby and has a part-time job there—she's actually a healer, but the store work gives her a regular income. She's amazing, Conn. We haven't known each other very long, but we really get each other. She..." He hesitated. "The thing is, she..."

Connie frowned. It wasn't like Kurt to be lost for words, or to ever be less than 100 percent sure of himself.

"What is it, Pa?"

He thought for a moment, then broke into a grin. "It doesn't matter. Anyway, I thought I'd invite her over to dinner next week, if you and Nate would like to join us?"

"We'd love to."

"Great. I'll make my butternut chili. Skye's a vegan, too."

A healer *and* a vegan—she sounded perfect for Kurt. Connie knew her dad though, and there was something he wasn't telling her about this woman. She was absolutely sure of it.

SIX

"There's no pillow menu in my room."

The woman standing in front of the oak table that served as the Covered Bridge Inn's front desk was giving Connie what could best be termed a death stare. Connie's heart dropped to her sneakers—though from the look on her face you'd think she was absolutely thrilled about this encounter. This particular guest—a Mrs. Hank Havers III—had only checked in that morning, but Connie had already had two run-ins with her. The first after she phoned reception to complain that her room didn't have a view of the mountain (when Connie came up and pointed out the unmissable hulk of Mount Maverick, the woman had groused that it was "too far away") and the second after she had ordered a slice of coffee pecan cake only to send it back because she "hadn't been informed it contained nuts."

"I'm afraid we don't have a pillow menu, but—"

"Well, why on earth not?"

"We're a small, family-run inn, it's just not something we offer, but I'd be very happy to change your pillows if they're not quite right for you. Would you like something softer or firmer?"

Mrs. Hank Havers III huffed. "What I'd *like* is an organic

buckwheat pillow. Failing that, a fifty-fifty blend of duck down and feathers."

"I'm so sorry, Mrs. Havers, but we don't have either of those. Perhaps I could ask housekeeping to send up a selection of pillows and you can see if any of those suit? Plus a jug of our fresh strawberry lemonade and some cookies—nut-free, of course—with our compliments, for the inconvenience."

The woman hesitated, but the lemonade and cookies had clearly worked their magic. Years of experience had taught Connie that the best way to deal with tricky guests was to love-bomb them.

"Fine," she snapped, and walked off.

Connie let out a relieved breath and only now noticed Spencer had been hovering nearby, watching the exchange. As their eyes met, he gave her a round of applause. The inn's young owner had the same distinctive wide-set eyes and thick brows that could be seen in the framed black-and-white photos of generations of Gridley ancestors lining the inn's corridors.

"You're a marvel, Connie. I'd have said you have the patience of a saint, but I'm not sure any of their torments match up to what some of our guests put you through."

"Thanks, Spence, but it's what you pay me for."

He glanced over to the stairs, where Mrs. Hank Havers III had disappeared a moment ago.

"Should we, um, be looking into these buckwheat pillows, do you think?"

Connie knew that Spencer worried about the little details—it was what made him so good at his job— but things had got out of hand since the arrival of a new hotel that was opening at the mountain later in the year. Maverick Lodge resort was promising six-star luxury for its guests, with a butler service and hot tubs in every room, and it was bound to have an extensive pillow menu; probably a comforter and mattress menu too. As much as Connie tried to reassure him that their respective hotels would be appealing to different guests, she understood why Spencer was worried.

"I can certainly do some research," she said.

"Thank you." He smiled. "Do you have a minute to discuss the candidates for the events manager role? We could grab five minutes in the gazebo."

"Sure. Let me just take care of Mrs. Havers and I'll see you out there shortly."

Connie made a call to housekeeping to arrange for the pillows and treats to be sent up the guest's room. There were twenty rooms in the inn, no two the same, each named after a bird native to Vermont. This woman was staying in Chickadee, a pretty room at the front of the hotel decorated in shades of pale blue. Connie liked to joke they should rename one of the rooms Wild Turkey or Common Loon, where they could house the trickier guests.

Her phone vibrated. It was a reply from Lana; she'd messaged her earlier to thank her for her birthday celebration.

Glad you had fun, sweetie! Theo's a hoot, isn't he? Hope Nate made it up to you over the weekend. Let's get together again soon. Love you.

Nate hadn't made it up to her—well, not in the way that Lana would have hoped. Their weekend had been much like any other: Nate had played golf, they had finished clearing out the basement in readiness for the lodger and Connie had spent far too much time ironing. After his weirdness on Saturday morning Nate hadn't mentioned wanting to talk to her again, but she couldn't help wondering what it had been about. She'd decided, though, that it was probably better to let sleeping dogs lie. Or should that be cheating husbands lie?

From the street, the Covered Bridge Inn seemed to occupy a modest block of Tansy Falls' main street, surrounded by a picket fence. Appearances were deceptive, though: behind the building the inn's grounds stretched all the way back to the woods that covered the hills beyond. Most of the guests ventured no farther than the pool terrace, with its loungers and tables where you could breakfast in the sunshine, but if you walked up the path away from the terrace and through a wrought-iron gate, you would be rewarded with the inn's best-kept secret: a traditional English walled garden, built over a hundred years ago by Spencer's great-grandmother. Now, in the summer, it was at its most riotously beautiful. The flowerbeds were overflowing with asters, day lilies and the broccoli-like heads of sedums, all set against weathered brick walls the golden-pink shade of sunset. Tucked away by the far wall was a gazebo, guarded by ranks of alliums and hollyhock spears, which was where Connie was headed now. The honeyed scent of flowers simmered in the heat and worked like a sleeping potion, yet even as she relaxed, she kept an eye out for plants that needed deadheading or scraps of garbage. It was second nature to her. At the inn she was always on duty.

Connie had worked all around the world, earning her service stripes at top hotels in London and Paris, but she and Nate had decided to return to Tansy Falls after Ethan arrived. When she first started working at the Covered Bridge, Spencer's grandparents, Mitch and Carole, had been in charge—and despite having "retired" to Florida a few years ago, to all intents and purposes they still very much were. They had passed the daily running of the inn onto Spencer and Piper six years ago, bypassing Spencer's parents, who had never been interested in the family business, but they were still refusing to sign over full control to their grandson. It was proving a challenge to balance Mitch and Carole's loyalty to tradition with Spencer and Piper's desire to modernize—and it was usually Connie who got caught in the middle. The senior Gridleys liked to remind everyone who was in charge by objecting to most of Spencer's ideas, most recently his plans to put in a charging station for electric cars in the parking lot. Worse still, they would occasionally turn up unannounced, invariably at the worst possible time—such as Christmas Eve—to criticize the latest developments. But with the six-star specter of Maverick Lodge looming over them it was vital that the inn attract new guests, and thanks to Spencer and Piper's efforts, they were succeeding. Not that Mitch and Carole would ever acknowledge that, though. The most recent edition of *Inns and Hotels of New England* had included a glowing review: "A few years ago the Covered Bridge Inn had seemed content to trade on past glories, but the new young owners have injected life into this venerable Tansy Falls institution." Connie grimaced at the memory of Carole yelling down the line from Boca Raton about *that* particular article.

Spencer was already waiting in the gazebo, the events manager résumés spread out on the table in front of him.

"You've done a great job of narrowing down the candidates, Connie."

"I think this one could be particularly good. Isabelle Bennett. Great hotel experience and excellent references. Would you and Piper like to interview the final three? I've arranged to meet them next week."

"No, we're happy for you to take care of it. How soon do you think we could have someone on board? I know you've got everything under control, but it would be great if they could be here in time to help with the press trip. Especially with the baby due so soon..."

Connie nodded, but a bubble of anxiety swelled inside her. The press trip had seemed like such a brilliant idea at the time. She had suggested inviting a group of journalists to stay at the Covered Bridge—all expenses paid—on the condition they would write about their stay in their publications, generating some free advertising and creating a buzz about the inn.

With his experience in the travel industry, Nate had suggested the names of some journalists, plus a couple of Instagram influencers for good measure, and Connie had planned a weekend of outings for the visitors to showcase the best of the Covered Bridge and Tansy Falls. She had planned everything meticulously; nothing could go wrong—unless, of course, everything did.

The first problem was that the journalists weren't actually obligated to write something positive about the inn. Yes, they would be staying for free, but there was no guarantee they would say nice things if the weekend was a disaster. Connie had taken to waking up at 2 a.m., fretting over insignificant details like the flavor of muffins they should serve at brunch.

Secondly, although Spencer and Piper were on board with the idea, Mitch and Carole were not. After getting wind of the press trip, Carole had called Connie and ranted about "freeloading journalists," accusing her of "cheapening the image of the Covered Bridge." Connie was beginning to feel like it was her own reputation that was on the line, as much as that of the Covered Bridge, and with Nate still out of work, she couldn't risk doing anything to jeopardize her job.

Finally, there was the issue of timing: the press trip was in a month's time and Piper's baby was due three weeks after that. But babies kept to their own schedule, and if Gridley junior arrived the same weekend as the press trip—well, that would be one of those aforementioned disasters. Not that she would voice any of these concerns to Spencer, of course.

"I'd be happy take care of the interviews," she told him. "It'll be tight, but I'll try to get someone to start as soon as possible. It would be great to have an extra pair of hands to help out."

Although what she *didn't* say was that if they had a professional on board, the press trip might at least have a chance of being a success.

SEVEN

Connie buffed pink blush all over her cheeks then paused to check her reflection. She had been aiming for "youthful glow," but the effect was more "dangerously high fever." Grimacing, she tried to rub it off, but that made her cheeks even redder, so she just covered her face with powder and left it at that.

She was a bundle of nerves about meeting her dad's girlfriend, Skye, at dinner tonight. Perhaps it was because it was entirely possible that this woman could end up becoming Kurt's wife. It was early days, but her dad certainly seemed smitten with her. Nearly fifty years old, and Connie could be getting a stepmother! An image of Maleficent appeared in her mind, complete with cloak and horned headdress, a taloned hand resting on Kurt's shoulder. She zipped up her cosmetics case, shaking her head at her imagination.

Downstairs she found Nate at the front door talking to Frank Whitman. The pair of them had been out together that afternoon fixing groundhog damage at their shared boundary fence, but while Frank was still in his overalls, his tanned arms covered with a fuzz of white hairs, Nate was fresh out of the shower in a white shirt and tailored trousers. It was the sort of thing he used to wear every day to the office, but after a year of nothing but sweats or shorts it was quite a contrast.

"Evenin', Connie." Frank touched the peak of his cap. "Don't you look as pretty as a pie supper?"

This was the problem with Frank: he was so charming it was impossible to be annoyed about his animals' antisocial habits, such as Jocelyn the giant donkey's 3 a.m. honk-a-thon earlier that week.

"How are you, Frank? All good?"

"Oh, you know. Gettin' by."

"Frank brought over some eggs for us," said Nate.

"You're a sweetheart, thank you," said Connie. "I've no idea why, but your hens lay the best eggs I've ever tasted."

The old man tapped a finger against the side of his nose. "I talk to 'em—that's the secret. Ask them about their day, what they've been up to. Hens like the attention, same as any woman."

Nate laughed, and Connie couldn't help thinking: *You should be taking notes, buddy*.

"Well, I better let you two young 'uns get on with your evening." Frank raised a hand in farewell. "You take care now."

Nate closed the door behind him and turned to Connie with an expectant smile.

"You look handsome," she said.

His eyes widened slightly. "Thank you. You do too—I mean, you look beautiful."

Not so long ago, this exchange would have been swiftly followed by physical contact: Nate would have pulled Connie toward him, she would have laughingly resisted, muttering something about smudged lipstick, but they'd have ended up kissing anyway. Instead, the moment was marked with half smiles and aborted eye contact. They were so far from the couple they used to be it made Connie's head spin.

"Shall we get going?" she said, to cover the awkwardness. "Kurt said to come over any time after seven."

"Sure," said Nate. "I'll drive."

. . .

As they pulled out of the driveway the sky was heavy with dark, gold-edged clouds, casting the landscape in an eerie glow, while the ranks of trees lining Cider Farm Road fidgeted and whispered as if spooked.

"Looks like there's a storm on the way," said Connie, gazing up at the brewing sky.

"Could be." Nate turned onto the mountain road. "Has your dad told you much about this woman?"

"Skye? Not really, no. He's clearly very taken with her, though."

"Well, I think it's great. I'm glad Kurt's got a girlfriend to join him on his crazy adventures."

"Girlfriend! Surely there must be an age limit to that word."

"Lady friend, then? Companion? Sweetheart? Current squeeze? *Wife?*"

"Whoa, let's not get ahead of ourselves!"

They drove past Lana's gallery, whisking Connie straight back to the evening of her birthday. Just remembering Theo's dark eyes fixed on hers was like getting an injection of self-esteem and feel-good hormones...

"By the way, I spoke to James Ortiz this morning," said Nate, dragging her back to reality.

"Who?"

"Our potential lodger, remember? I've gotta say, he seems perfect. Really nice guy. About our age, I reckon. Married with grown-up kids. He'll be working up at the Lodge during the week, but plans to head home to Manhattan on weekends. I've agreed he can move in on Monday, if that's okay with you."

Connie gaped at him. "Monday?"

"I thought you'd be pleased?"

"I am. It's just—so soon."

"I can put him off for a week if you like?"

"No, it's fine. Thanks for sorting it out."

It wasn't as if there was much work left to do to prepare the basement, just a few boxes of their son Ethan's old stuff to move to a new home, but Connie felt like she needed far more time to mentally prepare for the fact that a stranger was moving in.

"He offered to pay for a full week's rent, even though he won't be there at weekends," Nate added, sensing her disquiet.

The money would certainly help, and, who knew, perhaps this man—James Ortiz—wouldn't turn out to be a psychotic axe murderer after all.

They passed a roadside farm stall piled with baskets of strawberries and cherries and then the turnoff to Hoffman Creamery, the organic dairy farm that supplied the Covered Bridge with milk and cream. It was a favorite spot for tourists to stop for photos, thanks to the idyllic view of the barn and farmhouse by the duck pond at the foot of the driveway. Pictures of the Hoffman farm were even used by the Vermont tourist board to promote the state.

Moments later Nate swung off the main road and bumped along the track that led to Kurt's home. Lights were already blazing in the cabin's windows; the sun wouldn't set for at least another hour, but the moody skies had sent the world into an early twilight.

Sure enough, as they climbed the steps to the porch, there was a distant rumble of thunder and the first spots of rain began to fall. Connie was right about the storm—and it looked set to be a feisty one.

They knocked, and a few moments later the front door opened. Kurt looked younger than ever, his hair tied back in a ponytail and linen shirt artfully untucked.

He gathered Nate into a hug. "Great to see you, man. How have you been?"

"Hanging in there. Thanks for having us over tonight."

Kurt gripped his shoulder in acknowledgement, then turned to kiss Connie.

"Come on in, Skye's so looking forward to meeting you both." He leaned out to look up at the sky. "Reckon we're in for a wild night."

As they followed Kurt down the corridor toward the living room at the back of the house, Connie could hear the music of Joni

Mitchell, her parents' favorite singer, and she felt glad he had met someone who shared his tastes. She knew her mom would be happy that Kurt had found a companion. She wouldn't have wanted him to spend the rest of his life alone—she had said as much before she died.

When Kurt's home had been featured in the architectural magazine, the living room had been the focus of the article—and for good reason. It had a cathedral ceiling and stunning floor-to-ceiling windows that wrapped around the back of the house, making it feel like the room was a part of the forest behind. Rain was drumming on the skylights, almost drowning out Joni's wistful vocals. It was such a huge room that it took Connie a moment to notice the slight, dark-haired girl sitting in an armchair by the window. Her bare feet were scooted up beneath her, one arm hugged around her legs. She was so dainty it looked as if a strong gust of wind could whisk her straight back to Narnia.

Connie hovered in the doorway, trying to work out who she was. Had Skye brought along her daughter? She turned to Kurt for an explanation, but he was beaming at the woman with a besotted expression.

"Conifer, Nate—I'd like you to meet Skye Peters."

EIGHT

Connie's mouth went slack. *This* was his father's new love? Turns out the word "girlfriend" was appropriate after all. There was no time to process her shock, though, as Skye was already walking toward her. Her long hair fell around her shoulders and she was wearing a white vest and flowing skirt that looked exactly like something her mom would have worn in her hippie phase. Connie took a sharp inhale. Of course, *that* was who Skye reminded her of: her mother, the mid-seventies edition. It seemed Kurt was dating a ghost.

Outside, a rumble of thunder rolled around the valley.

"Conifer, I'm so grateful to meet you." Skye held out her hand. "You have such a pretty name."

"Thank you, but I usually just go by Connie." *Because my parents were probably high when they named me.* "It's great to meet you too," she added.

She watched as Skye turned to greet Nate with the Zen-like calm of someone who meditated daily, avoided gluten and never shouted at other drivers. Meanwhile, Connie's mind was racing frantically in a decidedly unenlightened fashion. Why would a young woman like this be interested in Kurt? He was certainly cool, but there was no getting away from the fact that he was a cool senior citizen. What could they possibly have in common? At this, Connie's eyes traveled around the room, taking in the expensive art, the latest tech gadgets and the jaw-dropping views from the vast, architect-designed window, and her mind instantly fixed on an explanation that she hated herself for even contemplating.

"We brought you some Rioja," she said, holding up the bottle. "I know it's one of your favorites, Pa."

"One of *our* favorites," said Kurt, putting an arm around Skye and gazing at her if she were the only person in the world.

Connie and Nate exchanged glances.

"Let me give you a hand in the kitchen, Pa," she said.

"Sure thing. Let's get that wine open."

As he walked out, his eyes snapped back toward Skye as if on elastic. "Back soon, honey. Nate, be sure to look after my girl."

In the kitchen, Kurt retrieved a bottle opener from a drawer and opened the wine, humming to himself, while Connie watched him, struggling to put her whirlpooling thoughts into words. He drew out the cork with a soft pop, then turned to get some glasses out of the cabinet. After a few moments, and without looking round, he said calmly: "Just say what you need to, kiddo."

Connie leaned both palms on the counter, trying not to let his tone rile her.

"How old is Skye?"

"She's thirty-nine."

Connie sucked in a breath. *Ten years younger than me.* "That's quite an age gap, Pa."

"Does that make you uncomfortable?"

"It's a surprise, that's all. I'm sure you can understand that."

"I'm not sure age is relevant when we have so much else in common."

"But do you—really? You grew up in completely different eras with different cultural references, different values. I know you consider yourself young at heart, but this seems a little, well, ridiculous."

Kurt sighed, as if he'd been expecting her to disappoint him. "I get this is a shock for you. Skye is younger than you'd anticipated, and perhaps I should have prepared you for that, but I didn't want you jumping to conclusions before you could meet her and see how fantastic she is. I'm really happy, she is too. Isn't that all that matters?"

"Of course, I'm just... She isn't what I was expecting."

Kurt put his hands on her shoulders. "I have no doubt that once you get to know Skye her age will seem as irrelevant to you as it is to me. Just give her a chance, okay? Now, why don't you put this to one side, park your reservations and let's have a wonderful evening."

The evening, for Connie at least, was the opposite of wonderful. She really was trying to keep an open mind about the relationship, but then she'd look at Skye twiddling her hair and batting her lashes at her father, and a voice inside her head would scream, *YOU ARE A DECADE OLDER THAN YOUR DAD'S NEW GIRLFRIEND!*

To make matters worse, Kurt hung on Skye's every word like she was the messiah.

"Skye, tell Conn and Nate about your work," he said, as they tucked into the butternut squash chili.

"Well, I work in Thompsonville's store part-time—"

"Which is where we met," added Kurt, leaning over to nuzzle her neck.

"Yes, which is where I met this wonderful man." She stroked his face. "But my real job—my calling, I guess you could say—is as a shamanic healer."

"Well, I don't have a clue what that is, but it sounds cool," said Nate.

"Skye has the ability to leave her body at will and enter the spirit realms to gain insight and seek help from her spirit guides," said Kurt reverently.

Connie raised her brows. "Wow, that's quite a skill set."

"It's not as far-fetched as it sounds." Skye said with a smile. "All of us leave our bodies at night to explore other worlds—when we dream, right?—but for most people this is an unconscious journey. I make the same journey but do so intentionally, and in order to help other people."

"What sort of things do you help with?" asked Nate, clearing half his glass in a gulp. He was hitting the wine hard tonight.

"People come to me for all kinds of reasons. Health issues, professional challenges, personal relationships." Skye's eyes fixed on Connie. "Maybe someone's just feeling a bit stuck? I find shamanic treatment can help with most problems."

Outside, the storm was rolling around the valley. Connie shifted in her seat, her skin prickling. This shamanic thing was nonsense, of course—just like all the other New Age fads that had consumed her parents—but the way Skye looked at her made her feel as if she was being dissected under a microscope.

"Excuse me," she said, pushing her chair back from the table and heading for the bathroom.

She wanted to get away from Skye, from Kurt—from the whole unsettling atmosphere. It didn't help that Nate was either oblivious to Connie's discomfort or indifferent to it. If only her sister, Everly, were here. She was the one person who would understand how she was feeling.

Connie hid in the bathroom for as long as she could without it being weird, and when she returned to the table, Skye was talking about a "womb energy cleansing ritual," the men hanging on her every word. Connie felt like saying that her womb cleansed itself quite effectively every month without having to pay someone to burn sage over it, but she didn't want to be childish—which was ironic, because right now it seemed as if she was the only adult in the room. Nate was drunk, while Skye and Kurt were like love-struck teenagers, their hands all over each other. Meanwhile, Connie sat at the head of the table, primly sipping at a glass of water, the disapproving maiden aunt.

It was blindingly obvious what was going on here: Kurt was

having another midlife crisis—his third by Connie's count. There had been the expensive Japanese motorbike, the trek through Tibet culminating in a three-month stint at a Buddhist monastery—and now he was dating a woman younger than both his daughters, a facsimile of his late wife, who was enabling his need to pretend he was still twenty.

Finally, the evening dragged to an end. As Connie was gathering her things, desperate to escape into the fresh air, Skye came over to speak with her.

"I know this must be weird for you, Connie. I'm probably a little younger than you were expecting. I told your dad he should warn you, but you know Kurt—stubborn as a mule!"

"Honestly, I'm pleased for you both."

"I do love your father, you know. We have a very intense connection."

"I'm happy if he's happy."

"I'm so glad." Skye hesitated. "I feel you should know that we've already talked about me moving in here."

"Oh?" Connie covered her shock with a smile.

"I hope it won't feel like I'm muscling in on your mom's territory? I sense her energy strongly here, but I do get the impression that she accepts me in her space."

Connie had no idea how to reply. "Um—well, that's great that my mom's cool with it," she managed.

"Perhaps you and I could go for a coffee sometime, get to know each other a little better?"

"Let's do that. Thank you again for tonight."

Then Connie headed for the front door like a diver using her final breath to reach the surface of the water.

Outside, the storm had blown itself out. Water was dripping from the trees and the sky was clear and thick with stars. Nate stumbled as they reached the car, giggling to himself as he swung himself into the passenger side. It really wasn't like him to drink so much.

"Well, that was a fun night," he said. "Typical Kurt. We should have guessed Skye wouldn't be a little old lady with bifocals and a walker."

Connie put the key in the ignition. "You don't think it's weird? She's thirty-nine, Nate. That's a whole lifetime younger than him."

"Your dad's a very good-looking guy."

"*And* a very rich guy."

Nate pulled a face. "Jeez, Connie..."

Connie's hands tightened on the wheel. Why couldn't Nate understand how weird this was for her? She just wanted him on her side, like he always used to be.

"It's taking me some time to get my head round it, that's all. Skye wasn't what I was expecting."

"I think we both know there's more to it than that." His voice was thick, the words slurring. "Let's be honest, Conn, are you jealous because she's young and pretty, or are you worried she's going to steal your inheritance?"

His words were designed to wound, and they did their job. Connie felt her throat tighten; for a horrible moment she would cry.

"Sorry," Nate mumbled. "That was uncalled for. I'm a little drunk."

They drove home the rest of the way in silence, sadness pooling inside Connie. *We're heading to the point of no return*, she thought, struggling to keep a lid on her tears. That place where they had no memory of the devoted couple they once were, and had become just two random people with nothing in common to glue them back together. *How had it come to this?*

At home, Nate belly-flopped onto their bed fully clothed and by the time she came back from the bathroom he was dead to the world, spread-eagled across the mattress, leaving no room for her. He was snoring so loudly she was surprised he didn't wake himself up. Connie went to sleep in Ethan's room, but as soon as she lay down she knew sleep would be impossible. She reached for her phone: it was past midnight—too late to make a call? After a moment's thought, she dialed a number, but it went straight to voicemail.

"Everly? It's me, Conn. Can you give me a call back? I need to discuss a Kurt issue with you. Nothing to worry about, but I'd appreciate some sisterly input. Thanks, honey. Bye."

NINE

Connie thought she might be falling a little bit in love. Isabelle Bennett was sitting on the opposite side of her desk, everything about her from the elegant suit to focused eye contact exuding a sense of capability and efficiency. She had answered each of Connie's questions as if she'd not only read the book *How to Be the Best Events Manager in the World*, but had written it, too. If she was a little robotic, Connie could definitely overlook that for the sake of her stunning résumé. The other two candidates she had interviewed had been pleasant enough, but they were no match for Isabelle Bennett's weapons-grade professionalism. It was like comparing a couple of fluffy Pomeranian puppies with an elite Doberman—and Connie knew exactly which of them she wanted by her side when the pack of Rottweilers turned up in a few weeks' time for the press trip. Sure enough, when Connie had mentioned the press trip Isabelle had reeled off a list of similar events she had been involved with, her anecdotes usually culminating with something like: "...and of course the write-up made the front page of the *New York Times* travel supplement," the words dripping like honey onto Connie's frazzled nerves. Which is why she had ended up offering the young woman the job on the spot.

Connie had given Isabelle a tour of the inn and as she watched her new employee running her eye over the facilities, as meticulous as a butler swiping a gloved finger across the furniture to detect specks of dust, she knew she had made the right choice.

When they reached reception they found Piper at the front desk. She looked tired and pale beneath her freckles. Connie had been worrying about her. It was so much to deal with—her pregnancy, the heat and the fully booked inn—and she hoped the news about Isabelle would help ease her burden.

"Piper, I'd like to introduce you to Isabelle Bennett. I've just offered her the position of our new events manager, and I'm happy to say she's accepted."

Piper's face lit up. "Welcome, Isabelle! It's great to have you on board."

"I'm looking forward to getting started. I already have some ideas to make the Covered Bridge an even more desirable destination."

"Isabelle will be able to start in two weeks' time," said Connie.

"So you'll be here for the press trip weekend?" Piper clapped her hands together. "Oh, that's the best news."

"I'll send the contract over to you tomorrow," said Connie. "We're thrilled to have you joining the Covered Bridge team."

Connie was still on an Isabelle Bennett high as she walked home later that afternoon, taking the scenic route along the banks of the Wild Moose River. Here on the valley floor the river ran wide and shallow, buffered on either side by silky willows and river birches. The farther she got from town, the less people she met, until she was alone on the path. She heard the distinctive call of a bittern, like the *plop* of a stone being thrown in the water, and watched as a little gray flycatcher skimmed over the shadowy shallows. She hadn't had time for lunch, but Piper had pressed a sweet potato and maple bacon muffin into her hands as she left (the result of her latest kitchen experiment) and Connie ate it as she followed the course of the river.

She was walking home today as Nate had needed the car, but regardless of that she was in no hurry to get back, because when she did James Ortiz would be ensconced in their basement. At least Nate had been home that afternoon to welcome the new lodger and get him settled in. Connie intended to have as little to do with him as possible. In fact she was hoping she could just pretend he wasn't actually living there. *Just focus on the extra income*, she reminded herself.

Her route home across the fields brought Connie out close to Frank's house, and as she skirted the paddock a piebald goat shot out from one of the sheds trailing a rope, chased by Frank.

"Hold up, Connie. I need a word!" he yelled, as the goat careened around him, kicking up its hooves. He eventually managed to catch the rope and came over to the fence leading the now sulky goat.

"Who's taking who for a walk there, Frank?"

"Gert ain't overly keen on being milked. You'd think the old girl would be used to it by now."

Connie reached through the fence to scratch Gert's flanks. "What did you want to talk to me about?"

"Well, I don't want to worry you, but I've seen a strange man hanging about your yard. He's been there for some time, just wanderin' about. You want me to come with you, check out who he is?"

"Thanks, Frank, but that'll probably be our new lodger."

"Ah, that's today, is it?" He yanked at the goat, which was trying to take a mouthful of Connie's skirt. "Nate mentioned you had some guy moving into the basement. New Yorker, ain't he?"

"That's right. Nate's at home, so he'll have settled him in."

"I don't think he is, Conn. Your car's been gone for a few hours."

"Huh." Connie turned and looked over at her house. "That's weird. I wonder where Nate could have got to? I guess I better go and rescue the lodger then. Thanks for keeping an eye out, Frank."

"No problem. You just scream if he turns out to be a bad 'un, and me and Gert will be there in a flash. She may look like a lady, but she can butt like a battering ram."

"Oh, I can well believe that," laughed Connie, but as she started across the grass toward the house, unease fluttered in her stomach. Where on earth was Nate? He had known their lodger was moving in this afternoon, so why wasn't he here? Talk about completely failing at first impressions.

It didn't take long for Connie to locate James Ortiz. He was down by the lake, lying in the long grass, his arms folded behind his head as if he was sunbathing. As she hurried down the slope toward him, apologies at the ready, she took the chance to check him out. He was a big man—broad-shouldered and thickset—with black hair and an olive complexion; basically, he looked as Spanish as his last name implied.

She kept expecting him to raise his head as she approached, but he didn't stir, and when she got within a few feet of him she realized he was asleep. She cleared her throat loudly, hoping he might, but nothing. He had a Goodfellas sort of face, with a substantial slab of a nose that had been badly broken at some point, heavy brows and a wide, downward-sloping mouth. His hair sprouted in thick waves, curling beneath his ears, but the stubble on his jawline had been immaculately groomed. His white shirt looked expensive too. He was clearly a man who cared about his appearance—although not enough to stop him from sprawling in the long grass. Then Connie noticed a spiral-bound pad by his side, open to reveal a sketch of a landscape. She crouched to look more closely. It was a picture of the lake and her favorite cotton-wood tree, rendered in a few delicate pencil strokes, and it was quite beautiful.

"Hey there."

With a start, she looked up to find James Ortiz propped up on his elbows.

"Oh—hi! I'm Connie. You must be James. I was just admiring your artwork."

He ripped out the page and offered it to her. "For you, Connie. A welcome present."

"Well, that's very kind of you, especially in light of our complete lack of a welcome. I'm so sorry nobody was here when you arrived. I've been at work, but my husband, Nate, was meant to be here." She looked around again, as if he might suddenly pop up from behind a bush. "He must have got held up. I can only apologize."

"Forget about it. I got a chance to relax and enjoy this awesome view." He got to his feet with a nimbleness that belied his size. "And now you're here," he added with a smile.

The tightness in Connie's chest began to ease a little. Contrary to Frank's worries, James certainly didn't seem like a bad 'un.

"Shall we go and get you settled in?" she asked. "I'll give you the grand tour."

"Sure. Uh, perhaps the first stop could be the bathroom?"

Connie laughed. "Of course."

They started up the slope together toward the house.

"So you're working up at Maverick Lodge?"

"That's right. My firm designed the interiors. I'm based in Manhattan, but I wanted to be on site to keep an eye on things now they're moving into the final phase of development." He looked up at the house as they approached. "Although if I'd known I would find somewhere like this to stay, I'd have begun working up here a lot sooner. You have a gorgeous home."

Connie smiled at the compliment, which meant even more coming from a professional like James. The house had been a labor of love for her and Nate, and every bit of the building, from the pale green walls to eclectic details like the round attic window and steeply sloping gables, had a story behind it.

"It was a wreck when Nate and I bought it twenty years ago," she told him. "It's actually an old cider farmhouse. Ethan—that's my son—reckons that you can sometimes hear the ghost of some drunk farmer crashing around at night." She unlocked the door.

"The interiors could probably use some TLC, though, so don't judge."

James held up his hands. "Don't worry, I make it a policy never to bring my work home with me."

After she'd taken him around the house, Connie led him down to the basement where he would be staying. The house was built onto a slope, like a traditional bank barn, so it was accessible both from the ground floor and via the French doors to the basement, which meant that even down here the room was flooded with the early evening light. Still, Connie was glad she'd taken the time to put some wildflowers into a vase and arranged one of her great-grandma's patchwork quilts on the bed. It looked welcoming at least, if not up to the standards James Ortiz was probably used to.

"Can I get you a drink while you get settled in? I can offer you iced tea, lemonade or..."

James pulled a bottle of tequila from his bag. "How about I make us margaritas?"

"Oh! Well, that sounds much more fun."

They went back up to the kitchen and she began opening the cabinets, showing James where things were kept. "Don't worry, I'm sure I'll find everything I need myself," he said. "You go sit outside. I'll bring the drinks out momentarily."

Connie hesitated; it felt odd letting a stranger loose in her kitchen. "You sure you don't want some help?"

"I promise I'm not gonna steal or set fire to anything. Okay?" He make a shooing gesture. "Out!"

It was the nicest time of the day to be sitting on their deck, as the sun didn't fully reach this spot until it was starting to set, and Connie settled into a chair, adjusting to the novelty of being waited on for a change. From inside the house, she heard James singing— was that Frank Sinatra?—and she smiled, marveling at how lucky they seemed to have got with their lodger. All that time she'd wasted worrying about it! Connie felt a pleasant heaviness creep over her as she finally took her foot off the gas and let herself relax. What a good day it had been: first she had hired Isabelle Bennett, which meant her press trip had a chance of actually being a success, and now her non-axe-murdering lodger was making cocktails. Even her concerns about Kurt and his girlfriend seemed less pressing. The only cloud on her otherwise clear horizon was the mysterious whereabouts of Nate. With that thought, Connie tried dialing his number, but it rang until it went to voicemail.

"Here we are! My world-famous Ortiz margaritas." James emerged from the house carrying a tray with the drinks and a large bowl of something that smelled warm and buttery. "I hope you don't mind, but I had a look through your larder and made a batch of chipotle popcorn too."

Connie forced her mind off her worries about Nate and smiled her thanks. She took a sip and her eyes grew wide. "Oh my gosh, that is delicious!"

"When I was in my early twenties I thought if I perfected a margarita it would help me get girls."

"And did it?"

"Depends how much tequila I used," he replied, with a lift of his eyebrows, and she laughed. "So tell me, Connie, what do you do apart from the landlady-ing?

"I'm a hotel manager. I work in town, at the Covered Bridge Inn."

"I've heard good things about that place. I hope the new resort isn't going to affect your business?"

"I think it'll be fine. We're catering to different markets. You'll have the private-jet crowd, and we'll have everybody else."

"Cheers to that."

Connie returned his smile. She liked the way his eyes danced, as if he was up to mischief. She imagined he'd be a fun friend to have.

Just then the sound of an approaching car caught her attention and she turned to see their silver Volvo coming down the drive.

"That'll be Nate," she said, relief and tequila mingling in a happy rush.

Her pleasure quickly faded though, when he got out of the car looking like he'd just been out to dinner at a big-city restaurant. What was with the shirt and trousers, the meticulously styled hair?

Nate bounded up the steps to the deck. "James! I'm so sorry, I didn't think you'd be here until later this evening. Welcome to the Old Cider Farmhouse. It's great to have you here. Everything okay for you?"

"Absolutely. I was telling Connie how lucky I feel to have found this place."

Nate was smiling, but Connie could detect of an edge of tension behind his eyes.

"Where have you been?" she asked lightly. "I was starting to worry you'd got lost."

"Oh, I went to see Tom Frost to borrow his pipe wrench to fix that leak in the top bathroom"—he waved a tool he was holding—"and we got talking. I completely lost track of time, sorry." He settled into the chair next to them. "What are we drinking?"

As James poured him a margarita, Connie turned over Nate's explanation in her mind. It seemed perfectly reasonable—he was golf buddies with Tom, Lana's husband, after all—but that didn't explain his appearance. She took a sip of her drink, her eyes fixed on the lake. Perhaps he had been to see Tom, but she would bet her last dollar that Nate's meticulous grooming hadn't been for his friend's benefit. In which case, wondered Connie, her stomach lurching—who had it been for?

TEN

The storm of two nights back had pressed the refresh button on Tansy Falls, sweeping away the haze and mugginess of the past weeks to reveal a brilliantly blue-skied morning. The air was as crisp and clear as the water at the nearby Smugglers Leap falls, while the local birds' philharmonic orchestra sang with a gusto that suggested they were all enchanted by the beautiful morning too. It was, in short, a picture-perfect summer day as Connie left the Covered Bridge Inn and strolled down Main Street, reveling in the sunshine rather than scuttling like a lizard from one patch of shade to the next as she usually did. It was wonderful to be able to take a few steps outside without dissolving into a puddle of sweat. She glanced toward Mount Maverick, enjoying the sense of calm the mountain always gave her. It was a sight that hadn't changed for millennia, and when life was particularly crazy she liked to look at the mountain to remind herself how insignificant her worries were. The new resort might be transforming the base of the mountain beyond all recognition, but at least it couldn't touch this view.

Connie turned off the sidewalk and headed up the path to a weathered clapboard building that looked as if it had been there for nearly as long as the mountain. The sign had recently been repainted though, FISKE'S GENERAL STORE now standing out in bright gold lettering, and the wooden steps up to the porch that used to groan and tremble when you climbed them now felt sturdy beneath her feet.

The changes continued inside the store too. Until recently, Fiske's had been like an Aladdin's cave—if, that is, Aladdin had been a compulsive hoarder with a fondness for llama-wool socks and artisan piccalilli. Every spare inch of the store's dimly lit space had been filled: not just with stuff for sale, but with random bric-a-brac, old magazines and stacks of cardboard boxes that threatened to tumble on top of you if you strayed from the main aisle. Goods had been scattered seemingly at random around the store with zero sense of logic, which was fine if you were a Tansy Falls local and knew that bubble bath was located alongside the fishing tackle, but tourists either needed a lot of help to find what they needed or took one look inside and fled, terrified, to the halogen-lit safety of the big-name grocer down the road.

Now, though, Fiske's looked exactly like the charming little village store it had always been beneath the dust and clutter. The floorboards had been stripped and polished, the tattered and bowed shelving replaced and the pared-back selection of stock beautifully (and logically) arranged on new varnished wood shelves. Yet despite these changes, the unique charm of Fiske's had been preserved, the ancient over-the-door bell greeting her with its comforting jangle as Connie stepped inside. The smell was the same too: lavender, furniture polish and a touch of woodsmoke. And all this—the renovations and thoughtful modernization—was the work of the redhead standing behind the counter in a spruce-green Fiske's–branded apron.

"Connie!" she called. "I'm so glad you're here. Perhaps you can help settle a little dispute between me and Darlene."

This was Nell Swift, who had moved to Tansy Falls from London last year after falling in love with both the town and one of its most eligible bachelors, the handsome forester Jackson Quaid. Nell had stayed at the Covered Bridge Inn on her very first visit to the town, when she arrived here on a pilgrimage to scatter the ashes of her best friend, Megan, and Connie had since felt protective of her—maternal, almost—even though she was in her thirties. Nell bought the store from Darlene Fiske, in whose family it had been for generations, but although Darlene had now retired, she was still often found here, perched on a stool at the counter just as she was today, her long white hair, elegant bone structure and piles of necklaces giving her the look of a mystic supermodel pixie.

"Hey, Conn, you wanna coffee?" asked Darlene, already heading toward the old machine at the back of the store. It produced famously strong and arguably terrible coffee, but everyone agreed it would have been a step too far to replace it, so it had stayed. Connie, like many of the villagers, had grown to like the potent brew, and now found normal coffee too weak.

"Thanks, Darlene, a coffee would be welcome. So tell me, ladies, what's this dispute about?"

Darlene's voice boomed out over the clank and hiss of the coffee machine. "It ain't a dispute if one party is right and the other one doesn't know what the heck she's talking about!"

Nell rolled her eyes fondly. "I've been explaining to Darlene that we have a dish in England called Yorkshire pudding that we eat with roast beef, which is almost the exact same thing as the dish you guys call a Dutch baby pancake."

"Are you listening to this craziness, Conn?" hooted Darlene. "A Dutch baby served alongside meat? Syrup or sugar, sure, but *beef*? I know you Brits have some weird habits, but honestly..."

"I showed Darlene the entry about Yorkshire pudding on Wikipedia, but—"

"And tell me why should I believe anything they put up on there?" scoffed Darlene. "Anyone can put any old codswallop on the internet. Don't mean it's actual fact... Connie, you know about this sort of thing. Will you please tell Princess Nell here that a Dutch baby is not the same as this... this *meat dessert* she's goin' on about."

"Um, I can't be entirely sure, but I actually think Nell might be right."

Darlene stared at her for a long moment. "Nonsense," she snapped, then whipped back to Nell. "I tell you what, young lady, why don't you make this 'Yorkshire pudding' and I'll whip up a delicious, all-American Dutch baby and we'll compare just how alike they really are."

"You're on."

"Hmph." Darlene cracked a smile; despite their bickering, she loved Nell like a granddaughter. She had never had children of her own—and her only niece lived in Los Angeles—which is why she was so thrilled when Nell offered to take over the store.

Connie heaved a large bag onto the counter. "Nell, I've been having a clear-out of Ethan's old stuff and wondered if Joe might like any of these toys?"

Nell now lived with Jackson and his six-year-old son, Joe, in their house in the woods outside town.

"I'm sure he will, thank you! He's still obsessed with trains and cars—anything with wheels, really—so these will be perfect."

"How's Ethan getting on at school?" asked Darlene. "Such a sweet young man. I do miss him dropping by the store for a Coke and a chat. Always so well mannered."

"He's good, Darlene, thank you. He's just finished his freshman year and judging by his GPA he's on course for a place at Penn Law once he's finished the undergraduate degree."

"You and Nate must be proud! Is he coming back this summer?"

Connie shook her head. "Not this year. He's got a vacation job in Pennsylvania. But I'm sure he'll visit at some point."

"Well, be sure to ask him to stop by the store," said Darlene.

"I will do."

Nell put her hands on the bag of toys. "Are you sure you don't want to hang on to these for sentimental value?"

"I would love to, but we needed to clear some space in the basement. We had a lodger move in yesterday. To help out with the bills, you know..."

"Well, you've certainly got the space," said Darlene. "The Old

Cider Farmhouse is a heck of a lot of real estate for just you and Nate. Who's the lodger?"

"His name's James Ortiz. He's an interior designer working up at Maverick Lodge, but that's about all I know." It only now occurred to Connie that it would perhaps have been sensible to have asked for references. They were lucky it had worked out so well.

At the mention of Maverick Lodge, Darlene snorted. She had almost been swindled by the company behind it—DiSouza Developments—whose boss had tried to hoodwink her into selling her the store for far below market value last year, until Nell had exposed their dodgy dealings.

"Don't worry, Darlene," said Connie. "James seems like a nice guy."

"Oh sure, they all seem like nice guys until they try to bulldoze your life's work and turn it into a sushi restaurant."

"Well, I'm sure James will be in here before long, then you can check him out for yourself." Connie headed for the door. "I'll see you soon."

"Thank you again for the toys, Connie!" Nell called. "Joe will be thrilled."

As she closed the door behind her, Connie's phone started to vibrate. She checked the screen, but the caller's number didn't appear.

"Hello?"

"Good morning, Connie, it's Patrick speaking."

It was her sister Everly's personal assistant. "Oh, hey, Patrick. How are you?"

"I'm good, thank you. I have Everly for you if could please hold?"

"Sure."

The line went quiet, and not for the first time Connie wondered why Everly couldn't just dial the number herself, but then this was typical of her sister. From a very young age she'd had Connie running after her while their parents had been off attending a peace march or festival. *My capable Conifer* her mother had always called her, blind to the pressure she was heaping upon her daughter's small shoulders. Meanwhile, Everly had grown up with a hefty sense of entitlement, perfectly happy for someone else to take care of the dirty work. A perennial over-achiever, she had effortlessly won at every aspect of life: she had twin daughters, a wealthy husband and a high-flying job, plus she'd got the lion's share of their beautiful mother's genes. If things seemed to have come effortlessly to her, though, Connie could never resent her sister's success. She was as proud of her as if she were her own daughter, even though she was just a few years her senior.

A moment later, Everly came on the line. "Don't tell me, Kurt's planning on climbing Mount Everest."

"Good guess, but no."

"He's taken up skydiving?"

"I'm sure he's planning to, but it's not that. He's got himself a girlfriend."

"Oh, well, that's hardly a shock. To be honest I'm surprised it's taken him this long."

"She's thirty-nine, Ev."

There was a silence at the other end of the phone. Connie imagined her sister swiveling in her leather office chair, staring out across the Manhattan skyscrapers, one stiletto-clad foot folded over the other.

"I'd like to think you're joking, but knowing Kurt I assume you're not."

"I met her the other night. Her name's Skye. She's a shamanic healer."

"Jeez. Didn't Mom dabble in shamanism at some point?"

"Probably."

"Yeah, it was somewhere between the gong-bathing and her tarot phase, I think. Does this woman have any kids?"

"Not yet. But I think she's moving into the cabin. I get the impression it's serious."

There was another pause. "Right, I'm coming to Tansy Falls."

"Oh, there's no need for that. I just wanted to talk to you about it because I knew you'd feel the same as me. Nate can't seem to understand why I'm finding this so weird."

He'd had a terrible hangover the morning after their dinner at Kurt's, and Connie's initial reaction was that he fully deserved it—but then instantly felt bad for being petty. She hated what was happening to their relationship, how it was changing them both for the worse.

"Connie, I'm coming to Tansy Falls and that's final," said Everly. "I want to check out this child bride for myself. I'll have Patrick look at the schedule and then get back to you with a date."

"Perhaps we're overreacting. Maybe they really are in love?"

"She's younger than both of us, Conn! No, we definitely need to stage an intervention. Leave it with me. I'll be in touch."

ELEVEN

"So how's the new lodger working out?" asked Lana.

Connie glided through the water, keeping pace with her friend, both of them swimming what they called "old lady stroke," a modified crawl that enabled Lana to keep her sunhat, chandelier earrings and cat-eye sunglasses dry.

"Surprisingly well, actually." Connie came to a halt, treading water, and gazed below the surface of the crystal-clear waters. It looked so inviting down there.

"Hold on a sec," she said, then took a breath and dived beneath the surface, kicking down until she touched the rocky bottom of the swimming hole eight feet below. She hovered down there for a moment, enjoying the muffled silence, and when she surfaced again the hum of insects seemed as loud as rush hour traffic. Connie smoothed the droplets of water from her face, then rolled onto her back, closing her eyes against the sunlight with a sigh.

Whenever they could, Connie and Lana got together on summer Sunday mornings at Moonshine Hollow, a natural swimming hole a way upriver from the waterfall that gave the town of Tansy Falls its name. Locally, there were a couple of different stories behind the pool's poetic moniker. One was that the water was as clear and dazzling as moonshine, but Connie preferred the alternative explanation, which claimed that bootleggers used to manufacture their hooch in a nearby shack, the ruined foundations of which could still be found amid the birch trees near the swimming hole. Whether or not this was urban legend, she felt it suited the secret feel of the place, which could only be accessed via a half-hour scramble over rocks and through dense forest off the Wilderness Trail. Most people—certainly the tourists—stuck to the well-marked swimming hole at the foot of Smugglers Leap, but it got busier than the French Riviera during the summer months.

"It must be weird, though," said Lana, "sharing your home with a stranger."

"To be honest I've hardly seen him. He comes and goes through the doors to the basement. He leaves early and seems to eat at work, then when he gets home, he keeps to himself downstairs. And now he's gone back to his home in the city for the weekend. You'd barely know he was down there at all."

In fact, after his arrival last Monday, she and James had spoken the grand total of once. She'd been in the kitchen a couple of mornings ago, just after 6 a.m., pouring coffee into her travel mug, when she'd heard footsteps on the stairs and looked round to find his broad frame filling the doorway. After decades working in hospitality Connie had become an expert at noticing small details about people, and she had taken in his tailored suit and shoes and could tell at a glance they were expensive and beautifully made.

"Morning, landlady," he'd said, running a hand through his hair, which was still wet from the shower.

"Hey there, lodger! How's the accommodation working out for you?"

"Extremely comfortable, thank you. I have zero complaints."

"Just let me know if there's anything else you need."

"I will."

James had hesitated, as if intending to say something more, and when he hadn't Connie had gestured to the pot. "Coffee?"

"I'll get some up at the Lodge, thank you. Well, you have a great day, Connie. I'll see you soon."

Then he'd held up a hand in farewell before vanishing back downstairs, and she had remembered thinking how huge his hand was, like the paw of a bear.

"Is he hot?"

"Lana!" Connie splashed back onto her front, the sound of her laughter echoing around the rocky walls of the hollow. "You're terrible."

"Well, is he?"

"He's... interesting looking."

Lana raised an eyebrow. "Married?"

"As far as I know, although Nate seems to think they're separated. That reminds me, did he come over to see Tom on Monday afternoon? Nate, I mean."

"Maybe. He didn't mention it, but then Tom's communication skills are about as good as my golf swing. Shall I ask him?"

"No, don't worry." Connie had answered automatically, but Nate's mysterious whereabouts on the afternoon of James's arrival was still playing on her mind. "Actually, would you mind?"

"Of course not. Are you still worried about Nate?"

"A little, yes. I feel like I don't know who he is anymore, and it's making me question my trust in him. I'm worried I'm turning into this suspicious, bitter person."

"I've got two words for you, Conn: male menopause. I know it's not meant to be a thing, but believe me, it's *definitely* a thing. Nate's an idiot, he needs to appreciate what he's got before it's too late." She pushed out toward the bank, and called over her shoulder: "He probably needs to take HRT."

Connie laughed. "I think I need some of that too."

"Yeah, you do. *Husband* replacement therapy."

When they reached the banks they pulled themselves out of the water and climbed up onto a flat boulder at the top end of the pool where they lay in the sun to get dry, Lana looking camera-ready in a fifties-style lemon-print bikini, Connie in her functional black one-piece.

"I wish I had your body, Conn," said Lana. "You've got such

fabulous legs. Must be all that time you spend on your feet running around the inn."

Connie looked at her, surprised. When she looked in the mirror her eye always went straight to the bits of her she didn't like: the saggy knees or witchy hands. "You think so?"

"Uh-huh. No wonder my young friend Theo was so keen on you. He's been asking after you, but I've told him you're married and he needs to give it up."

Connie laughed, but the compliment made her feel good. It was nice to be told you were pretty, and she was a little ashamed to admit how much she missed the feeling of being admired, especially because at her age she was pretty sure she was well past her best-by date.

They didn't stay out on the rocks for long; it was desert-hot today, without even a whisper of a breeze, and it was a relief to get under the shade of the trees for their walk back to the Wilderness Trail. As their route was unmarked, they oriented themselves by signposts hidden in the landscape: a pillar-shaped rock, the gnarled tree trunk that Ethan used to pretend was a dinosaur when he was a kid, a gulch edged by plumes of ferns. In some parts they had to thrash through the undergrowth to keep to their path; it was hard going in the heat, but at least the canopy of leaves overhead provided some relief.

They weren't far off the main trail when Lana put her hand out to stop Connie.

"Look over there."

Following the direction of Lana's gaze, Connie saw a clearing through the trees, inside which was a group of people sitting in a circle. There were probably about a dozen of them; on closer inspection, Connie realized they were all women. They were watching one of their number who seemed to be performing a sort of ritual. She raised something to the sky, a curl of smoke emerging from her clasped hands.

"What do you think they're doing?" said Connie.

"Beats me. Human sacrifice?"

The group started passing whatever it was from one to another, accompanied by chanting, and a moment later Connie caught a waft of a familiar smell: incense. She peered a little closer and with a jolt realized that the ringleader was Skye.

"You'll never believe this, but that's Kurt's new girlfriend. The woman in the middle."

"Isn't she a bit young to be dating your dad?"

"Not just dating—she's moving in with him."

Lana turned to her, open-mouthed. "That *child* is going to be your stepmom?"

"Maybe. Oh, I don't know. But it is a little odd, right? She's ten years younger than I am." Connie watched as Skye started to wave her arms. "I phoned Everly to tell her about it and now she's threatening to come and stage some kind of intervention."

"Wow, little sis must be worried if she's deigning to leave Fifth Avenue."

"I really wish I hadn't said anything to her now."

In the days that had passed since dinner at Kurt's, Connie's shock about Skye's age had begun to fade and she'd come to the conclusion that the only thing that mattered was her father's happiness. Besides, Skye had seemed perfectly nice, and surely it was none of her (or Everly's) business if the pair of them moved in together. Unfortunately, though, Everly seemed to be on a mission: she had already messaged Connie on several occasions to get updates on the situation.

"Well, for what it's worth," said Lana, "I'd say it's pretty much certain she's after your dad's money. Don't get me wrong, Kurt *is* a stone-cold fox, but he's also extremely rich—and Carrie Krishna over there has got 'gold-digger' written all over her tie-dye kaftan."

Connie gave her a shove. "You're as bad as Everly." They watched the group for a moment. "Skye wants to go out for a coffee with me, to"—she made finger quotes—"'get to know me better.'"

"You should go, find out what she's up to."

"That's the thing. I don't think actually she's up to anything. You're right though, I *should* meet with her. I'm not sure how friendly I was to her at dinner the other night, and I've been feeling bad about it."

"Well, let's go and join in with Mom and her merry band of disciples now! I could do with getting my chakras rebalanced."

"Absolutely no way!"

"Gah, you're no fun anymore, Conifer," said Lana, hooking her arm around Connie's. "Come on then. If you're not up for meditation, I'm taking you for brunch."

TWELVE

The phone on her desk was already ringing when Connie arrived at work the next morning. She dashed in, nearly tripping over the sleeping Boomer, and made a grab for the receiver.

"The-Covered-Bridge-Inn-this-is-Connie-speaking." The words came out in a breathless rush.

"Who in heaven's name is Mimi's Dreamy Destinations and why are they getting an all-expenses-paid weekend at my inn?"

Connie sank into her chair, closing her eyes. It was Carole Gridley, Spencer's grandmother and effectively her boss (even if in name only), and it looked like she had finally gotten round to reading the list of invitees for the press trip.

"Good morning, Carole, I—"

"I thought you were inviting journalists from respectable publications." Connie heard a muffled voice in the background of the call—no doubt Carole's husband, Mitch. "Quite right," replied Carole tartly. "Mitch wants to know why we aren't having people from the *Washington Post* or *Reader's Digest*. Proper journalists, not this vulgar website person."

"Mimi's Dreamy Destinations is a very well-respected Instagram travel page. She has over 300,000 followers, so her reach is comparable to mainstream media, and in her letter of agreement she's contracted to do four permanent posts and ten stories on her page, so that will definitely—"

Carole cut her off to speak to Mitch again. "Connie says this Mimi character is popular on Instagram." There was an inaudible response. "Yes, like the Facebook, I think." Another pause, more muttering. "You could well be right, dear." Carole boomed back down the phone again. "Mitch is worried that this Instagram lady will attract the type of guest who gets drunk and uses profanity, and I have to say I share his concerns."

Connie rubbed her temples. With hindsight it had been a mistake to have sent them a link to her page, which had a profile photo of Mimi in a tiny bikini cuddling a Pomeranian, and a bio that read "Wanderlusty twenty-something travel babe." The media landscape had changed so much over the past few years that it was confusing enough for her, let alone the octogenarian Gridleys.

"Carole, I do understand your worries, but the list of invitees was put together with Nate's input and we only approached publications and accounts that we believed were an excellent match for the Covered Bridge brand."

"So Nate okayed all this?"

She sounded mollified; as Connie had hoped, the mention of her husband had worked wonders. Carole had always liked Nate and trusted his judgement because he had been editor of *Roam*, a well-known travel journal. But she didn't have a chance to take a breath, as Carole snapped: "Why isn't there a journalist coming from his magazine?"

"Well, Nate's not actually working at *Roam* anymore. He's gone freelance."

Carole's voice shot back up an octave. "Then how in blue blazes does he know the right people to invite on this darn press weekend of yours?"

"You're going to have to trust me, Carole. We're planning a really exciting weekend and I'm confident we're going to get lots of positive publicity for the inn. I know we've never done anything like this before, but Maverick Lodge will be opening their bookings soon and it's important we step up our promotion so we don't get forgotten. Our new events manager, Isabelle Bennett, will have joined us by then, and she's had a huge amount of experience working on similar projects."

"Well, I hope you know what you're doing, Connie... Now, while I've got you, I wanted to double-check whether Piper is still using my family recipe for the banana muffins?"

"Yes, of course." Connie thought it better not to mention that Piper had improved the original recipe by adding cardamon and chia seeds.

"Good, because as I told Piper, people come to the inn purely for those muffins. Right, can you put Spencer on now?"

"I'm afraid he's not here at the moment."

"Well, can you please tell him to return my call? We need to discuss this year's Halloween menu and he's ignoring me."

"I'm sure he's intending to call you back. It's just we're at full capacity right now and he's been preparing for the baby's arrival so he's been busy with..."

"We're *all* busy, Connie dear." Carole gave a huff of impatience. "Anyway, I can't stay chatting all day, I've got aqua-Pilates in ten minutes and I need to dig out my noodle."

And with that she ended the call.

With Carole's phone call having piled on the pressure, Connie spent the rest of the morning working on the itinerary for the press trip. It was proving to be a full-time job—on top of her already full-time job, managing the inn—and she was having to delegate many of her usual tasks to any staff member she could grab. There had already been an awkward moment when Connie had asked Pam, the head housekeeper, to briefly cover reception, and Pam had made an error on a guest's bill and ended up charging them $42.50 for a two-night stay instead of $425. At least Isabelle Bennett would be starting soon; it was the only thing stopping Connie from giving in to full-blown hysteria.

It was midday before she finally managed to get away from her desk, just as Piper and Spencer arrived back from their routine prenatal check.

"All okay with Junior?" asked Connie.

"Piper needs to rest more," said Spencer, steering his wife toward the couch.

"The doctor didn't say that," said Piper.

"He said you need as little stress as possible because your blood pressure is high."

"A *little* high." Piper sighed as Spencer plumped the couch cushions behind her. "Connie, the baby is absolutely fine, thank you—as am I. And Spencer, I love you but you need to chill out. Women have been having babies forever. It's what our bodies are designed to do. And this is our busy season at the inn. I can't just spend the next few weeks lying on the couch while you feed me grapes."

Connie smiled at the tenderness between the two of them. It brought back a flood of memories of when she had been pregnant with Ethan, and the way Nate had doted on her too. That had been such a blissful time: just the two of them locked in a bubble of happiness and wonder at this tiny being kicking inside her, their love for each other intensified by the love they felt for their unborn child. Mother Nature was so clever: it was as if she was shoring up the foundations, making sure their relationship was as strong as it could be to help them weather the storms of early parenthood. Piper and Spencer had no way of understanding how much their lives—and more to the point, they themselves—were about to be transformed. It was a special time, those weeks before your first baby arrived, and Connie felt a pang of envy that she'd never get to experience those heady emotions again.

"I'm so pleased that everything is okay," she told Piper. "But while I have no doubt you could go on working just as hard as usual until your water breaks, we've got everything under control here and the most important thing you can do now is look after yourself. Do you hear me, Miss Piper?"

"Okay, Mom."

"Good—and don't you forget it. Now, if you guys can cope here, I'm just going to head out for an hour or so. I've got to stop by Tansy Falls Fine Cheeses."

Vermont was famous for its gourmet cheesemaking, and this was the best place in town to sample the produce of the local dairies. It was run lovingly (some would say obsessively) by a tall, Q-tip-skinny man named Edwin Catesby who had hair the color of aged cheddar and ears so prominent it looked as if he were trying to pick up a signal from passing satellites.

"We're still taking the journalists there for a cheese tasting, right?" asked Spencer.

"Yup, Edwin knows all about it, but he's getting his apron strings in a twist about the details, so I need to go calm him down. You know what a perfectionist he is. Can I get you anything while I'm there?"

"I would kill for a large slice of raw-milk Camembert," said Piper.

"Sorry, honey." Connie well remembered those pregnancy cravings all too well. For her, for some crazy reason, it had been oysters; it wasn't even as if she liked them that much. "I tell you what, after you've given birth, I'll treat you to a selection of the stinkiest, runniest, most disease-ridden cheeses Edwin can find. Okay?"

"Mmm. With a bottle of red wine?"

"Done," she said, heading for the door, then paused. "Oh, Spencer, your grandma called. She's extremely keen for you to phone her back."

He looked up at the ceiling and exhaling heavily. Connie understood exactly how he felt: Carole was hard work, and the poor guy had too much on his plate at the moment.

"Thanks, Connie, I appreciate the nudge. I'll call her now."

THIRTEEN

Tansy Falls Fine Cheeses was located on the mountain road, a little way past Lana's gallery, at the point where the asphalt began to curve upward into the foothills of Mount Maverick. From the outside the store looked just like one of the state's famous red barns, but inside it was fitted out like a chic city deli with prices to match. Edwin had moved from Boston to Tansy Falls a decade ago to set up his store, but he was still considered a newcomer—a "flat-lander," as out-of-towners were known. You had to be at least third generation to be considered a local in these parts.

Nearly all the spaces in the parking lot were occupied, as were most of the café-style tables packed in the decked dining area at the side of the store. Connie was pleased to see that business was booming. Edwin worked hard, he deserved the success. As she walked into the flagstone-floored interior her skin prickled into goosebumps at the sudden drop in temperature. She remembered bringing Ethan here when he was little and how his face always scrunched up at the sharp, damp whiff of cheese. "Yuck, Mom!" he would say, his hand flying to his nose. Connie's heart lit up at the thought of her son, followed by the ache of missing him.

The store was busy with shoppers browsing the aisles, mostly well-heeled tourists (locals tended to buy cheese direct from the dairies at half the price), and it took Connie a moment to locate Edwin, but she eventually spotted a telltale shock of orange hair behind the sandwich counter, where he appeared in deep conversation with a customer. Not wanting to disturb, she made the most of a rare moment of free time to explore a display of European rosé wines, marveling at the colors that ranged from flamingo to the merest whisper of pink, and it wasn't until she glanced back to see if Edwin was free that she realized that the customer he was speaking to was none other than James Ortiz.

Actually, it wasn't so strange James was here, Connie supposed, as this was one of the nearest places to the mountain to get lunch, and her surprise gave way to an unexpected jolt of pleasure at seeing him. She stayed where she was for a moment, taking the opportunity to study her lodger from behind a pyramid of gourmet cracker boxes.

For all the expensive clothes and sharp grooming, James wasn't at all how Connie would have imagined an interior designer from Manhattan to look. In fact, as she watched him in conversation with Edwin, it occurred to her that what he reminded her of most was a boxer. It wasn't just his broken nose and heavy-set build, but the way he carried himself, like a fizzing ball of energy. There was an unpredictability about him: standing in front of him, you'd have no idea whether he was going to kiss you or punch you.

Edwin loved nothing better than sharing his knowledge of cheese with a captive audience, and it quickly became obvious that James had been taken hostage.

"Now this one," he was saying, handing over a sliver of cheese, "is from a little dairy in Thompsonville, just up the road. I'd describe it as quite a throaty goat."

James tried it—then pressed the back of his hand to his mouth. "Wow. Yes, that is certainly"—he coughed—"bold."

Edwin was already lining up the next sample, holding it out on his mother-of-pearl-handled sampling knife. "And this is one of my favorites, a raw sheep's Manchego. A little shy on the palate perhaps, but with a wonderfully well-articulated finish. Notes of honeycomb, nettle and barnyard."

At that moment, Edwin spotted her hovering nearby. "I'll just be a couple of moments, Connie," he called.

At the mention of her name, James swung round. "Connie! This is a nice surprise."

"Hi," she said, walking over. "Are you here for lunch?"

"I am. I was just getting some expert advice on what to order."

Edwin beamed. "Always a pleasure to share my passion with a fellow enthusiast. Oh, I've just taken delivery of the most sublime Gouda. Aged for five years! Back in two ticks..." And he disappeared out the door behind the counter.

After he'd gone, James dropped his voice. "I only came in to get a sandwich, but I made the mistake of asking what he would recommend and since then I've been stuck in this... this infinite cheese loop. I like cheese as much as the next guy, but I get the impression your cheesemonger buddy is testing my manliness with the most extreme cheeses he can find. It's like Russian roulette, but with Brie instead of bullets."

Connie laughed. "Edwin means well, but he can be a little overenthusiastic."

At that moment the store owner reappeared, bearing a large wheel of cheese.

"Don't worry, leave this to me..." Connie beamed at Edwin. "Why don't you make James your incredible Tansy Falls cheddar with fig jam on sourdough? In fact, am I right in thinking it won quite a prestigious award?"

"It did indeed! It was first runner-up in the sandwich class of last year's Vermont Foodie Awards."

"Well, in that case I will definitely take one," said James. "In fact, make that two—that is, Connie, if you'd like to join me for lunch?"

Her first instinct was polite refusal, but then her stomach reminded her that she hadn't even had breakfast yet.

"Thank you, I'd like that. Edwin, can we catch up about the press trip after my sandwich?"

"Absolutely. Take a seat outside and I'll bring your food out momentarily."

The only seats available were at a tiny bistro-style table right at the edge of the deck. It had clearly been ignored by the rest of the store's patrons as there was barely room for a small child to sit there, let alone two fully grown adults, one of whom was built like a Hummer. Connie skirted her way awkwardly around the tiny table, apologizing to the person sitting directly behind as she slammed her chair straight into theirs, and when she finally managed to sit her legs pressed up against James's.

"Sorry, it's a little cozy," she said, pulling away.

James turned to the table next to them. "Guys, would you mind moving your table a few inches back that way? We're kinda cramped here."

He had the kind of laidback charm that instantly made people warm to him, and sure enough their neighbors were happy to oblige.

"Is that better?"

"It is, thank you."

James smiled, then took a breath and let it out in a happy *whoosh*, closing his eyes and tipping his face up toward the sun, and his ease made Connie start to relax too. It was so rare for her to grab some time off during the day that she felt like she was playing truant from school. She gazed up at Mount Maverick. You wouldn't have a clue that a huge hotel was lurking in the woods nearby. The only hint it was there was the occasional construction truck thundering past on the mountain road.

"How's it going up at the mountain?" she asked James.

"Well, I've never given birth, but I imagine the experience to be somewhat similar."

"Tears, nausea and agony? Extreme terror interspersed with hysterical euphoria?"

"Yeah, that's about the size of it. Have you had much to do with DiSouza Developments, the company behind the resort?"

"A little. The woman in charge, Liza DiSouza, hasn't made many friends around here. Let's just say she's not conducted her business with a great deal of integrity."

She was thinking specifically about the drama over Fiske's General Store, but there had been many other incidents too, which had made it clear that Liza DiSouza's one and only concern was her business's bottom line. Despite her promises, the issue of preserving the town's character wasn't even on her radar. She had certainly made a sworn enemy of Nell, the new owner of Fiske's, who was the loveliest, most easygoing person Connie had ever met.

"It's not the most enjoyable project I've been involved with, that's for sure," said James. "It's a stunning development, but it doesn't feel like it's got anything to do with Tansy Falls and its surroundings. It would be more at home in Vegas or Dubai."

Just then the sandwiches arrived, and they tucked in.

"Mmm, this is excellent," said James. "Good choice, thank you."

They ate in silence for a little while; Connie hadn't realized just how hungry she was.

"I've got a favor to ask to you," said James.

"Shoot."

"Would you mind if I stayed at the house on Friday night this week?"

"No problem. Are you needed up at the resort on Saturday?"

"No—quite the opposite actually. I so enjoyed sketching the scenery at your house the other day, I thought I'd check out the local sights. Go for a hike, maybe take my sketchpad with me."

"Where are you thinking of going?"

"Well, that was part two of the favor. You must know this place as well as anyone, so could you give some suggestions?"

"Of course. I can give you a whole list of places with stunning views. It's something we're not short of round here."

James looked at her, his head to one side. 'Would you...?'

"Would I what?"

He held her gaze, as if weighing something in his mind, then shook his head, smiling. "It doesn't matter."

The atmosphere at the table was very different that evening when Connie sat down to eat with Nate. She had cooked dinner as usual, heading straight to the kitchen to get started on a lasagna after getting home from work, and not for the first time Connie had found herself wondering why she was the one making their dinner when Nate had been home all day. There was no point in making a fuss, though. It would just make the atmosphere between them more tense than it was already, and Capable Conifer could certainly handle it.

"This is delicious," said Nate.

Connie just nodded, mechanically dipping her fork to her plate. She took a sideways glance at him. He looked, she thought, like a surfer: his face golden-brown and his hair bleached by the sun. It suited him not being in an office, working outside with Frank. He looked as handsome as ever, but the surge of longing she felt for him—the physical ache of missing her husband and best friend—was swept aside by the memory of the conversation she'd had with Lana earlier that evening. Her friend had finally got back to her about whether Nate had come over to speak to Tom on the day of James's arrival, and while she confirmed that he had, he'd only stayed long enough to pick up the wrench. None of which explained where he'd been for the rest of the afternoon, nor why he'd been so dressed up.

"I spoke to Ethan earlier," said Nate, breaking the silence.

"How is he?"

"Fine. Really good."

"I miss him so much."

"Me too." Nate stared at his plate. "It's not the same without him round here."

Just then they heard the sound of a car pulling up on the driveway, shortly followed by the sound of the French doors to the basement closing. Their lodger arriving home.

"By the way, James asked if he could stay an extra night this week," said Connie.

"Fine by me."

She paused. "What do you think of him?"

"He isn't at all what I was expecting. When we first talked about getting a lodger, I imagined we'd get a student, not some glamorous New York designer. From what he's said to me, he's not even that busy up at the lodge. I mean, does he really need to be up here all week?"

"Well, I'm glad we found him. He's responsible, he keeps the room neat, he's very low-maintenance—I don't think we could have asked for a better lodger."

The phone on the kitchen wall started to ring.

"I'll get it," said Nate, getting up from the table with surprising swiftness, but Connie was sitting closer and reached out to grab it.

"Hello?"

She got the feeling there was somebody at the other end, but then the line went dead. She frowned and replaced the handset.

"Who was that?" asked Nate.

"I don't know. I think whoever it was put the phone down."

"Must have been a wrong number," he said, getting back to his food.

Sometime later that night, Connie woke with a start. She must have been asleep for only an hour or so because Nate still wasn't in bed, although these days that wasn't unusual—their schedules were as out of sync as their emotions. It took her a moment to realize what had disturbed her: it was the sound of raised voices downstairs. She lay still and listened, trying to work out where the noise was coming from. The basement perhaps? But it had now gone quiet, and Connie let herself drift back to sleep. It must have been the TV.

FOURTEEN

"There's a toad in the swimming pool!"

A woman in a hotel robe had come tearing into the lobby, her shrieks so piercing that even Boomer stirred from his nap—and this was a dog that routinely slept through the fire drill. Connie, who was checking in some new guests, piled on the apologies and phoned the number for the maintenance team. Nobody picked up.

Robe woman was still standing next to the desk, glaring at Connie while she waited on the line.

"You do know how unsanitary it is to have an animal in the pool?" she said. "It could be diseased. Toads carry syphilis, you know."

She announced this to the entire lobby with admirable self-confidence.

Connie muttered more apologies and tried phoning the kitchen instead. To her relief, Piper was there and happy to take over at check-in while she dealt with the toad.

Out at the pool, a clutch of people was gathered at the shallow end, pointing and swapping advice. Connie immediately saw that it wasn't in fact a toad, but a tiny, jewel-like frog.

"You should use a net," a man stated.

A net would be the worst thing to use, as the frog's legs could get tangled, but Connie thanked him for his advice and, grabbing a bucket, scooped the poor creature out. With calm restored around the pool—apart from robe woman telling anyone who would listen that the pool should now be drained *in case of syphilis*—Connie took the frog to the walled garden, where she rinsed it in fresh water and then plopped it into the ornamental pond. She really needed to talk to the maintenance guys about building a critter-proof fence around the pool area—that is, if they'd ever pick up their darn phone.

When she got back to the lobby Piper was still at the reception desk, but the guests had now gone. Instead, sitting in their place, Connie was surprised to see Skye. She was wearing a white dress that looked like a nightgown from the pages of *Little House on the Prairie.*

"Ah, here she is, our fairy frog-mother," said Piper, with a lift of her brow. Connie had told her all about Kurt's new girlfriend, but judging by Piper's expression she was still taken aback by how young Skye was.

"Skye! This is a surprise." Connie glanced around the lobby. "Is Kurt with you?"

"Nope, just me. I was hoping you might have time for that coffee we talked about last week?"

"Oh! Thank you, that's kind, but I'm not sure if I can get away right now."

"As indispensable as you most certainly are," said Piper, "I don't think the Covered Bridge Inn will go into receivership in the time it takes you to drink a flat white."

"Promise you won't go into labor?"

"I will keep my cervix firmly closed."

"Okay." She turned to Skye. "Looks like I'm all yours. Shall we go to Mistyflip Coffee? It's just around the corner."

"Sure, lead the way."

As Skye stood aside to let her go first out the door, Connie caught a waft of her patchouli-heavy perfume, a scent so familiar from her parents' hippie phase that it instantly whisked her back to a moment from her childhood. Bright sunshine, the damp coolness of long grass, a soft breeze: she was snuggled in her mother's arms, blissfully content. But then she became aware of other adults' voices and suddenly she felt cold. Her mom had gone and with it her happiness, in its place the all-too-familiar chafe of worry at being alone, and being responsible for herself and her sister. As a mom herself now, Connie's heart ached for that little girl who'd had to grow up so fast.

"I wanted to apologize if I was less than welcoming the other night," said Connie, as they walked alongside each other. "My relationship with Kurt is, well, complicated. And I admit you weren't at all what I was expecting."

"Please, Connie, there's absolutely no need. I was well aware how strange it must have been for you. And I felt like Kurt wasn't as sensitive as he could have been to the fact that I—"

They were interrupted by someone shouting Connie's name. Darlene was on the other side of the street, waving at them. "Connie, a word!"

The old woman hurried across the road, forcing an approaching bike to swerve.

"Watch where you're going!" she snapped at the cyclist, who was wobbling away, struggling to stay upright.

"Morning, Darlene," said Connie. "What's up?"

"You won't believe this, but that Yorkshire pudding Nell was talking about is almost *exactly the same* as a Dutch baby! And don't tell Nell I said this, but it was actually very tasty with beef. Turns out those Brits aren't so crazy after all..." She glanced at Skye, frowning. "This a friend of yours, Conn?"

"Sorry, yes, this is Skye Peters. And Skye, I'd like you to meet Darlene Fiske, local legend and unofficial mayor of Tansy Falls."

Darlene snorted. "I'd make a better job of it than the official one, that's for darn sure. You staying at the Covered Bridge, Skye?"

"No, I recently moved to town."

"Skye is, um, dating my dad."

Darlene looked as if she'd been slapped. "You do know Kurt

Wilson's knockin' seventy? I don't mean to be rude, but you're swimmin' in my pond, honey."

Skye laughed. "I appreciate that people will notice the age gap, but somehow it just works."

"Well, good luck to you," she muttered. "Honestly, Conn, the day your father finally grows up will be the day the devil ice-skates to work."

Connie and Skye took a table on the sidewalk outside Mistyflip, a snowboarders' hangout during the winter season that served excellent coffee all year round.

"Were you up in the woods near the waterfall last weekend?" asked Skye, after they had got their coffee. "I was leading a healing circle and I thought I saw you through the trees."

"Oh! Um, yes, I was there. I'd just been swimming with my friend Lana."

"You would have both been very welcome to have joined our circle."

"That's kind, but we were going for brunch, and—well—it's not exactly my thing. I don't think I inherited Kurt's hippie gene."

"I understand. It's not for everyone."

Skye flashed her a quick smile, then took a sip of her drink. Connie got the impression she was nervous, and softened a little more toward her.

"So, Dad tells me you're hoping to open a healing practice here in Tansy Falls?"

"That's the idea, yes. I'm looking for a premises at the moment." Skye paused, then put down her cup. "Connie, can I speak plainly?"

"Of course."

"Okay. I wanted to say that I understand if you're uncomfortable about me being with your father."

"I was a little at first," she admitted. "The age gap, you know?"

Skye nodded. "You must have wondered about my intentions,

but the truth is Kurt and I just clicked. It's like we're... twin souls. He's a very special man."

"That he is," agreed Connie.

"And he really doesn't seem his age."

"Also true."

"I get the impression he's been a far from a conventional father figure, though. I imagine that must have been tough."

"At times. But he was the most devoted and loving husband to my mom. And I can see how much he cares for you."

Skye's cheeks dimpled. "Obviously things have moved pretty fast, but I have no end game, Connie, I assure you. I'm just enjoying the time Kurt and I spend together. And I'd really like to spend more time with you too. Friends?"

"I'd like that," said Connie with a smile—and she meant it.

As she walked back to the Covered Bridge, Connie typed out a message to Everly.

Hey, sis, just to let you know, I met Skye for a coffee just now. She's genuinely sweet and will be good news for Dad. No need to come to Tansy Falls. All under control.

FIFTEEN

"Yup, it's definitely a giant hogweed."

Connie was standing in the woodland bordering their yard with the local forester, Jackson Quaid, glaring at an evil-looking monster of a plant. Admittedly Connie didn't go into the woods that often, but it seemed as if this thing—at least twice her height and giving off seriously moody Star Trek vibes—had appeared overnight. With its thick, bristled stems covered with purple splotches, spiky leaves and umbrella-shaped clusters of white flowers, you could almost believe that aliens had dropped it off by spaceship.

Frank had been the one who had first identified the intruder. When Connie had taken her neighbor to see it, curious if he might know what it was, he had taken a sharp intake of breath and physically pulled her away, as if the plant could lunge and attack at any moment.

"We better call Jackson Quaid," he'd said, his voice dark. "If it's what I think it is, this thing is as mean as a scalded bandicoot."

Sure enough, Jackson confirmed that the giant hogweed was highly toxic; just touching the sap could cause painful skin blisters, third-degree burns, even blindness. Connie was just relieved that she hadn't got round to cutting some of the striking-looking flowers to put in the kitchen, as she'd planned.

"It's a good job you called me," said Jackson. "This is going to need careful removal."

"I know it's not really your area of expertise, but can you recommend somebody who might be able to help?"

"Of course. There's a couple of specialists I can put you in touch with."

Connie stared at the plant. "How on earth did it *get* here?"

"The usual way—wind, animals. It grows fast and produces a much higher than average amount of seeds, so they'll have to clear the whole area."

More expense that they would struggle to afford. "Thanks, Jackson," said Connie. "I appreciate the advice."

They walked back across the grass toward the house, where Jackson had left his truck. The forester had only moved to Tansy Falls a few years ago, but he had quickly become popular with the locals, especially among the town's female population, who appreciated the single father's brooding good looks as much as his professionalism—although he was now happily settled with Nell.

"Thanks for sending Ethan's old toys over for Joe," said Jackson. "He's obsessed with that fire truck with the flashing lights—takes it everywhere with him."

"Gosh, it feels like yesterday that Ethan was carrying that truck around! Time plays tricks on you when you're a parent."

"Sure does. I'm still trying to work out how my baby will be going into first grade in September." Jackson's face softened into a smile. "You gotta cherish every moment, right?"

"Absolutely." She beamed at him. Joe was a sweet kid; Jackson had done a great job of raising him.

They had now reached Jackson's truck.

"Connie, I've got some news. I'm going to ask Nell to marry me."

"That's wonderful!"

"I'd like to propose over dinner at the Covered Bridge. It's where she stayed on her first visit here, and she's so fond of you and Piper."

"We would love that. When are you planning on doing it?"

"The weekend after next, if that works for you guys."

The weekend of the press trip! Connie tensed up at the thought of it, but then forced herself to relax. Everything was under control, and Isabelle would soon be there to help out.

"I'll make sure you have our best table," she told Jackson. "Just let me know what we can do to make the evening as special as it can be. Oh, I'm so thrilled for you both! This is just the best news."

"Let's just hope she says yes."

"Seriously? That's something you're even worrying about?"

They both laughed.

"Thanks, Connie," said Jackson, climbing into the truck. "I'll be in touch about your poisonous pal in the woods back there."

After she had waved him off, Connie sunk into one of the Adirondack chairs on the deck. She was still wearing the old T-shirt and shorts she'd put on first thing that morning, intending to fit in a workout before having a shower, but it was now early afternoon and she was as yet unexercised and unwashed. She hadn't slept well last night, having been disturbed when Nate came to bed (they seemed to keep very different hours these days) and then again around 2 a.m., when a noise woke her up. She wasn't sure what it had been—a door slamming perhaps? Then again, the tiniest thing seemed to disturb her these days. She was like the princess and the pea.

Struck by a wave of weariness, she relaxed against the headrest and her eyes drifted shut...

"Connie?"

She opened her eyes to find James standing over her. He was wearing technical gear and had a backpack over his shoulder. Even his hiking gear looked designer. "Were you asleep?"

"I think I must have been." She rubbed her face, sitting up. "How was your hike?"

"I only managed to get lost twice, so I'd say it was a great success. Would you mind?"

He gestured to the chair next to her.

"Not at all. I clearly need help staying awake." She scraped her hair behind her ears, conscious of what a mess she must look.

James pulled his backpack onto his lap and retrieved two bottles of beer, holding one out to Connie.

She laughed. "Do you always carry alcohol around with you? You're like a one-man mobile bar."

"I stopped by the Wild Moose microbrewery on the way back, thought I'd try out your local craft beers."

Connie took a sip. It was somehow still ice-cold (perhaps James kept a cooler in his bag too?) and she let out a long *aaaah* of happiness, stretching out her legs in front of her. James told her about his hike, making her laugh with descriptions of the different people he'd passed on the trail and asking questions about local landmarks, and Connie reveled in the unusual sensation of having nowhere she needed to be and nothing she needed to be doing.

As they talked, she stole glances at James from behind her sunglasses. When Lana had asked her last weekend if her new lodger was hot, Connie had been confused how to answer. After all, with his heavy brow and wide mouth—plus that crooked nose— James wasn't exactly conventionally attractive. Not like Nate, who most people would agree was a handsome man. Yet looking at James now, it occurred to Connie that his face was a bit like a vintage wine, or one of the works of modern art in Lana's gallery. You had to work harder to appreciate it, but your effort would be amply rewarded.

Their conversation lapsed into an easy silence. Across the field Connie caught sight of Frank out in his paddock. From this distance, it looked a lot like he was trying to put a small saddle on a very large pig.

James had noticed this too. "What's up with your neighbor and all his animals? I can't work out if that place is a rescue shelter, a farm or a circus."

"Pretty much a combination of all three. Frank's a character, that's for sure, but I couldn't ask for a better neighbor. Just this week, for instance, he saved me from a killer plant."

James looked at her quizzically.

"Long story. Just don't go poking around the woods for the next week or so."

"Got it. Where's Nate today?"

"Golf. He always plays on a Saturday. It's his thing."

Connie cursed the edge she could hear in her voice and hoped James hadn't noticed.

"He seems to leave you on your own quite a lot."

"Excuse me?"

"I'm sorry, it's none of my business. I just—recognize some of the signs."

Connie shifted in her seat, nervous about where this was headed. "What signs?'

"Me and my wife, Jessica, we're separated. Getting divorced, actually. But it was a long time coming. We were growing apart for years, but we didn't do anything about it until one day we woke up and then—*bam!*—we were strangers. And by then it was too late to fix it. Our daughters had gone to college, and we couldn't remember who we were before we'd become parents." He exhaled heavily. "Irreconcilable differences, the lawyers called it."

"I hope you don't mind me asking, but did anything particular happen to make you decide to separate?"

"Nope. Exemplary spousal behavior on both sides. Isn't it crazy how you can love someone so deeply you would kill for them, yet even a love that intense can just—fade away." He shook his head, then turned to her with a grin. "Sorry, this is getting way too heavy, must be all this mountain air. How long have you and Nate been married?"

"Twenty-two years. Actually, it's our anniversary this week."

"Well, I hope he treats you as wonderfully as you deserve, Connie."

Connie was starting to feel the effects of the alcohol, which perhaps explains why she said what she said next.

"I feel like Nate and I might be reaching a similar place. To you and your wife, I mean. We've lost that closeness we used to have."

"I did get that impression. I'm sorry. Do you think it's over?"

She paused, wondering how to answer. She didn't want to put her fears into words, because that would make it more real, but at the same time it was a relief to speak to someone neutral about her worries.

"I don't know. I appreciate that you need to work at a marriage to make it a success, but it feels like we've got nothing left to work *on*. I just don't know what's happened to us."

Then to her horror, Connie started to cry.

"Hey, it's okay." James shuffled his chair toward her and put his arm around her back. "I understand. It's tough."

Connie was close enough to feel the warmth of his body and smell the muskiness of his skin. Muttering apologies for the tears, she glanced up to discover that he was already looking at her. Rather than their usual humor, though, his eyes burned with a strange intensity. Unnerved, she pulled away.

"Daytime drinking really doesn't agree with me," she said lightly, wiping her eyes. "I blame you and your backpack bar. I better get on—thank you for the beer and the pep talk."

James shook his head. "I gotta say, Connie, you're the best darn landlady I've ever had."

She laughed. "Aren't I the only one you've ever had?"

"Yes, you are. The one and only." James drained his bottle. "I should be getting back to the city, but I'm thinking of doing this again next Saturday. If you don't have plans, would you like to join me?"

"Oh, I..." She trailed off, unsure how to answer. Whatever had happened between them a moment ago had left her rattled.

"Just to clarify, I'm talking about a hike, not the daytime drinking."

He chuckled, and Connie was pleased to see his usual light-heartedness restored. She had probably been reading far too much into what had been a moment of kindness in response to her tears.

"It would be more fun with you there. Probably not so much getting lost, but much more fun."

"Sure. I'd like that," she said.

After all, what harm could it do? She liked James's company. She had always enjoyed hiking. And, though she hated to admit it, she really liked the feeling of someone noticing her again.

SIXTEEN

The following Monday, while Connie was in the kitchen before work, James came up from the basement to see her.

"Oh—hey," she said, surprised to find him awake at this hour; she had got up thirty minutes earlier today to get a start on her emails while the inn's guests were still in bed. "Everything okay down there?"

"I heard you moving around and thought I'd get out of bed and wish you a happy Monday."

Judging by his worn gray T-shirt and disheveled hair, James had literally just got out of bed. He yawned and stretched, his shirt riding up to explode a strip of tanned stomach. Connie looked away, busying herself with the coffee machine. "Can I get you one?" she asked.

"Sure, why not. Thanks."

She heard him pull back a chair at the kitchen table.

"What's that bird I can hear?" asked James, after a moment.

Connie had propped open the front door to enjoy the fresh morning air before the mugginess set in, and the accompanying birdsong was her favorite morning soundtrack.

"The loud one that sounds like it's playing a flute? It's a wood thrush. They're known as swamp angels because they sing so beautifully."

"Swamp angels! How d'you learn this cool stuff, Connie?"

"I grew up here. Country kid."

James nodded. "I guess that's why I can tell the difference between the sound of an Oldsmobile Cutlass and a Chevrolet Cavalier." He grinned. "City kid."

Connie laughed, any lingering self-consciousness fading away. While she finished making her coffee, he quizzed her about what her week had in store. It felt good to be checking in with someone before getting started on her day, just as she used to with Nate before he lost his job, and that morning Connie left for the inn with a spring in her step.

The same thing happened when she was making her coffee on Tuesday morning—although this time James was dressed and ready for work—and again on Wednesday.

On Thursday morning, rather than falling out of the shower and scribbling on her face with whatever makeup she had on hand, Connie found herself making a little more of an effort, styling her hair and taking time over her mascara and blush. When she got downstairs, though, James wasn't around, and he hadn't appeared by the time she left the house. Swatting away the disappointment that buzzed around her like a mosquito, she walked out to the car, and as she got closer she noticed something tucked under the windshield wipers. It was a bunch of meadowsweet, together with a note written in a looping, artistic hand. "Sorry to miss you, Connie, early start for me up at the mountain this morning. Have a wonderful day."

She held the flowers up to her nose, breathing in the scent, the image of James stumbling around the meadow at dawn to pick flowers bringing a smile to her face. Thank goodness he hadn't come across the giant hogweed and tried to make a posy out of that.

. . .

It was now only ten days until the press trip and the inn was booked to capacity. Nevertheless Connie was feeling more relaxed than she had in weeks. Perhaps it was the knowledge that Isabelle Bennett's first day was fast approaching, but even when she received an email from Mimi of Mimi's Dreamy Destinations informing her that she was now vegan and asking that her dietary preferences be updated accordingly, Connie didn't break a sweat. The cheese tasting would be challenging in light of this new information, true, but she was sure she would sort something out; she always did. Connie's Zen mindset must have been outwardly visible too, because when she went to meet Lana after work, her friend took one look at her and asked, "What's got you in such a sunny mood?"

"What do you mean?"

"You look all sparkly. Like you're nine years old, it's Christmas Eve and you've just found a stash of sugar cookies."

They were walking along Main Street, checking out the stalls for the annual Tansy Falls Foodie Festival that was happening that week.

"I guess I just had a good day at work."

Lana studied her for a moment, narrowing her eyes. "Uh-huh."

The sidewalks were gridlocked with tourists moving at an ice-cream-eating pace, and Lana and Connie let themselves be swept along by the crowd, enjoying the carnival atmosphere and the scent of barbecued ribs and hot candied nuts, while the Tansy Falls High School marching band belted out Ariana Grande hits. The local food producers had put on a particularly fine show this year, and Connie was proud to see so many visitors in their town.

They came to a stall displaying pots of cream and milk, under a sign featuring a dancing cow with curly red script reading HOFFMAN CREAMERY, which was manned by Santa Claus's slightly slimmer brother and a young woman whose freckled cheeks and overalls attested to a life spent working outside.

This was Dewitt Hoffman, a third-generation dairy farmer in Tansy Falls, and his daughter-in-law Mallory.

"Ladies!" Dewitt beamed, beckoning them over. "Wonderful to see you both."

"Hey, guys," said Connie. "The stall's looking great this year. Is that a new sign?"

Mallory nodded. "There are so many new suppliers here this year we needed to do whatever we could to stand out." She held out some a couple of paper cups. "Try some yogurt. It's from our new line."

Like many of the small dairy farmers in the area, the Hoffmans were always searching for ways to diversify and compete against the bigger operations.

"Gosh, that's delicious," said Connie.

"What flavor is it?" asked Lana, licking the spoon.

"Date and maple. I was going to check if Piper wanted some for the inn."

"I'm sure she would," said Connie. "I'll take some for me and Nate too. How's business been today?"

"Not bad, although it's a shame that we've been put next to these guys."

Mallory nodded at the next-door stall, around which the biggest crowd they'd seen all afternoon was gathered. Connie looked at the sign and it all made sense: MAVERICK HANDMADE CHOCOLATES.

"They're giving away so many samples I'm surprised they've got anything left to sell," said Mallory.

Dewitt stared forlornly at the chocolate stall. "If only the organizers had let us bring Merlin," he muttered.

"Merlin?" asked Lana.

"Dewitt wanted to bring along one of our calves to help drum up business," said Mallory.

"I thought it would be nice for people to bottle-feed him," he explained. "Get some hands-on farming experience, you know? Lana, you're good at marketing and so forth—don't you think that's a clever idea?"

"Dewitt, the day I touch a cow is the day I quit lipstick, but I would have thought the kids would love it."

"Exactly." He folded his arms—case closed.

"Merlin is quite a *big* calf, though, isn't he, Dew?" said Mallory. "More like an adolescent bull."

Dewitt ignored her. "The organizers said it was a health and safety issue! Ridiculous."

They talked to the Hoffmans a little while longer, then moved on. There was another gridlock around the stall run by the Lazy Knoll Sugar Shack, a local maple syrup producer that was handing out samples of maple fudge—although it appeared that the price for the free fudge was to listen to a lecture on the process of syrup production. They passed Mistyflip Coffee, where their famous banana peanut butter donuts and fried chicken grinders were being sold from a stall out front. Connie recognized the guy manning the stall and waved as they passed.

"Hey, isn't it your wedding anniversary soon?" asked Lana.

"Well remembered. It's tomorrow."

"What are you doing to celebrate?"

"Nate's taking me out for dinner. I'm really looking forward to it. I haven't been at to a restaurant with him in ages."

"Well, I'm glad he hasn't forgotten this time. How are things between the two of you? Any better?"

"Not great, but then I've barely seen him lately."

"Perhaps you could talk to him tomorrow, tell him your worries."

"Should I do that on our anniversary? It might be a bit of a downer. Besides, I'm not sure if I *want* to talk to him about it. I don't think it'll do any good."

In truth, Connie was terrified about what she might find if she dug too deep. Since Lana had first planted the seed of doubt about Nate's fidelity, Connie had been just about keeping her worries under control, but now she knew that he'd lied to her about his whereabouts on the afternoon of James's arrival it didn't take a great leap of imagination to think he had been cheating. Connie wasn't sure what was worse: not knowing or finding out that it was true.

"I'm hoping it will all blow over, and he'll get over whatever's been troubling him," she told Lana, although that seemed less likely with each passing day.

She realized they were approaching the Tansy Falls Fine Cheeses stall. Edwin Catesby was behind the counter, stooped to fit under the low awning, dismembering a large cheese into sample-sized shards.

"Hey, Edwin, I don't suppose you stock vegan cheese?" Connie called to him.

The look on his face was enough of an answer.

"Never mind," she said. She would just have to find another solution to Mimi's dietary issues on the press weekend.

"Ooh—hot dogs!" Lana beelined for the stall run by the Black Bear, the local bar and skier hangout. Connie took a seat on a nearby bench that a couple had just vacated. While she was waiting, another stall caught her eye. It had a sleek black awning and behind the counter a Japanese chef, also in black, was slicing raw fish into sashimi, his knife flashing at astonishing speed. It looked like it belonged in a glitzy Los Angeles mall, not stuck between Fred's Dirty Dogs and a clown selling balloons.

Moments later, Lana reappeared with the hot dogs. "Well done for getting a seat."

"Do you know who's running the sushi stall?" asked Connie, nodding in its direction.

"Maverick Lodge. Apparently that guy is some famous Japanese chef they've recruited for their main restaurant."

At the mention of Maverick Lodge, James popped into Connie's mind.

"Lana, can I ask your opinion on something? It's about our new lodger—James."

"Ah yes, how is Mr. Interesting Looking?"

"He's fine, but the thing is, we've been kind of—hanging out."

"'Hanging out'?"

"He comes up to talk to me when I'm making my coffee in the morning."

Lana raised an eyebrow. "I see."

"What? We just talk."

"And do you and Nate talk much these days?"

Connie bristled at Lana's tone. "Would you be asking me that if James were a woman?"

"He's not though, is he? And quite frankly you're all lit up like a Fourth of July firework and I'm betting this talkative lodger is the reason why."

"It's just nice to have someone pay attention to me for a change. Is that so bad?"

"Of course not."

"And he's very charming. He seems interested in everything about me."

"That must be nice."

"We're going on a hike together next weekend—on Saturday, so it won't interfere with our swim."

"Well, I look forward to hearing all about it."

They ate their hot dogs, watching the parade of passersby.

"The thing is," said Connie after a while, "I worry that I'm somehow betraying Nate."

"Oh, honey, you're not. Just relax and enjoy the attention! There's no harm at all in a bit of flirting." Lana patted her leg. "Come on, let's see if we can sweet-talk ourselves some of that sushi..."

But that was just it, thought Connie, as she followed Lana through the crowd. Whatever was happening between her and James, it didn't feel like just "a bit of flirting," and she was beginning to worry where it might end up. Flirting was fun when it couldn't go anywhere, like with Lana's artist friend Theo, but with James it wasn't just close to home—it was home.

SEVENTEEN

Years ago when Connie was working at a hotel in London, a Hollywood actress, renowned as a great beauty, had checked in. Connie remembered being surprised by how ordinary the woman had looked; with her messy hair and sweats you wouldn't have given her a second glance in the street. Just a few hours later, however, Connie watched the same woman leave for her movie premiere and had been left speechless by how stunning she looked. It had been a master class in the transformative power of grooming and a killer outfit, and it was a lesson that had stayed with her.

Looking in her bedroom mirror now, Connie thought she must be feeling just a tiny bit of the magic that actress must have felt before stepping out onto the red carpet. In readiness for her and Nate's anniversary dinner tonight she was wearing red lipstick, high-heeled sandals and a new silk dress that was the exact green of the maidenhair ferns by their lake. It was the sort of dress, Connie had thought, spotting it on the rails of her local boutique, that would be worn by a woman who was perfectly happy and in control. It had cost far too much money, but she had been seduced by this fantasy of a perfect life as much as the fit and fabric; besides, it would be more than worth it if Nate took one look at her and fell in love with her again.

As Connie headed downstairs carrying her gift for Nate—taking it slowly in the heels—she felt as giddy as if this were their first date. He had told her to meet him on the deck at seven, but beyond that she had no idea what he had planned. Perhaps he had booked that new place in Thompsonville that had just opened? The chef was some young hotshot from Chicago and the food had been getting incredible reviews. She had a vision of Nate sitting opposite her in the candlelight, handsome in his navy suit, while they were presented with a succession of plates, each one a miniature work of art. Her breathing quickened, warmth flooding her cheeks. She was sure that tonight was just what they needed to help get their relationship back on track.

Twenty-three years of marriage. It was a lifetime, yet she remembered the day Nate proposed as vividly as if it were yesterday. They had been living together in London, sharing a tiny apartment near the hotel in Piccadilly where Connie was working. The apartment was in the attic of a rundown Victorian mansion block; the elevator was broken the whole time they lived there, they had to wear coats indoors during winter (which seemed to last a good eight months in England) and the water pressure was so weak they couldn't use the shower, but they were young and dizzily in love, so none of this mattered.

One evening, after a particularly long shift, Connie had wearily climbed the four flights of stairs to the apartment, planning on taking a long bath in the iron tub and then falling into bed, but when she opened the front door the hallway had been completely transformed. Instead of the usual single bare bulb, rows of tealights provided a soft light, by which Connie could see that the walls had been covered, from floor to ceiling, with photos from their travels. There were dozens of them, all taken during their backpacking adventures around Thailand, Chile and India, and their travels in Europe. Moving slowly so she didn't miss a single image, Connie had walked down the corridor, entranced by the memories that she and Nate had shared, and at the end of the corridor, surrounded by rose petals, she found an envelope. "Are you ready for our next big adventure?" it said on the front, and inside there was a note that read: "The journey starts in the bedroom." She had run in and there found Nate clad in a rented tuxedo, in the midst of yet more candles and petals, down on one knee and holding out the diamond ring that was still on her finger today.

Nate was out on the deck, sitting with his elbows propped on his knees, staring out at the lake with a bottle of beer in hand. As she approached, he turned to look at her and for a moment seemed lost for words.

"Wow," he managed finally. "You look incredible."

"Well, it's not every day you celebrate twenty-three years of marriage."

"Are we really that old?"

She laughed. "Yes, we really are." She sat down next to him; he was still in the clothes he'd been wearing earlier to cut the grass, but it didn't take him long to get ready. "What time is our table?"

"I'd say it will be ready in about..." He checked his watch. "Half an hour."

She glanced at his grass-stained shorts. "Shouldn't we get going then?"

"No need. We're already here."

Connie blinked. "I thought we were going out for dinner?"

"We are—to this fabulous little spot called Chez Nate. And the best part is we don't even have to get in the car to get there!"

"But... but I *wanted* to get in the car. We haven't been out to a restaurant in months." She looked down, hands spread. "I bought a new dress."

"And I love that you did." Nate shook his beer bottle, clocked it was empty and got up. "Can I get madam a drink?"

Connie's mind was racing. Perhaps, she thought desperately, this was all part of an elaborate surprise, and Nate had booked a restaurant after all? But then she looked at his old clothes again, and her stomach dropped.

She made herself smile. "A drink would be lovely, thank you. What does Chez Nate have on its bar menu?"

"I think there's a bottle of rosé in the fridge?"

There is, she thought, the smile fading at her lips. *I bought it last week.*

As Nate disappeared into the house, Connie sank into the chair and closed her eyes, fighting the waves of disappointment that were crashing over her. She'd been so looking forward to tonight. It had felt like a chance at a new start, but now it would be just like every other night: avoiding each other's gaze across the kitchen table, the same old tensions souring the atmosphere and twisting at her gut like indigestion.

Perhaps, though, this was the problem? She had been piling so much pressure on tonight, imagining it would be a magic pill to cure their problems, while the best thing for their relationship would be if she just relaxed and enjoyed herself. Besides, who knew what Nate had in store? He may well have gone to a lot of trouble, and her acting like a spoiled child certainly wasn't going to help their relationship.

"Here we are," said Nate, returning with the wine. "Happy anniversary, honey. Here's to us."

"And to being very, very old." Connie clinked his glass. "This is for you," she added, holding out the gift.

"Oh, thank you! You shouldn't have."

"I always do," she said, smiling to make it a joke rather than a rebuke. *And so do you, usually*, she added in her mind.

"It's a vintage cocktail shaker," she explained. "I found it in a thrift shop in Burlington. The twenty-third wedding anniversary is traditionally silver plate, just in case you were wondering why I chose it."

"What a thoughtful gift. Thank you, honey. Guess I can finally throw out that peanut butter jar."

In the absence of a proper shaker, it was what Nate had always used to make cocktails.

"It'll be a novelty to have a martini without an aftertaste of Skippy," joked Connie.

Nate gave a flat chuckle, but looked ill at ease. "I meant to get you something, but—"

"Please, don't even think about it. You've arranged a lovely dinner, and that's more than enough."

Connie now wished she hadn't got him anything, but they had always exchanged gifts on this day. Just something silly to fit the tradition of whatever anniversary it was for less than fifty dollars. For their twenty-first anniversary—nickel—Nate had got a five-cent coin mounted as a key chain and had got the words I STILL DO engraved on its face. Connie used it on her house keys to this day.

Nate drained his glass. "Well, the chef is needed back in the kitchen. I hope you're hungry!"

After he had disappeared, Connie kicked off her sandals and wandered down to the lake. She had a sudden urge to break into a run and just keep going across the fields, to escape this whole claustrophobic situation. Instead she took a slow walk around its perimeter, letting the softness of the grass beneath her feet and the sound of the water calm her.

"Dinner is served!" Nate waved to her from the deck.

Inside, the kitchen looked much like it did every other evening: a hastily laid table with kitchen towels as napkins, and not even a few flowers to liven the atmosphere. Connie felt glaringly over-dressed in her lipstick and new dress.

Nate had made steak and fries with creamed spinach. It was his signature dish and as always he'd cooked it perfectly, but the atmosphere was so tense that each mouthful was a challenge.

"This is delicious," said Connie.

"I'm glad you like it."

The clank of their cutlery just emphasized the silence between them.

"How's work?" asked Nate.

"Busy. It's the press trip the weekend after next."

The old Nate would have peppered her with questions—after

all, this was his area of expertise—but he just nodded. "I'm sure you'll do a great job."

Connie ate another mouthful in silence, and then another. Nate drained his wineglass and filled it again. There was already one empty bottle and the second was almost finished, but she'd had no more than two glasses.

"Talking about the press trip, have you heard back from any of those magazines you contacted about freelance possibilities?" she asked.

"Not yet."

"Perhaps you should call them, just to remind them you're still looking?"

"Maybe..."

"Oh, I meant to tell you! I was talking to Edwin at Tansy Falls Fine Cheeses and apparently *Cheese Connoisseur* magazine is looking for a new editor, and—"

"For pity's sake, Connie, I don't want a job writing about cheese!"

He swept out his arm and his wineglass was sent flying, red wine spreading across the table and spilling on her dress, spreading like blood over the pale green silk.

Connie jumped up, while Nate scrambled to stop the tide. "Darn it! I'm so sorry, I—"

"It doesn't matter." Her throat was tight. "I'll just go upstairs and get changed."

When she came back down, Nate had cleaned up the mess and laid out dessert: brownies and ice cream. They ate quickly, stewing in their own thoughts. Connie heard James come home at some point and hated herself for thinking how different the evening would be if she were sitting opposite him instead.

A little later Connie was at the sink, washing up, when she felt Nate's arms snake around her waist. She froze, her whole body tensing. Surely he wasn't trying to seduce her after the excruciating evening they'd just had?

"How about you leave that and we go upstairs?" he whispered, kissing her neck. She could smell the stale alcohol on his breath and tried not to flinch.

"Nate, I'm sorry, but I'm tired," she said, edging out of his arms. "Work is so busy right now, you know..."

He nodded, but there a wounded look in his eyes. "Of course. Thank you again for the gift." He gestured to the sink. "I can finish up here."

"Thanks," said Connie.

They looked at each other and she was hit by an overwhelming rush of sadness. "Happy anniversary, Nate," she said.

"Happy anniversary, Conn."

It felt like the last time they'd ever say it.

EIGHTEEN

Mia Callaghan: that was her name. Connie had checked her in yesterday morning and had wondered at the time why a heavily pregnant young woman was staying at the Covered Bridge on her own for two weeks. Mia had been sweetly polite, but when Connie had asked if she was here on vacation she just shook her head and looked away, shutting down any further questions.

Now, however, coming across the young woman alone in the gazebo, in floods of tears, Connie didn't hesitate to approach her.

"Hi there, are you okay?"

Mia looked up, startled. "Oh—yes, sorry. I'm fine, thank you. Just a little hormonal, I guess."

"Would you like to talk?"

"No, it's okay."

"It's an emotional roller coaster, isn't it? I was in tears every day for the final months of my pregnancy. I called it the third cry-mester."

Mia attempted a smile.

"I tell you what, why don't I bring you out a glass of iced tea and a slice of today's cake? It's a mille crepe cake, which is a basically a stack of chocolate crepes layered with vanilla ganache and covered with strawberries. It's pretty good." When she didn't reply,

Connie added: "I've found cake helps most things, even if it's only a tiny bit."

Mia looked up, her eyes still shining with tears. "How about broken hearts?"

"Perhaps. And time helps with that too."

"Thank you, I really appreciate it, um?"

"Connie." She shot her a warm smile. "I'll be right back with that cake."

Connie had spent the rest of the afternoon helping Harold from the maintenance team clear out the storage room that was to be Isabelle Bennett's new office. For as long as Connie had worked at the Covered Bridge, this had been an unofficial dumping ground, crammed with old furniture, boxes of holiday decorations and archived files, so she'd never managed to get a foot beyond the doorway, but now that it had been cleared out she was delighted at the gem of a room that they'd uncovered. It had been well worth the three broken nails, bruised shins and constant stream of grumbled complaints from Harold (who apparently felt that room-tidying was beneath his pay grade) to get it perfect.

As well as a new desk and office chair, Connie had furnished the room with a few treasures they'd unearthed beneath the junk: a carved wooden bench that looked like an old church pew, which she'd prettified by adding cushions from the lobby couches, and an antique coffee table with elaborately turned legs. She'd also found a framed sepia photograph of farmers cutting hay next to a cart drawn by a pair of horned cattle that she'd asked Harold to hang over the desk. The date in the corner of the photo said 1906; Connie wondered who they were—perhaps Dewitt Hoffman's ancestors on their dairy farm? She made a mental note to ask next time she saw the farmer.

Afternoon tea was being served in the dining room by the time they finished getting the office ready. Connie sunk into the office chair, closing her eyes to enjoy a moment's break, but as soon as she did so memories of last night's anniversary dinner rushed into her mind. She flinched, remembering the moment that Nate had kissed her neck, and how every fiber of her being had been desperate to get away. The same horribly familiar thoughts began ticker-taping through her mind: How had things between them gone so wrong? How could they fix it? It would be easier if one of them had done something terrible, as at least then they would know what needed fixing, but it was as if their relationship was simply fading away. Connie jumped up from the chair. *Better to keep busy*, she told herself, throwing open the window to banish any lingering mustiness. The room faced directly onto the inn's rose garden and with the blast of warm air came the scent of the showy pink flowers that were strewn over the trellis like drunken ballerinas. Leaning on the window sill, Connie visualized Isabelle Bennett sitting at the new desk, busy planning the destination weddings that the Covered Bridge would hopefully become famous for. The guests for the press trip would be arriving a week from today, but just this mental image helped calm Connie's nerves. Between the two of them they would make sure it would be a success, she was sure of it.

She was just deliberating whether to pick some roses to put on Isabelle's desk when Spencer's head popped around the door.

His mouth dropped open. "Wow! Where did you find this place?"

"Looks great, doesn't it?"

"You've outdone yourself, Conn. What have you done with all the other stuff that was in here?"

"Put it this way—just be careful how you open my office door."

"Well, I'm sure Isabelle will appreciate all your hard work. And talking of our new events manager, I've got her on the line for you just now."

"Can you put her through to this extension to check it's working?"

"Sure." Spencer disappeared, and a moment later the phone on the desk trilled.

"Isabelle, how are you?"

"Good afternoon, Ms. Austen. I'm well, thank you. And you?"

"Please, you must call me Connie. Funnily enough I'm actually just sitting in your new office, admiring the view. I hope you like the smell of roses, because it's like a flower bomb exploded outside the window in here!"

Isabelle cleared her throat. "I'm afraid I won't be able to start on Monday."

"Oh." Connie's smile faltered. "Well, when can you start? It would be great to have you here for at least a couple of days before the press trip starts on Friday, so I can get you up to speed on what's planned."

"I've been offered a job at Maverick Lodge. It's a bigger role, a better salary, more responsibility. You'll appreciate that I couldn't turn down such a fantastic opportunity."

Connie felt like she'd been slapped. "What?"

"I'm sorry if this puts you in a difficult position," Isabelle went on, sounding far from it, "but you'll understand that I have to think about what's best for my career."

"But what about the press trip? I was counting on you being here to help."

"I'm afraid that's no longer my problem," said Isabelle.

Connie had an urge to slam the phone down, but desperate times required desperate groveling.

"Is there anything I can do to persuade you to join us? I'm sure we could take another look at the salary, perhaps give you a different job title?"

"I appreciate your offer, but I've made up my mind. Working for a luxury global brand like Maverick Lodge is far more in alignment with my career goals than at a small family-run inn."

Connie bit down the words she really wanted to say and plastered on her most dazzling smile. Isabelle might not be able to see it, but she would certainly be able to hear it—and while they might not have Maverick Lodge's money at least this "small, family-run inn" had manners.

"Well, in that case, all that's left is for me to wish the best of luck in your new role."

"Thank you. Goodbye, Ms. Austen. I'm sure our paths will cross again."

And you better watch out when they do, fumed Connie.

As the surge of anger faded away and panic rushed in to take its place, Connie stared blankly at the wall. Her mind was zipping all over the place, and she made herself take a couple of deep breaths. The press would be arriving a week from today and were expecting a full weekend of activities, which they would then write about for thousands of people to read—and while they might be getting a complimentary stay, that wouldn't stop them pointing out anything that was less than perfect. Piper and Spencer would be helping, but they were going to have to their hands full with the day-to-day running of the inn. She supposed she could call back the other two candidates she interviewed for the events manager role on the off-chance they were still available, but it was highly unlikely they'd be in a position to start by next week.

Just then there was a tap at the door.

"You can come in, Spence. I've finished the call." Connie spun round in the swivel chair to face the door. "You are never going to *believe* what just..."

But she trailed off as in walked the very last person she was expecting to see.

NINETEEN

Everly paused in the doorway, glowing as if she traveled under her own personal spotlight—although this was probably thanks to her diamond ear studs and the glossy sheen imparted by face creams that cost more than Connie's weekly wage. Today, in a pair of pale jeans, glossy ponytail and an Hermès handbag (that probably cost more than Connie's *annual* wage), Everly had the look of an off-duty model, but then she broke into a grin and she was her muddy-kneed kid sister once again.

"Hello, sis. Do I get a hug?"

"It's so good to see you!" Connie flew into her arms. "Did I miss a call from Patrick? I had no idea you were going to be here today."

"Spur-of-the-moment decision. I had a last-minute schedule opening and thought I'd come up for a flying visit to surprise my favorite sister." Everly scrutinized her. "You look tired, Miss Conifer."

"And you absolutely *don't*. In fact you look like you've just come back from two weeks in Barbados."

"That would be the laser facials. I've discovered this fabulous clinic. I'll give you the number."

"That's sweet of you, but the only facial I can afford right now would be a tube of Neutrogena clay mask and a couple of slices of cucumber in the bathroom."

"My treat, then—a late birthday present." Everly checked her watch. "Honey, when I say this is a flying visit, I literally mean it. I'm booked on the late flight back to the city from Burlington. The twins have got a party on Shelter Island on the weekend and we're driving up to the Hamptons first thing tomorrow, so we better hustle if we're going to meet up with Kurt to discuss his sugar baby situation."

"I'm really sorry but I can't leave work early today. Our new events manager has just dropped out and we've got this big press thing next week, which I..."

Her sister swept this away with a wave. "Oh, I'm sure you'll sort that out. But I came all this way to speak to Kurt and I can't do it alone. It's a sensitive issue, and he's far more likely to listen if you're there too—plus you've actually met this witch doctor woman."

"Skye's a shamanic healer. And she's very sweet. She genuinely likes him."

"Come on, there's no way a woman in her thirties is with a seventy-year-old for his six-pack and sparkling conversation. You know what Kurt's like. He's in denial and we need to save him from himself. More to the point, we need to save our inheritance."

"Skye's not with him for his money, I'm sure of it."

"Well, I'm afraid I don't have your sweet trusting nature." Everly started for the door. "Where are you parked?"

Connie hesitated, cursing all over again her knee-jerk decision to get Everly involved in Kurt's love life. This was *exactly* why she preferred to handle things by herself! If only she'd have kept quiet until she'd actually got to know Skye then she could have avoided all this drama. As much as she loved her sister, though, Everly was as stubborn as their father, and Connie knew it would be pointless trying to persuade her to drop it now she'd got the bit between her teeth. Besides, what more could she do about the Isabelle Bennett situation right now? Bottom line, she had two options: crawl into bed and hide for the next ten days, or handle the whole press trip single-handed.

"Fine, we'll go," said Connie. "But I need to speak to Spencer first to let him know that I'm heading off early."

"You're a marvel. Thanks, honey. I'll wait for you in the lobby."

Twenty minutes later they were heading up the driveway through the forest to Kurt's cabin.

"Hey, what's happened to Mom's hawthorn?" Everly's head swiveled as they passed a clearing that had recently been slashed into the undergrowth. "I loved that tree!"

"Dad's planning to build a Japanese Zen garden."

"What—raked sand, rocks, pagodas and stuff?"

"Yep."

"What's the betting he loses interest after the first ton of sand is delivered?"

"I think it's good for him to have a project. Keeps him out of mischief."

"Yeah, but it hasn't worked this time, has it?"

She gazed out of the window, her chin cupped in her hand.

A moment later they pulled up outside the cabin. Everly reached for the door handle before the engine had even cut, but Connie put out a hand to stop her.

"Listen, Ev, you do realize that Dad probably isn't going to welcome us interfering in his love life. You will handle this sensitively, won't you?"

"Of course! I'll be my usual tactful self," she said, slamming the door behind her.

"That's what was I afraid of," murmured Connie.

Her sister had already bounded up the steps and banged on the front door by the time Connie had got out of the car.

"Come on, come on..." muttered Everly.

"Looks like he's out," said Connie, relieved.

Everly gave it another moment and then skipped back down

the steps. "Let's check the yard." She disappeared around the side of the house; with a sigh, Connie followed, breaking into a jog to keep up. They passed the bank of lilac under which they had both been born, the last of the season's flowers still clinging to the branches like snow, and skirted the outbuilding where Kurt kept his midlife crisis motorbike, then took the path through the woods that led to the meditation platform that their father had built after his visit to Tibet. And it was here that they found him, sitting cross-legged in front of the little gold Buddha statue, eyes closed and hands resting on his knees. His bare chest was draped with wooden beads, and his lips moved silently.

"Oh, for goodness sake," grumbled Everly. "Yo, Kurt! Look smart, you've got company."

He opened his eyes as if waking after a long sleep.

"My girls! To what do I owe this pleasure?"

"Hi, Pa," said Connie, "we thought we'd come round and—"

"Connie's called a family conference," said Everly.

"What?" Connie whipped her head round toward her. "No I haven't!"

"Well, whatever the reason, I'm very happy to see you both," said Kurt. "Shall we go inside? I've just brewed a batch of ginger kombucha."

"Sounds delicious," said Connie, anxious to keep the peace.

"I'll take a coffee if you've got some," said Everly. "*With* caffeine."

Once Kurt had prepared the drinks, the three of them gathered in the den. As she passed their father's desk, Connie noticed what looked like a real estate agent's property brochure among the paperwork, but he swept it into a drawer before she could get a proper look. Her curiosity was piqued, though. Was he thinking of buying a new house?

"So you're gonna have to bring me up to speed," said Kurt. "What's this family conference about?"

"It's *not* a family conference..." muttered Connie.

"Connie has told me about your new girlfriend," said Everly.

"I thought she might have done. And as I've already told your sister"—Kurt flicked Connie a look of irritation—"Skye and I are very happy together."

"Dad, she's younger than both of us!" gaped Everly. "How do you think that makes us feel?"

"Well, I guess I hoped you might be pleased that I met someone who loves me as much as I love her. I assumed, clearly incorrectly, that her age wouldn't come into it."

"Of course it's going to come into it!"

Kurt tipped his head to one side, his fingers steepled. "And why do you think you might feel this way?"

Everly growled in frustration. "For pity's sake, we're not here to have therapy!"

In the silence that followed, Everly glowered at Kurt while their father sipped his kombucha. As usual, it was left to Connie to play the role of peacemaker.

"Dad, I think I speak for both of us when I say that of course we want you to be happy, and we're thrilled that you've met someone, because we know how much you've missed Mom. I do admit that I was a little shocked when I first met Skye, which is why I called Everly to discuss it with her, but I—"

"It does look kind of fishy," her sister interrupted. "A young woman dating someone old enough to be her grandfather."

"Fishy?" repeated Kurt.

"Yeah. I mean, how can you be sure she's not with you because you're rich?"

Kurt's expression remained calm, but tension flickered in his jaw. "Is that what you're concerned about?"

"Yes," said Everly. "We are."

Connie cut in. "I think what Everly's trying to say is—"

"That could be taken as quite an insulting suggestion," said Kurt, "that the only reason Skye's with me was because of my money. That she couldn't possibly be interested in me for any other reason."

"We don't want you taken advantage of, that's all," said Everly.

"I think I can take care of myself. I haven't got involved in any of your relationships."

"You haven't got involved in our lives period," said Everly.

Kurt gave a martyrish sigh. "Look, all I can say is that I'm happy for the first time since your mother died. Who knows what will happen in the future? I'm sorry you feel this way, but Skye is going to be in my life, with or without your blessing."

Everly rolled her eyes. "What's that saying—there's no fool like an old fool?"

Connie froze, expecting her father to explode at the word "old," but instead his eyes crinkled with amusement. "And this old fool loves you both dearly but would prefer you to mind your own business. Okay?"

"That's fine with me," said Connie. "Everly?"

Her sister took a moment to respond, but eventually she gave a resigned shrug. "I've said my piece, Dad. You're old enough to make your own mistakes."

"Hey, enough with the 'old'! Come here, my darling Evergreen." She loped over and let him hug her. "I can hear that you're worried about me, and I appreciate you caring, but quite honestly you don't know what you're talking about."

"Don't push it, Kurt," she muttered—but she was smiling as she said it. That was the way it always was with these two. Quick to temper, but it usually blew over as fast as it had begun.

"Well, as delightful as this has been," said Everly, "I've got to get back to the city."

"Can't you at least stay for dinner?" asked Kurt.

"Sorry, Pa, I'd love to but we're off to the Hamptons tomorrow. Can you get me a car to the airport?"

"Of course. But you'll come and see me again soon? Perhaps bring the girls and Charles, stay for the weekend?"

"I will."

"I better get going too," said Connie. She gave Everly a long hug, the pair of them holding each other tight. "I'll speak to you soon, Ev."

"Love you, Conn."

Connie blew a kiss at Kurt, who was on the phone to the car service. "I'll see you soon, Dad."

"Sure thing, honey."

What a day, thought Connie wearily, as she turned onto Cider Farm Road. What she needed right now was a cold shower and a soothing stroll around the lake, but as the house came into view she saw there was a strange car parked outside. She felt a flicker of irritation—yet another thing to deal with!—before realizing whose car it actually was. Connie let out a cry. Surely it couldn't be...? Speeding up for the last few yards, she stamped on the brakes, swerving to a halt in a cloud of dirt outside the house, and leapt out of the car.

TWENTY

There he was. Lounging on the steps to the deck, his face maybe a little bit thinner than when she last saw him—his blond hair definitely longer and shaggier—but her baby all the same.

"Ethan!"

As she rushed to greet him he got to his feet, his father's smile lighting up his handsome features.

"Hey, Mom," he said, the grown man's voice even now a surprise to Connie.

There were shadows beneath his eyes, he looked pale and hadn't shaved for a few days, but then she supposed there was too much fun to be had for sleep.

She pulled him in for a hug. "Oh, honey, it's so good to see you!"

Wrapped in his arms, Connie closed her eyes, her insides glowing with happiness, and even though Ethan usually disentangled himself from a hug after a couple of seconds, today he held on to Connie as if he was just as pleased to see her. She couldn't stop smiling. *This* was what really mattered, not work or silly family disagreements. Nothing could be that bad with Ethan home.

"This is such a wonderful surprise." She beamed. "What are you doing here?"

"I needed to get some washing done," he said, with a lopsided grin. "Nobody irons my socks like you do, Mom."

"Well, whatever the reason, I'm thrilled you're here." She looped her arm through his. "Come on, you'll need something to eat."

"Thanks, but I got a burger on the way."

"A drink then." She unlocked the front door. "How was the drive?"

"Not bad. I took the I-91 and it took about seven hours plus burger stoppage time."

"What would you like? Iced tea? Soda?"

"Just some water would be good." He took a seat at the table, stretching his long legs out in front of him.

"Coming right up, sweetie." She filled a glass and brought it over, taking a seat next to him. "You know, this has been quite the day for surprises. First your Aunt Everly turned up, and now you. I hope you're going to stay a little while?"

"If that's okay with you, Mom?"

"Of course! I'd love that."

Ethan took a sip of water, and it was only now that Connie noticed a small bruise on his cheekbone. Narrowing her eyes, she examined her son more closely. He actually looked more than just tired; he looked utterly exhausted, as if something was eating away at him inside. She knew better than to give him the third degree though, so she asked lightly: "How are things in Pennsylvania?"

He shrugged, avoiding her eyes.

"Ethan?"

He chewed his lip, clearly wrestling with how to respond, and Connie's insides lurched to see that his eyes were brimming with tears. She grabbed his hand, squeezing it in hers. "It's okay, honey, you can talk to me."

A tear trickled down his cheek; Ethan immediately swiped it away. Connie could see he was on the verge of breaking down, and as the silent seconds ticked by her head spun with the all the possibilities of what might be wrong. It was agonizing, like the breath was slowly being squeezed out of her.

"Something happened the other night," he said finally. "At a party."

Connie waited for him to go on.

"We were playing this stupid drinking game. I—I was really drunk."

"Okay..."

"Someone filmed the whole thing on their phone..." Then he broke into sobs. "People are saying these terrible things, claiming that I was one of the people involved, but I didn't do anything, Mom! I was stupid and drunk, but I *swear* I didn't hurt that girl!"

Connie's stomach twisted into a knot of fear. "Shh, it's okay, honey," she said, gripping his hand as much to force herself to stay calm as to comfort him. "Take your time and tell me what happened..."

Three days ago Ethan had gone to a party thrown by a group of seniors from his college. He didn't know them, but he'd been invited by Ben, the kid whose family he was staying with, and there were some other friends from his year at college, including a girl called Kayla. There was a lot of alcohol at the party—not just beer, but spirits—and as the night went on Ethan had got swept up in a drinking game, knocking back shots of vodka, until he was so drunk he barely remembered getting home—"although I do remember falling up the stairs to my bedroom," he said, indicating the bruise on his cheek. He woke the next morning with enough of a hangover to make him swear off vodka for good, yet the worst was still to come. When he turned on his phone it began pinging with messages, sharing the shocking news that Kayla had been sexually assaulted at the party and was currently with the police. Then moments later, he received a link to a video that had just appeared online. The footage was dark and blurry, rowdy with shouting and laughter, but among the chaos you could plainly see Ethan, swigging from a bottle of vodka, his arm draped over Kayla's shoulder. The video had immediately gone viral, gaining traction as an example of the toxic "frat culture" on college campuses. Commenters piled on to attack the boys in the video and clamor for their arrest. Whether or not they were guilty, the fact that they were there, partying with a girl who would later be a victim of an assault, was more than enough to condemn them.

When he'd sobbed out the last of the details, Connie gathered Ethan into her arms, clutching him as if he were still six years old. But this wasn't a bruised knee that she could kiss better. Connie didn't for one second doubt her son's innocence—he had always been a gentle, sweet-natured boy—but she was aware just how devastating trial-by-internet could be, how merely the spark of a rumor could ignite an inferno that would destroy everything in its path.

"I keep expecting the police to turn up on the doorstep and arrest me," said Ethan. "Do you think I should turn myself in?"

"Oh, honey, you're not a criminal! All college students get drunk sometimes. It's stupid but it's not that big a deal."

"Maybe I should speak to my faculty advisor?"

Connie thought for a moment. "Do you know who actually assaulted that poor girl?"

"I have no idea. I didn't know most of the people who were at the party. I think it was one of the seniors, but that's just one of many rumors."

"But this girl—Kayla—*she'll* know you weren't involved, won't she?"

Ethan gave an anguished shrug. "Everyone was so drunk. I haven't spoken to Kayla, and I don't know what happened after I left. I thought about messaging her to offer my support, but that's probably the last thing she needs right now... I feel terrible even thinking about myself after what Kayla has gone through, but you should see what people are saying about me online, Mom." He raised his head to look at Connie, and the pain in his eyes broke her heart all over again. "What's going to happen to me?"

Connie had no idea, but she had no doubt that this video would be enough get him thrown out of his class; worst-case scenario, it would put an end to his future legal career before it had even begun. Right now, though, her only concern was to comfort her child.

Much later that night, when Ethan was finally asleep in his old bedroom, Connie and Nate sat in the kitchen discussing what they should do. Once upon a time there would have been hugs, hand-holding, murmured reassurances. They would have tackled this as a team, drawing strength from each other, secure in the knowledge that they could handle anything because they were together. Now, though, Connie was sitting alone at the table while Nate stood across the room, leaning against the kitchen counter, emotionally as well as physically distant.

"Do you think we should contact the police?" asked Connie.

"Of course not! Apart from the drinking—and come on, which college kid hasn't done that—Ethan has done nothing wrong."

"But maybe he should go and tell them what he remembers about the evening?"

"What would be the point? You heard what he said, Conn. It's all a blank."

"Yes, but if he went to speak to the police voluntarily, they could at least—oh, I don't know—count him out of their enquiries?"

"This party was three days ago, right? I'm sure Kayla will have already given them the names of anyone involved. Ethan would have been brought in for questioning if there was even the hint of suspicion."

"But that video, Nate..." Connie trailed off.

Ethan had showed them both the footage. With the foresight of what would happen to Kayla later that night, it made for very distressing viewing. Ethan was almost unrecognizable in it: falling-down drunk, his eyes unfocused and head lolling, clinging onto Kayla as if for support. At one point he had stuck the bottle of vodka in her face, encouraging her to drink, and she had laughingly batted it away. It was the briefest of moments, but it made Connie flinch. She had started to read the comments beneath the video, but what strangers were saying about her boy was too painful to read.

"It will blow over," said Nate firmly. "These things always do."

"It's not like when we were young, Nate. All the stupid things you do as a kid are now immortalized forever. You read about people losing their jobs over one stupid tweet they made in their teens."

"Connie, I promise it will all be forgotten by next semester."

"But what if it's not? What if the college administrators see it and decide to make an example of him? In the current climate they're not going to be tolerant of anything that looks remotely toxic. They can't be seen to condone this kind of behavior." She leaned toward him, trying to get him to grasp this severity of the situation. "He wants to be a lawyer, Nate. This could destroy his future."

"You're overreacting."

"Or perhaps it's you who's underreacting." She bit down her anger. "Sorry, I'm just really worried about this. Can't you at least understand that?"

"And I'm telling you that you don't need to worry."

"But it doesn't work like that, Nate!"

Here they were once again, hovering at the brink of an argument. It was familiar territory these days.

"Look, it's late," said Nate. "I guarantee things will look better in the morning. Let's get some sleep."

"Are you going to play golf in the morning?"

"I am, yes. I think the best thing is if we go on with life as normal. Ethan doesn't need us fussing around him."

Connie bristled at the perceived insult.

"Anyway," Nate went on, "Ethan is bound to sleep in until at least midday. Shall I see you upstairs?"

But he had already gone before she'd had a chance to reply.

TWENTY-ONE

These days, Saturday was the only day of the week Nate set an alarm, to make sure he was awake in time for golf with Tom or his early run. Connie usually got up with him, but today she pretended to be asleep. She was still angry with him for sweeping aside her concerns last night; besides, she'd been lying awake for hours, agonizing over how to help their son, and even the thought of speech was exhausting.

Once she heard Nate drive off, she pulled on a wrap over the vest and boxers she slept in and went downstairs to get a coffee. It wasn't yet 7 a.m. and she was lightheaded from the lack of sleep. What she really needed was a giant cup of the extra-strong brew from Fiske's General Store—but then she remembered that Nate had taken the car, so she would have to try to recreate it at home instead. Somehow, though, it never tasted quite the same, or gave her the same turboboost. She wasn't sure what Darlene—and now Nell—put in their coffee at the store, but it wasn't known as Fiske's Jet Fuel for nothing.

Connie was just mixing up a batch of Ethan's favorite cinnamon breakfast muffins, a recipe she'd made so many times it was the work of seconds, when she heard a car pulling up outside. It must be Nate, coming back for a forgotten nine iron or pitching

wedge or whatever. When it came to golf, Connie was in agreement with whoever said that it had too much walking to be a good
game and just enough game to spoil a good walk. She readied
herself to be pleasant (though not too pleasant, as she was still
smarting over last night's row) but when the door opened it was
James who appeared.

"Morning, Connie. Beautiful day out there."

"Oh—hi!" She pulled her wrap about her, conscious that she
was wearing so little. "Where have you been so early?"

"I've been getting refreshments for our morning's hike," he
replied, and she only now noticed he was wearing his trekking
gear. *Of course, they were meant to be going on a hike this morning!*
"That is, if you're still able to join me?"

"I'm so sorry, I completely forgot. My son—Ethan—came home
yesterday for a surprise visit and I've been a little preoccupied."

"Is that whose car is outside?"

She nodded. "He's asleep upstairs, and probably will be until
way after lunch. You know what teenagers are like. He's having a
few problems right now."

"I'm sorry to hear that. Do you want to take a rain check on the
hike?"

Connie thought this over. There were plenty of reasons why
she shouldn't go. She was tired, Ethan was here and her mind felt
like a honeybee, frantically buzzing from one problem to the next.
Perhaps, though, these were all the reasons why she *should* go?
Fresh air and nature were probably just the medicine she needed,
and chances are she would be back before Ethan had even stirred.

"No, I'd like to come. You'll have to drive, though. Nate has
taken our car."

"Great, I'm so pleased." His eyes ran over her, and even though
she was covered up, Connie felt exposed under his gaze.

James's car was exactly like its owner: expensive, immaculately
groomed and very smooth. As they purred along Cider Farm Road,

Connie relaxed into the plush leather seat, which cradled her as perfectly as if it had been designed to her dimensions.

"Take a left up here," she said, as they approached the junction with the mountain road.

"Where are we headed?"

"I thought we could hike up to Sunrise Ridge. It's a popular spot with rock climbers, about halfway up Mount Maverick. We can take the scenic route, though, so no ropes or harnesses required."

"That's good, because I left my crampons back in the city."

"Crampons are for ice climbing, you know."

"Well, obviously I knew that. I was just testing you."

Connie smiled, the tightness in her chest easing a little.

They left the car in the parking lot at the foot of the mountain and followed the signs to the trailhead, pausing at the State Forest board so Connie could show James the map, the route of the Sunrise Trail marked in a red zigzag up Maverick's left flank.

At first the path cut a broad swathe through the woods, wide enough to accommodate a car, but as the gradient steepened it narrowed until it was little more than a rocky path fit only for mountain goats. The morning was oppressively hot, but it was cooler beneath the trees, the worst of the stickiness filtered out by the leaves overhead. To start they chatted away easily—the trail was well maintained, with wooden walkways bridging the most precarious parts—but as the path wound upward more steeply they fell silent, the only sound the trudging of their boots. The trail was clearly signposted, so Connie let James take the lead and set the pace. She considered herself to be pretty fit, but he was in another league, striding ahead at a speed that made conversation impossible, leaving her alone with her thoughts.

Like an itch she couldn't stop herself scratching, Connie kept returning to the image of Ethan's stricken expression when he told her about the video. The memory of him brushing that tear away, trying so hard to hold it together, caused her physical pain. *My poor, sweet boy*. She thought back to when Ethan was little and how hard motherhood had felt at times—the early waking, exploding diapers and grocery store tantrums—but right now she would give anything to go back to those simple times. Gone were the days when she could make everything right for her son just by loving him fiercely, and that knowledge troubled her like a sharp stone in her shoe.

Then, of course, there were all the other disasters waiting in the wings: her relationship with Nate, in which she increasingly felt like a passenger who had fallen overboard into the ocean while the ship sailed on regardless, and the prospect of next weekend's Isabelle Bennett–less press trip. As much as she knew Mitch and Carole Gridley were fond of her, it had taken a huge effort to persuade them of the value of the trip, so if it didn't garner any positive press—or worse, if it turned out to be an expensive fiasco—it was feasible they would be angry enough to fire her. Spencer and Piper would fight for her, she knew that, but it was the senior Gridleys who were still in charge, and in recent years they had seemed to want to assert their status more than ever.

"Hope for the best, prepare for the worst" had always been Connie's motto, but was it even possible to prepare for losing both your husband and your job at once?

TWENTY-TWO

After an hour of climbing they emerged from beneath the trees onto a rocky ridge, where the only vegetation was the occasional wind-stunted pine or scrubby shrub clinging to the stone. James sprinted up onto a jutting rock, offering Connie his hand to help her up, and together they looked out at the landscape below. Below their feet lay a sea of trees and beyond that the Tansy Falls valley, so vivid with color it looked like a Van Gogh painting.

"Now *that* is a view," he said.

Connie just nodded; she loved being up here, on top of the world.

James turned to her. "Breakfast?"

"Yes please."

They went back down to the trail and found a spot to sit. This route was usually quite busy, but today they had it to themselves— perhaps because it was still so early.

James unpacked his backpack: he had brought bagels, yogurt with granola, sliced mango and coffee.

"What—no mimosas?" gasped Connie, mock-horrified. "No Bloody Marys?"

James jumped up. "For you, I'll go back and get some. What'll you have?"

She laughed. "No need, this is wonderful. Thank you."

They ate for a while in silence, then James said: "You mentioned Ethan is having some problems—would it help to talk about it?"

"Maybe."

"I'm a good listener. And I've dealt with a lot of teenage problems over the years."

So she told him everything, the words pouring out of her. And when she had finished, she felt a little lighter; as if just putting her fears into words had lessened their grip on her.

"I understand why you're so worried about this video," said James. "You must be concerned about who might see it, and how it might affect Ethan's future."

"I am, yes."

"The bottom line, though, is that he didn't hurt that girl. That's what you should hang on to."

"But he was in that video. I worry the college will make an example of him."

"They'll be well aware that drinking goes on. If they make an example of him, they'd have to make an example of all the other students. They wouldn't have anyone left on campus if they started kicking kids out for getting drunk."

"Possibly..."

"Look, if this were my son, I'd do exactly what you're doing. Keep him home for a few days, wait to see if the police get in touch, reassure him as best you can."

"Thank you," said Connie. "That's helpful."

A couple of hikers passed them on the trail, and said good morning.

When they had gone, James glanced at Connie. "Can I ask you a personal question?"

"Shoot."

"How old you are?"

"Forty-nine."

"Hey, me too!" He held up his hand for a high-five.

"I still can't believe I'm that old," said Connie. "When I read something about a forty-nine-year-old in a newspaper I think how ancient that person must be."

"Oh absolutely. I'm like, 'well that's basically the same age as my dad.' But we're in our prime, Connie Austen, and don't you forget it."

The food finished, they tidied everything away into James's backpack. Connie stood up. "We better get going," she said, keen to be home when Ethan woke up.

"Connie—just wait a moment. I need to tell you something."

She hesitated; it sounded serious.

"I shouldn't say it," James went on. "It's not fair of me, and this is clearly a bad time. But I'm going to go mad if I don't tell you. Will you sit back down?"

She did as he asked. "What's up?"

"The thing is..." He paused, as if getting up his nerve for whatever was coming next, then looked her straight in the eyes. "I'm deeply attracted to you, Connie. I can't stop thinking about you. And quite frankly it's driving me nuts."

Connie felt as if been smacked in the face; she even raised her hand to her cheek. She was too shocked to even respond.

"And the reason I wanted to tell you is that I was hoping you might feel the same way about me."

"James, I'm married," she said, finally finding her voice. "I take those vows seriously."

"Nate's not treating you like you deserve," he said fiercely. "Your marriage might have been worth fighting for once upon a time, but now anyone can see that it's over."

She opened her mouth to protest, but feared that he was right.

"James, I'm forty-nine. I'm perimenopausal. I have a grown-up kid and a ton of baggage. I'm flattered, but I'm struggling to see what exactly is in this for you."

"Well, I'll tell you," he said. "I think about you the whole time. I love the sound of your voice and the curve of your neck. You look so good first thing in the morning it takes my breath away. There's nobody I'd rather hike up mountains or drink margaritas with." He tipped his head to the side, studying her. "I could go on. Why is this so hard for you to believe?"

She lifted a shoulder and let it fall.

James's brow creased. "This is too weird for you, isn't it? I'm so sorry, Connie. I can move out if I'd made you feel uncomfortable."

"No! No, not at all. I'm sorry. I'm just in shock."

"Why? Any man would be lucky to have you."

She gave a hopeless shrug. "I'm sorry, James. I just don't know what to do with that information."

"You don't have to do anything with it. For now, just think about it. You've got a lot of other things on your plate right now. And I'm a patient man."

Then before she knew what was happening he reached for her hand and pressed it to his mouth. It was over in an instant, but she was as aware of every moment as if it were freeze-framed: his warm breath, the touch of his lips against her wrist, her breath catching in her throat. She pulled her hand away, but something had stirred inside her, unfurling like the petals of a flower. Connie knew she wanted more, and that knowledge terrified her.

They barely spoke on the hike back down, but James occasionally glanced behind him, and whenever their eyes met, the spot he'd kissed on Connie's wrist throbbed as if she'd been branded. She'd always found James such easy company, but she had no idea how to act around him now. The atmosphere between them was like the air just before a thunderstorm. On the drive home they spoke about the weather and traffic, the sort of thing you talk about to a person you'd met at a party rather than one who'd just asked you to leave your husband for them, and by the time they got back home it seemed far more likely that she had imagined the whole conversation.

As they parked, Connie glanced up at Ethan's room and was

relieved to see that the drapes were still closed. She had hoped he would have a long sleep. It would do him good.

James pressed a button on the dashboard and the car instantly fell silent—not like her old Volvo, which grumbled long after the engine had been turned off. Connie's brain was ordering her to get out of the car, to put some distance between them, so she could process what happened before she did something she'd regret. At the same time, though, she felt irresistibly drawn to him, as if pulled by a magnet at her core.

"I better get back to the city," he said. "I've got meetings in the Manhattan office, so I won't be back in Tansy Falls until Thursday this week."

Connie just nodded. There was a pause, and when James spoke again his voice was low, and sharpened by an urgency she hadn't heard before.

"Will you at least give what I said to you some thought? Because I promise you, Connie, I won't stop thinking about you."

Once again, there was a flicker deep inside her.

"I will," she said—and the breath caught in her chest as those two words triggered an avalanche of guilt.

"I have to go," said Connie, and fled into the house without a backward look.

TWENTY-THREE

For the rest of the weekend, though, Connie could think of nothing but Ethan. In any other circumstances the conversation with James would have hijacked her every waking moment, but her son took priority over everything. As she was powerless to fix his problems, she threw herself into making him feel as loved as possible: cooking his favorite meals, encouraging him to play tennis with Nate and letting him sleep as long as he wanted. By Sunday there was at least a bit of color back in his cheeks and, with each hour that passed without a call from the police or college, he seemed to relax a little more. He visited Frank and the animals next door, and when he came home he was as full of stories about their neighbor's menagerie as he had been as a little boy.

Connie's fears started to ease too, until on Sunday night she made the mistake of going back online to check the video. Her stomach plummeted to see it had now been viewed millions of times. With a trembling hand, she scrolled down to the comments; they were still pouring in, as vitriolic as ever. Her eyes blurred with tears. *That's my sweet, gentle son you're calling an evil rapist.* There was a link to a blog post too, in which the writer denounced the boys in the video as "odious examples of toxic masculinity" and repeated the call for police action. Connie felt like a weight was crushing down on her chest. There were no signs of this "blowing over" as Nate had so confidently predicted; if anything, it seemed to be gaining momentum.

"I really think Ethan should speak to his college advisor," Piper said to Connie.

It was first thing on Monday morning, and they were sitting in the lobby, catching up after the weekend. Piper had just returned from a walk with Boomer, who was sprawled at their feet, panting heavily after some overenthusiastic rabbit chasing.

"I'm sure his college is already aware of the video," Piper went on, "and at least Ethan can then tell them his side of the story. Has he tried to contact this girl—Kayla?"

"Not yet. I think he's embarrassed by how drunk he was, and worried that he somehow failed her."

"But they're friends, right? Leaving aside everything else, I think it would be good if he checked up on her." Piper suddenly winced, her hand flying to her belly.

"Sweetie? Are you okay?"

"Just a bit of cramp. I'm fine."

"You don't look fine. Should I get Spencer?"

"Don't you dare! Any excuse and he'll have me confined to bed all day, and that would really drive me crazy. This baby loves sugar just as much as his mama, and today's cake isn't going to bake itself."

"Surely Rosa and the guys in the kitchen can take care of that?"

"Connie, I *want* to do it! Besides, I'm making my white chocolate and blueberry cake today, and there's no way I'm letting Rosa get hold of my recipe. She's been trying to steal it for years."

Connie held up her hands in surrender; she knew better than to get between Piper and her cake pans. Then at their feet, Boomer's tail started to thump on the floor, as if he was expecting company, and Connie looked up to see Mia

Callaghan, the young woman she had found crying in the gazebo last week.

"Morning, Miss Callaghan," said Connie, glad to see her smiling. "How are you today?"

"I'm good, thank you." Her hand was cradling her bump. "Struggling a little in this heat, though."

"Oh, I hear you," said Piper. "Is there anything we can do to help?"

"No, thank you. I just wondered if there'd been any messages for me while I was out?"

"I haven't taken any calls this morning," said Connie. "Piper?"

She shook her head.

Mia Callaghan's smile faltered. "Well, thank you anyway. Enjoy the rest of your day."

Connie and Piper watched as she trudged wearily up the stairs.

"I do hope she's okay," said Connie. "I found her in tears the other day and she said something about a broken heart. I didn't want to pry, but I can't bear the thought of her having been abandoned with a baby on the way."

"We spoke on the weekend," said Piper, "sharing bump stories, you know. She lives in Manhattan now, but she's originally from San Francisco. I don't know all the details, but I got the impression that the father of her baby lives in Tansy Falls. Reading between the lines, I think he might well be married."

"Ah, well, that would explain the broken heart. Poor girl..."

Piper eased herself up to standing. "Well, I better go and make a start in the kitchen."

"You will take it easy, won't you? Make sure you ask for help with any heavy lifting."

"I'm making a cake, Connie, not changing a carburetor."

"Point taken." She smiled. "Oh, and put me down for a slice of that cake, won't you?"

. . .

When Connie arrived home that evening, Ethan's car was gone from the driveway.

"He's out with some of the gang from high school," Nate explained. "I think they've gone swimming at Smugglers Leap."

"That's so good to hear."

"Yeah. I feel like he's finally beginning to believe this might all just go away."

Connie just nodded; she had given up trying to convince Nate that he should be taking the situation more seriously. "Well, I think I'll go and shower before making a start on dinner, it's so sticky out today."

But as she headed for the stairs, Nate called out: "Connie, wait up."

She turned to look at him.

"I need to talk to you," he said.

"About Ethan?"

"No, about something else. Will you come and sit down?"

"What's this about?" she asked, trying to keep her voice light as she joined him at the table.

"I've been offered a job."

Connie felt a great rush of relief. "Oh, that's fantastic!"

"It's a two-year contract with a small travel publisher, overseeing the production of a new series of guidebooks for 'midlife adventurers.' It's a really interesting role. I'll have lots of creative input, and moving into book publishing could be a really good direction for my career."

"It sounds perfect! This is so exciting. I presume you're going to accept it?"

"Yes. They want me to come into the office later this week to meet the team."

"This is wonderful!" Before she could think, Connie leaned across the table and threw her arms around him, just like she would have done in the past. "Oh, I'm so happy for you, honey."

She beamed at him and although Nate returned the smile, he seemed on edge.

"The thing is, there's a bit of a complication. The publisher is based in San Francisco."

"So you'll be working from home? How long's the flight to San Francisco—about eight hours? I guess you could do that once a month or so, to check in with your team, but so much can be done online these days with video conferencing. You could definitely make it work, for sure."

"No, Connie, the job is *based* in San Francisco."

She looked at him blankly. "What are you saying?"

"I'm saying I'd have to move there."

Her stomach convulsed. "*What?*"

"It would only be for two years. And I would fly home to see you as often as I could."

"I don't understand. You're going to move to San Francisco—without me?"

"Well, I would never ask you to leave your job at the Covered Bridge, that wouldn't be fair."

She was shaking her head, as if she could physically rearrange the information he'd just told her to get it in an order that made sense. "But—I can't—when was your interview?"

"I spoke to the publishing director over Zoom. It was on the day James arrived, do you remember?"

Connie tried to focus; of course, that was the day he'd looked so inexplicably smart. "But that was weeks ago!"

"I didn't want to say anything to you until I knew I'd got the job. I didn't want to jinx it."

"But you were perfectly happy to jinx our marriage! You didn't think it would be considerate to tell your wife you were thinking about moving to the other side of the country?"

"As I said, it wasn't a done deal until today, which is why I'm telling you now," he said, defensiveness creeping into his voice.

"And you just assumed I'd be okay with it? Isn't that a little selfish?"

Nate's eyes flew wide. "Connie, for the past few months our relationship has been falling apart and it's like you haven't even noticed. Every time I try to speak to you about it, you just brush me off. So yes, I thought you'd be as fine about this as you appear to have been about everything else in our relationship recently. To be honest, I wasn't sure you'd even care."

She gaped at him. "How can you say that?"

"Because that's how it feels! You never ask how I am, how I'm doing. I've been falling to pieces and you haven't even noticed."

"Well, maybe that's because I've been too busy holding everything together, trying to keep a roof over our heads! I'm sorry if I haven't been holding your hand, but you're a grown man. Nobody ever asks me if *I'm* fine. I just get on with it, like I always have. I thought maybe that was your approach too. Looks like I was wrong."

Nate's eyes were glazed with pain. "Do you have any idea how badly losing my job affected me? It nearly destroyed me, Connie. It killed my self-esteem. I felt I was too old, washed-up and worthless. I've been so down about it."

"Then why on earth didn't you tell me?"

"I tried!" His voice was shrill with anguish. "And I kept trying, but you never wanted to listen!"

Connie glared at him, her heart racing. "So I've been a terrible wife, have I? This is all *my* fault?"

"No! Of course not. But it's not all mine either." He tried to reach for her hand, but she snatched it away, so whipped up with emotion she felt like a cornered animal. "What's happened to us, Connie?" he asked, his voice breaking with emotion. "Where did it go so wrong? We used to be the best of the best. We were the couple who everyone wanted to be. And now... it's like we're broken. Can we fix it? Can we fix *us*?"

"I don't know, Nate." Her voice was steely. "But I do know that I'm not the one who's running away."

TWENTY-FOUR

Nate left for the airport early on Thursday morning. He had decided to stay on in San Francisco after his meeting with the publisher, visiting a college friend who lived in the city, and wouldn't be back to Tansy Falls until the following week.

"It will do us both good to have some time and space to think," he had said—although with the press trip starting on Friday and Ethan still at home, Connie very much doubted she'd have any time left to ponder the inexorable collapse of their marriage.

Since the argument, they had avoided each other as much as possible in the day and clung to opposite sides of their bed at night, the silence between them as impenetrable as a brick wall. Once upon a time it would have been unthinkable that they would have gone to sleep on an argument, let alone leave it festering for days afterward, but hadn't it also been unthinkable that Nate would move across the country without consulting her? She knew things were bad, but she couldn't believe they had ended up here. Ever the trooper, Connie went through the motions every day, but beneath her bright smile and bustle she felt as hollowed out as if her world was being dismantled brick by brick.

On Friday morning—the morning of the press trip—Connie

opened the drapes to find clouds blotting the horizon, sucking the color out of the landscape. The one day she needed Tansy Falls to dazzle, and it looked like all the countryside wanted was to hop back into bed for a duvet day. "You and me both," she muttered, sloping off to the shower.

On her phone she found a message from Nate.

Good luck today, Connie. I know you'll be brilliant as ever.

She deleted the message without replying.

Connie tried to make up for the grayness of the day by putting on a poppy-red dress and lots of jewelry. The guests would be arriving for the press trip in less than six hours, and if the sun wasn't going to shine, then she would have to instead. But when she caught her reflection in the mirror at the top of the stairs her skin looked dull beneath her makeup, and her eyes as flat as the sky outside. She headed downstairs to the kitchen and in the dim light it took her a moment to realize that James was at the table, his hands clasped in front of him, as if he had been waiting for her there all night. He was dressed for work, his hair swept back and his shirt perfectly pressed. He seemed larger than life, almost unreal, as if a movie star had just wandered into her kitchen.

At the sight of her his face lit up, but his smile faded as he studied her.

"Connie? Is everything okay?"

"Is it that obvious?"

"Has something happened with Ethan?"

"No." She let out a breath. "Nate."

James didn't comment.

"We had an argument. He's gone away for a week."

As soon this was out of her mouth she regretted it. It was a simple statement of fact, but it felt loaded with implication, as if she was issuing an invitation. Judging by the arch of his brow, James had certainly taken it that way.

"I'm sorry to hear that. I'm not going back to the city this weekend, so if you want to talk...?"

"Thank you, but I think I'm going to be busy with this press trip. It starts today and I've got so much to do."

A moment passed, then James pushed back his chair and walked over to where she was standing until he was close enough to touch her. He filled up her senses; his height, the delicious scent of his cologne, the sheer size of him.

"You're so beautiful," he murmured. "I burn for you, Connie."

She held her breath, waiting for whatever might unfold, wrestling with her emotions.

Touch me, touch me not...

"I'll let you get on, but I'll be here on Sunday evening. We'll talk then."

Then he turned and went downstairs, and she finally released her breath in a shaky exhale.

The weather might not be playing ball, but at least the Covered Bridge was looking as gorgeous as it possibly could. Connie spent the morning finishing the preparations with her usual meticulous attention to detail. In each of the journalist's bedrooms she put a box of maple fudge from the Lazy Knoll Sugar Shack, a hand-drawn map of Tansy Falls by a local artist and a folder of information about the inn and town, plus a bottle of sparkling wine chilling in an ice bucket. In Connie's experience, free stuff made everyone happy—even cynical journalists.

After reviewing the itinerary with Spencer, who would be leading the group's hike up Maverick tomorrow and then accompanying them on a paddleboard safari around the reservoir, Connie headed for the kitchen to check on Piper.

She found her slumped on a stool, still wearing her apron. She looked up as Connie came in, her expression defeated. "Please tell me that when your ankles get swollen they do go down again," she said.

"They do. Now will you please go and put them up for the rest of the afternoon? I need you to be on top form for this baking master class with the journalists on Sunday."

For once, Piper didn't argue. "Okay." She called over to the head chef. "Rosa, will you get my sponges out of the oven when they're ready?"

"Sure thing."

Connie watched Piper go, shuffling along the corridor like an old woman. It wasn't like her not to argue; she must be feeling terrible. Well, at least she would be able to rest now. Connie tried to shelve her worries and hurried away to make the final checks.

Just before midday, the driver of the minivan that Connie had arranged to collect the press trip guests from the airport messaged to say they were ten minutes away. Right on schedule.

Connie positioned herself at the front desk and Boomer trotted over and settled by her feet, as if knowing she would appreciate the support. A few minutes later Spencer came and sat with her too, looking every inch the welcoming New England inn host in a plaid shirt and khakis.

"It'll be fine," he said, squeezing her hand. "We're a great team and you've planned a wonderful weekend."

Connie returned Spencer's smile. She had run through her mental checklist countless times this morning and was confident that everything had been taken care of. Her family might tease her for being Capable Connie, but at times like these it came in handy.

Her phone vibrated with another message. "They're just parking," she told Spencer.

To occupy her restless hands, Connie adjusted the vase of roses on the table in front of her, so that the press trip attendees would get its best angle when they entered the lobby. As she did so, the front door swung open.

"Here we go," muttered Spencer, getting up to greet the arrivals.

Connie stood alongside him, putting on her most welcoming smile—and then her heart plummeted, as if she'd just crested the highest peak of a roller coaster, as into the lobby, wearing matching BOCA RATON baseball caps, marched Mitch and Carole Gridley.

TWENTY-FIVE

At the sight of his grandparents, Connie heard Spencer take a sharp intake of breath.

"I'm really not convinced by those hanging baskets on the deck," announced Carole, by way of a greeting. "The colors are awfully clashy."

"Come here, Boomer, old boy!" Mitch squatted down and put out his arms; the dog lolloped happily toward him. "Great to see ya, champ..."

Connie's mouth flapped open and shut like a beached fish. "Mitch, Carole, I—we—weren't expecting you."

"Mitch told Spencer we were coming," said Carole, tweaking the vase of roses. She was wearing a violet-colored sweatshirt that read, NOTHING SCARES ME, I'M A VERMONTER.

Mitch, who was rubbing Boomer's tummy, glanced up. "No, dear, you said you would take care of it."

"I most certainly did not. I clearly remember saying to you—Mitch, you must let Spencer know we'll be in town for the weekend of that dreadful circus of Connie's."

Spencer finally recovered his voice. "Um, it's great to see you, Grandma, Grandpa, but—why are you here?"

Carole kissed him on both his cheeks. "It's our hotel, honey, and as you well know we're perfectly entitled to stop by anytime we like."

"Of course, but I mean, why *now*?"

Mitch leaned on the table for support as he stood, knees creaking. "We thought we'd come and check out these press hoodlums. They're getting a free weekend in our hotel, so we wanted to check they were the right sort of people. Look 'em straight in the eye and see what they're made of."

At that moment there was a sudden frantic yapping and they all swung round to see a young woman in a plunging crop top and baggy jeans stumble through the doorway, dragged by a Pomeranian on a glittery leash. Connie recognized her immediately: it was the influencer Mimi, from Mimi's Delicious Destinations. There was no mistaking that tumbling scarlet hair, which made her look like the flashier sister of Ariel from *The Little Mermaid*.

At the sight of Boomer, Mimi's dog went mad, lunging and snarling with a viciousness that would have been terrifying in an animal that was larger than a donut.

"Ooh, look, Mitch, it's that vulgar Facebook woman," Connie heard Carole say.

"Pikachu, no!" shrieked Mimi. "Leave that big dog alone!"

When the dog didn't quit, a young man with astonishingly muscular arms dropped the bags he was carrying and lunged for the still-yapping dog, then handed it back to Mimi.

She tapped it on its nose. "Bad Pikachu! Mommy is *not* happy with you."

Elbowing his way past Mimi and her pile of bags, a middle-aged man wearing a gray sweatshirt that matched his hair and face strode up to the desk and dumped his luggage. Connie got a whiff of ashtrays and regret.

"That rat of a dog did not shut up the whole way here," he muttered. "Jerry Whitlock. Global Media Group."

After weeks of preparation, Connie knew their résumés off by heart. Jerry was an old school journalist who had been commissioned by a news syndicate that sold stories and features to regional newspapers across the country. His review would appear in hundreds of local newspapers, so it was crucial that he enjoyed his time at the Covered Bridge. Judging by his expression it hadn't got off to a flying start.

"Welcome to the Covered Bridge Inn, Jerry!" Connie went into charm overdrive. "If I may call you Jerry? It's so wonderful to meet you, how was your journey?"

"Perfectly fine, until we got to Burlington and I encountered *that woman.*" He threw a dark look at Mimi. "Now, I need a stiff drink. Which way's the bar?"

Out of the corner of her eye, Connie could see the other guests struggling to maneuver around Mimi's oversized bags which were blocking the doorway. To her relief, Spencer noticed this too. He stepped in and introduced himself to Jerry, freeing up Connie to deal with the logjam.

"If you can just allow me a minute to get you checked in, Mr. Whitlock," Spencer was saying, "I'll show you the way to the bar and pour you a triple myself."

Connie hurried over to help the other guests, passing the Gridleys who were watching the unfolding drama with expressions hovering somewhere between horror and glee. She felt like she should be handing them popcorn.

"Why don't you guys go and see Rosa in the kitchen?" Connie suggested, trying to keep the pleading note out of her voice. "She'll be so pleased to see you! Then I can introduce you to the journalists over lunch once Spencer and I have taken care of the paperwork."

"Didn't I say you should have invited *Reader's Digest*?" muttered Carole, but she allowed Mitch to lead her off to the kitchen, her eye running over everything as she went, no doubt gathering ammunition for her barrage of complaints at a later date.

As she approached the guests, Connie performed a quick mental triage. Mimi seemed happy enough canoodling with her muscled escort (who on earth *was* he?) while a thirty-something woman with a frown, black hair and a cellphone clamped to her ear had made it around the blockade and was heading for the front desk. That would be Andie Ferguson, a freelancer who was writing an article on New England inns that would appear in several prestigious women's magazines. Their final guest, however, was still struggling to get through the doorway, puffing like a steam engine climbing a steep hill. She was a small, round lady, her white hair waxed into spikes. The bright orange frame of her glasses matched the swoosh on her Nike high-tops, though she must have been at least seventy-five.

"Here, let me give you a hand," Connie called over.

This was Elaine Easton, editor at large of *Cakes, Rakes and Lakes*, a popular magazine targeted at seniors that covered, with pleasing literality, baking, gardening and travel.

"Elaine, welcome, I'm Connie Austen, manager of the Covered Bridge."

She pumped her hand. "Connie, hello! Wonderful to meet you. What a charming lobby this is! Our readers would just love that fireplace. I must take some photos—we have a lot of Instagram followers, you know."

"Well, we're thrilled to have you here. Let's get you checked in, then we've arranged lunch for you in the restaurant, where I'll talk you through the weekend's itinerary. We've got some wonderful activities planned." Although having now met her, Connie was unsure whether Elaine would be up to the hike, let alone the paddleboard safari.

"Right you are, Connie. Ooh, you have a Labrador!" She bent to pet Boomer. "Aren't you a handsome boy? Why, I feel right at home already!"

Back at the front desk, Spencer was trying to check in Andie Ferguson, although it didn't look like he was having much success. She was sitting opposite him, but her attention was entirely focused on her cell. Connie overheard snippets of her conversation.

"No, the pumped milk is in the freezer.... Well, that's because they don't like the formula... I got it for emergencies, okay!" Andie slapped a hand against her forehead. "Kevin, I wrote all this down for you. They have two naps in the morning and two in the afternoon, but that last one must be before 5 p.m. otherwise they won't go down at seven... Yes, *of course* you give them milk first, otherwise they'll be too hungry to sleep! Jeez, we have done this twice before, you know... Look, I've got to go... Yeah, yeah. Okay. Bye. Bye." She ended the call, then looked wearily up at Spencer. "Sorry, what was that?"

"I was just saying I need to get your signature here, please," he said, tapping the guest registration form. "Sounds like someone's got their hands full back home," he added, while Andie scribbled her name.

"That was my husband. We have three-month-old twins and this is the first time I've been away from them."

"Goodness, that sounds full-on."

"We also have a two-year-old and a five-year-old." Her shoulders crumpled, as if even just this thought was sapping her energy. "Do you have kids?"

"My wife is about to have our first baby."

"Congratulations, but for everyone's sake please stop there. We had two, decided we'd have go for one more and got a bonus baby for our troubles. I'll be honest—it's pushed us all over the edge. It's like some kind of... living hell."

Spencer's eyes grew wide; Connie could tell he was wrestling with how to respond.

"Well, hopefully you'll be able to relax and enjoy your stay with us," he managed, his smile over-bright.

"Did you hear *any* of that conversation I just had? I won't be relaxing, I'll be parenting via Zoom. I'll be lucky to get any sleep at all."

Connie came to Spencer's rescue. "That sounds extremely stressful," she said to Andie. "What can we do to help you get a few moments of peace? Would you like us to arrange a massage in your room? A yoga class? A large slice of chocolate cake and a temporary Wi-Fi outage?"

Andie laughed. "That might be good, thank you."

Spencer took Andie and Elaine to their rooms, while Jerry had already made a beeline for the bar, so that left only Mimi to deal with. She had been on a video call since the dog drama, the tinny voice of whoever she was speaking to echoing around the lobby. When Connie tried to catch her attention, Mimi gestured for her male companion to deal with it instead. He slouched over, his loose tank revealing bulging pecs.

"Welcome to the Covered Bridge." Connie said with a smile. "I'm sorry, I don't think I have your name?"

"I'm Glen. The Glute Guy?" He said this as if it would mean something to Connie.

"And you're here with Mimi?"

"Yeah. But I have over 34,000 followers," he added, flexing defensively. "And I've just launched my own brand of protein powder."

Connie very much doubted that the followers of an account called Glen the Glute Guy would have any interest in staying at a charming New England inn famed for its cakes and walled garden, but she couldn't exactly ask him to leave.

At that moment, Mimi ended her call and trotted over, still carrying her dog.

"Hiii!" She shook Connie's hand. "Enchanté! This place is just so cute and old-timey, I absolutely love it. And so does Pikachu. Don't you, baby?" She waved the Pomeranian's paw and said in a squeaky voice: "Yes, mommy, I weally, weally wuv it."

"Can I just check, will you and Mr., um, Glute Guy be sharing a room?"

"Absolutely," purred Mimi, tracing a nail down Glen's bicep.

"Well, in that case I'll show you both to your room, then we have lunch for you in the restaurant."

"I think I'll skip that and check out your gym," said Glen.

"I'm afraid we don't have one in-house, but I'd be happy to direct you to the town gym."

He looked as if he'd just been told they were on a sinking ship and the last lifeboat was full.

Mimi stuck out her bottom lip. "We're on vacay, babe. Surely you can have a couple of days' break?"

He muttered something about it being "leg day" but let it drop.

Lunch, at least, went well. Everyone enjoyed Rosa's enchiladas —and Mimi was thrilled with her vegan version—and Andie managed to put down her cellphone long enough to listen to Connie's talk about the inn and Tansy Falls. Jerry had cheered up and got some color in his cheeks—although this was probably down to the bottle of red wine he'd just downed—and Elaine was enthusiastic about everything, from the kale Caesar salad to her server's "darling" hairstyle.

By 3 p.m., with the visitors either relaxing by the pool or browsing the shops on Main Street, Connie finally had a chance to switch on her cellphone—and was horrified to discover five missed calls from Ethan.

Frantic with worry, she called him straight back.

"Ethan?"

"The police called me, Mom. They want me to go back to Pennsylvania to speak to them."

"Okay, honey." Connie's heart was galloping, but she had to stay calm for Ethan. "Did they say why?"

"I'm not sure—maybe. I can't remember, I was kinda freaking out, y'know?"

"I'm sure they just want to ask if you witnessed anything, that's all. When are you going back?"

"Right now. I was just about to get in the car when you called. They want me to come into the police station on Tuesday, but I need to get back and see if I can find out what's going on." He took a breath. "Do you think I need, like, an attorney or something? That's what happens in movies, right?"

"Oh no, I'm sure that isn't necessary," said Connie, although she had no idea if that was true. "Do you want me to come with you?"

"No! I mean, thanks, Mom, but I'd rather deal with it on my own." She heard the sound of a car door slam. "I still haven't heard back from Kayla. I messaged her to see if she's okay—and I can tell she's read it—but she's not replied. What if she somehow blames me, Mom? So much of that night is a blank."

"Try not to worry. Kayla's dealing with a lot right now, you can't expect her to respond to messages. Everything will be okay. Call me when you get back to Pennsylvania, okay?"

"Okay, Mom. I love you."

"I love you too, honey—so much. Everything's going to be okay."

Perhaps if she kept repeating this, it might actually come true.

TWENTY-SIX

Edwin Catesby was holding the evening's cheese tasting in his "cave," a climate-controlled storeroom at the back of Tansy Falls Fine Cheeses. Connie remembered it as quite a sterile space, basically a walk-in fridge, but thanks to the addition of an old farmhouse table and an assortment of vintage candelabras, embellished with rivulets of molten wax, the room now had a surprisingly romantic atmosphere. Cut-glass decanters of wine glittered in the candlelight, while the flickering light gave glimpses of giant wheels of cheddar stacked on wooden shelves around the walls.

As well as the extensive samples of cheese that had been presented with Rothko-like artistry on slate platters, there were also a number of salads, plates of charcuterie and an entire bakery's worth of different breads. As they walked into the room Connie muttered a silent prayer of thanks to Edwin, who had clearly gone to great lengths to make the evening a success.

"Ooh, a dimly lit French cellar and a mysterious gentleman," cried Elaine, blushing as Edwin bowed. "How thrilling! It's like a scene from *La Reine Margot!*"

"Or like that bit in *Beauty and the Beast*," said Mimi, breaking into song. "Be our guest, la-la-la, something-something-da-de-da!"

Only Glen seemed unmoved. "Dairy has been proven to significantly reduce testosterone production," he said, eyeballing the cheese as if it might bite him.

"I reckon those tight shorts of yours would be more of a problem," said Jerry, making Andie—who had pulled up a chair next to him—snort with laughter.

Edwin was an engaging host, with a joke for every type of cheese they sampled ("What music does cheese listen to? R and Brie!") and everyone seemed to be enjoying themselves. After picking at celery sticks for the first half hour, enviously watching the others tuck into the food, Mimi suddenly announced that she was now a vegan "who occasionally eats cheese, and also this particular sort of truffle salami." Edwin kept the Beaujolais flowing and by the end of the night everyone piled happily onto the minivan back to the inn, with Jerry and Glen bringing up the rear, staggering out of the store with their arms wrapped around each other, one of Edwin's HONK IF YOU LOVE CHEESE! bumper stickers stuck to Glen's fanny pack. Connie got home well past midnight and fell into bed without taking off her makeup, which— as she used to tell Nate when they had a social life—was the mark of a successful night. Tonight, though, she just wanted to find the oblivion of sleep as quickly as possible; at least then she'd be able to put a stop to the carousel of worries—Nate, Ethan, James—spinning endlessly in her mind.

Six hours later, as the sun peeked over the horizon, Connie was heading back through the doors to the Covered Bridge. She'd covered up the shadows beneath her eyes and tried her best to muster a smile, hoping that would perk up her spirits too, but the constant worry about Ethan was leaching the positivity from her. Just staying on her feet required effort, and the dazzling morning sunshine and birdsong that would usually bring her such pleasure felt more like an assault.

After the success of last night's cheese tasting, Connie was at least feeling a little more confident about today's activities. This morning Spencer would be taking the group on a gondola ride up Mount Maverick and a guided stroll around the mountain's plateau, and then after lunch he would lead a stand-up paddle-board safari at the reservoir, leaving Connie time to prepare for the gala Taste of Vermont dinner in the inn's restaurant tonight. Thinking about the dinner reminded Connie that she still had to collect the menus from the printers—perhaps she could pop out when she got back from Maverick...

"There you are!"

Connie had barely set foot in the lobby when Carole bustled over to her. She was wearing a lilac sweatshirt emblazoned with the words MY INN, MY RULES in curly pink writing.

"You'll never guess what's happened," said Carole, jowls quivering as if the news was about to explode out of her. "Spence came in and woke us up at 2 a.m. this morning and announced he was taking Piper to hospital. Apparently she'd been bleeding and in pain. That's not good, is it? But then that girl is such a tiny slip of a thing, I'm not really surprised. As I said to Mitch, it's really no wonder she's had a difficult pregnancy. When I was expecting, I ate three pork chops every single day for the entire last trimester. I always used to joke that Spencer's daddy was half man, half hog!"

Connie's body had gone cold. "But how's Piper now? Are they still at the hospital?"

"Oh yes, and Mitch is with them too. I phoned him just now and said, 'You really should come home and get some rest.' But oh no, he *insists* on staying with them. He's always been like that. Such a family man, it's one of the reasons that I—"

Connie almost yelled at her. "For pity's sake, Carole, just tell me if Piper's okay!"

The old woman's lips pursed. "As I just told you, she's in hospital, so I'm sure she's getting all the attention she needs."

Connie had already grabbed her phone and was dialing Spencer's number. He answered on her third try. "Hey, Conn, I'm so sorry about all this, the timing couldn't be worse."

"Don't even think about it. How's Piper? The baby?"

"We don't know. They've got her on a drip. She's sleeping now, but she was in a lot of pain. They're trying to work out what's wrong with her. Her blood pressure is too high, but they're not sure what else might be going on." He faltered, tripping over his emotions. "I'm afraid we're going to be stuck here for the time being. The press trip—"

"We will cope without you. Do you want me to send someone round with a bag of things for you and Piper?"

"Thank you, Connie, but we're good for now. Mitch has offered to come back to the inn for a change of clothes."

"You will let me know when you have any news?"

"Of course. And, Conn?"

"Yes?"

"Thank you so much. We couldn't do any of this without you."

"Don't be silly! Don't give us or the inn another thought, just take care of Piper."

By the time Connie ended the call, Carole was still looking affronted.

"Well, I suppose you're going to need my help running the inn while you run around sorting out this ridiculous press trip of yours," she sniffed.

"Yes," said Connie, her heart sinking. "I suppose I will."

TWENTY-SEVEN

Brody Knott was well known around Tansy Falls for two reasons. Firstly, for his knowledge of Mount Maverick and expertise as head of the mountain rescue team, which was the reason that Connie had phoned him in a panic and asked him to take over as their guide on the morning's hike; and secondly, because he was the town's answer to Brad Pitt (though arguably hotter). His floppy blond hair, boyish grin and chiseled jawline were matched by a nuclear-grade charisma—although regrettably he didn't possess a similarly superior moral code. He mopped up pretty female tourists like a human sponge, and was famous for leaving a trail of broken hearts in his wake.

Connie had arranged to meet him by the gondola station at the foot of Maverick for the morning's guided tour, and even as the group approached she could see Brody clock Mimi's mermaid hair and tanned legs, which were showcased in a pair of shorts so brief they may well have been the bottom half of a bikini. Glen clocked Brody's interest too, and circled a meaty arm about his girlfriend's waist, nostrils flaring like a charging bull. Connie could almost smell the testosterone in the air. She would have to do her best to keep the two of them apart.

For much of the year Mount Maverick was blanketed in snow,

but now the lower slopes were covered in knee-high grass, with splashes of color from a riot of wildflowers. Where snowboarders once took flight over moguls, butterflies now dipped and danced. One thing remained the same, though: just as in winter, the red bubbles of the gondola cars bobbed sedately up the slopes, disappearing into the brightness above.

"Are we going all the way up there?" asked Andie, shielding her eyes as she gazed up at the peak that jutted above the treeline. She had spent the whole drive up to the mountain on the phone explaining to Kevin how to burp two babies at the same time.

"We most certainly are," replied Brody. "Ma'am?" He offered her his arm and Connie saw Andie flutter her lashes; it seemed even hard-nosed hacks weren't immune to the famous Knott charm. Hopefully today he would be happy to stop at flirting.

The group split into two for the ride up to the top. Andie and Jerry went in a car with Brody, while Connie accompanied Elaine, Glen and Mimi. The group had clearly bonded at last night's cheese tasting, and as they set off Glen was chatting to Elaine.

"Have you ever thought about adding 'Snakes' to the name of your magazine?" he asked. "Like, I'd totally buy a magazine called *Cakes, Lakes, Rakes and Snakes*."

Elaine gave him a playful slap. "Oh, Glen, stop it! Personally, I've always thought we rename it *Cakes, Lakes, Rakes and Aches*. Now *that* would be a more accurate title for our readership."

Glen beamed at her, and she patted his arm like he was a favorite grandson. Meanwhile, Mimi was shuffling her way around the gondola's benches trying to find the best light for her selfie.

Once they had got up to the plateau, Brody guided them on a stroll along the ridge, pointing out landmarks in the valley below such as the town's church spire, which could be seen as a white needle against the green, and the silver ribbon of the Wild Moose River, while recounting a history of the mountain and ski resort. He was knowledgeable and entertaining, and as Connie took in the group's smiles and laughter—with even the terminally hungover Jerry perking up—her tension started to ease. Brody had had been an inspired last-minute replacement for Spencer. Perhaps she should ask him to guide the paddleboard safari that afternoon?

They stopped at a grassy patch beneath the shade of a cliff, where Connie spread out picnic blankets and got out the banana and peanut butter donuts and coffee she'd bought from Mistyflip that morning. She was relieved to see Brody pick a spot on the blanket sitting next to Andie and Jerry, and she felt her face relax into a smile for the first time that morning. She'd been worrying unnecessarily about him pouncing on Mimi. Perhaps Brody wasn't so keen on redheads? Or maybe Tansy Falls' most eligible bachelor had finally grown up?

After they'd finished eating, Connie was reclining against her backpack, enjoying the song of a mountain warbler somewhere nearby, when Brody said: "If you look just over there, guys, you'll see the track that leads up to the very top of the peak."

"Goodness, that looks treacherous," gasped Elaine.

"It is." Brody nodded thoughtfully. "In fact, every year there's a famous race starting from this very spot up to the highest point of the mountain. It's called the Maverick Muscle Challenge."

Connie narrowed her eyes at Brody. She'd never heard of the Maverick Muscle Challenge; in fact, she had a strong suspicion he had just made it up.

"Yeah, it's a *totally* hardcore event," Brody went on. "The record to the top is fourteen minutes, but that guy was, like, super fit." He ran an eye over the group, lingering on Glen. "I can't imagine anyone will ever be able to beat his time."

In one swift move, Glen was on his feet. "I will take that challenge," he growled.

"Whoa, are you sure, dude?" asked Brody. "It's pretty gnarly up there."

"I'm not called the Glute Guy for nothing."

Brody broke into a lazy smile; this was too easy.

"Okay, man. I'll time you. Best of luck." He made a show of setting his watch as Glen assumed a racing stance. "Ready, set—go!"

As soon as Glen powered around the bend, Brody got up, stretched, and then casually wandered over to where Mimi was preening against a rock. Connie's heart sank. She had been wrong about Brody not being interested in Mimi; he'd just been playing the long game.

"Hey." Brody treated Mimi to the signature Knott move: dropping his gaze, then looking up at her through his blond bangs, his smile suggesting a world of possibilities.

"Hey there, mister." Mimi licked her lips.

From an anthropological point of view, it was fascinating—like watching a documentary on gorillas' courtship rituals—but Connie was pretty sure this would not end well. Not for poor Glen, at least.

Brody dropped on his haunches next to Mimi. "I was wondering whether you like waterfalls?"

"I do! They are the absolute *best* for Insta."

"Well, if you'd like, I could take you to see one now. It's not far from here."

"I would totally love that," squealed Mimi.

"Neat." He held out his hand to help her up. "Back soon, Connie," he threw over his shoulder.

"Make sure you take lots of photos!" Elaine called. "Our readers love waterfalls!"

Andie rolled her eyes, having clocked what was going on, while Jerry was softly snoring, sleeping off last night's wine and whiskey.

"Don't be long, guys!" called Connie.

But if they had heard her, they didn't acknowledge it.

Twenty minutes later, a red-faced Glen came tearing back down the path and slowed to a halt by the group. He bent over, his hands on his knees, sucking in lungfuls of air.

"What was my time, man?" he said, still breathless.

When there was no reply, he straightened up and looked round. "Where's Mimi?"

"She went to look at a waterfall with Brody," said Elaine. "They do seem to be taking their time, though. Do you think we should go and look for them, Connie? Perhaps they're lost."

Glen's expression turned from confusion to shock to fury as it dawned on him what had happened.

"Where the heck has he taken her?" he growled, the veins in his neck and temples all standing out. "Which direction did they go?"

Connie jumped up, reluctant to lose another member of the group. "Let's just wait for them here, shall we? I'm sure they won't be long, and Glen, you must need to rehydrate after all that running. I reckon you've definitely set a new record in the Maverick Muscle Challenge, though!"

"Oh, how wonderful!" Elaine broke into applause. "Bravo, Glen! What a tremendous achievement!"

Connie would have to find the poor guy a medal. It was the very least she could do.

TWENTY-EIGHT

Another half hour passed, and the waterfall party still hadn't returned. Connie had been sending increasingly frantic messages to Brody's cellphone telling them to get back RIGHT NOW. She wasn't worried for their safety—he knew Maverick better than his backyard, after all—but she *was* concerned for Glen's blood pressure. Since getting back from his run he had spent the entire time pacing back and forth, muttering to himself, fists clenched.

"You'll wear a hole in that rock, Glen," said Jerry. He was still stretched out on the scrubby grass, dozing off his hangover.

"I do hope that young man is behaving himself," said Elaine, oblivious to Glen's brewing fury. "He had the look of a lothario, I thought. Don't you agree, Glen? My mother would have said he had shifty eyes, and she would have been absolutely right."

Just then Connie's phone buzzed with a message. Thank goodness, it was Brody.

Sorry, took a wrong turn. Don't worry, will get Mimi back to inn later!!

He'd even had the cheek to sign off with a wink face emoji and a thumbs-up. Cursing Brody Knott—and herself for trusting him in the first place—Connie turned to the group.

"Good news, everyone, Mimi is fine! They've just got a bit lost. Let's get back down the mountain and grab some lunch, then Mimi will join us at the inn."

Glen growled and punched a nearby bush.

Back at the inn, Connie hurried to speak to Carole at the front desk, anxious for news of Piper.

"Any word from the hospital?"

"Did you know that Piper has changed my banana muffin recipe?" Carole thrust a half-eaten muffin at her. "What in the name of all that's holy are these black specks?"

Connie forced herself to take a breath. "I think they're chia seeds, Carole. But—the hospital? Have you heard from Spencer?"

"Not as yet." She looked back down at the offending muffin, a groove forming between her brows. "I'll be having words with Piper about this. She promised me she wouldn't mess with that recipe. It's been passed down through generations of Gridley women." She gave an exaggerated huff and dropped the muffin in the wastebasket. "Housekeeping tells me that Facebook woman's dog has made a mess in her room. I was going to add a damage fee to her bill, but then I remembered that Connie, in her *infinite wisdom*, had decided to let her stay for free."

"Don't worry, Carole, I'll deal with it," said Connie, wearily.

"Make sure you do. Where is she anyway?"

"Mimi? She's been kidnapped by Brody Knott."

Carole rolled her eyes. "That man is a walking sexual harassment suit. You should have asked Mitch to take the mountain tour. He'd have been a far safer pair of hands. They certainly don't wander as much as the Knott boy's, that's for sure."

"Thank you, Carole, that's very helpful," muttered Connie.

. . .

Mimi still hadn't reappeared by the time they headed off for the paddleboard safari after lunch. Connie had never been on one in her life, but asking Brody to lead the group was clearly completely out of the question, even if he wasn't still MIA. Still, Connie was a strong swimmer, so she was sure she could at least manage to lead the group on a sedate paddle around the reservoir.

As they all filed back onto the minivan again, Connie checked her phone. Still nothing from Spencer, although there was a message from Jackson Quaid. She took a seat next to the driver and clicked it open.

Hi, Connie. Just checking all ok for dinner later? Wish me luck! Jackson.

Connie frowned at this for a long moment, then her eyes went wide. "Darn it," she muttered. How could she have forgotten about Jackson's plan to propose to Nell in the inn's restaurant tonight? She typed out a reply.

Everything is fine! See you later.

Connie was beginning to feel like she should have these words tattooed on her forehead. I'm having a complete breakdown, my family and career are in jeopardy and my life is spiraling out of control, but—*everything is fine!*

"What exactly is an SUP?" asked Elaine, who was sitting behind her looking at the itinerary. "Is it a type of car?"

"Stand-up paddleboard," explained Andie, from the seat opposite. "It's kind of like a windsurf without a sail. Oh—sorry, Elaine, I've gotta take this..." Her phone had started to ring again. "Kevin? What's happened now?"

"Well, that sounds like tremendous fun," announced Elaine. "Our readers love water sports."

Thank goodness for Elaine's relentless positivity, thought Connie, as she bashed out a message to Rosa in the kitchen alerting

her to Jackson's marriage proposal plan. At least it was straightforward: the ring was to be displayed on Nell's dessert plate, around
the edge of which would be written "Will you marry me?" in
chocolate sauce. The server would place the plate in front of Nell
and as she looked at the plate Jackson would drop to his knee, then
it would be all tears, smiles and happily ever after.

Within moments Rosa had replied to say that she was on it,
and Connie gratefully ticked this off her mental to-do list and
turned her attention to the world outside the minivan window.
Just the sight of the trees and meadows calmed her. Green was
such a soothing color, she thought, resting her forehead on the cool
glass, grateful for a moment to herself. In time, though, she became
distracted by a low muttering somewhere behind her. She turned
to see Glen sitting on the back seat of the minivan, cradling
Pikachu (who was no longer trusted to stay in the room on his
own) and staring blankly ahead, his lips moving as if repeating a
mantra.

Jerry had looked around too. He was nursing a takeaway cup of
black coffee and had an unlit cigarette behind his ear. "You okay
back there, Glen?"

"I'm gonna kill him," Glen was saying, seemingly oblivious to
Pikachu methodically licking every inch of his face. "I'm gonna
find him, and then I'm gonna kill him."

Jerry just raised an eyebrow. "Whatever you say, son."

The Tansy Falls reservoir formed a hammock of water between
Maverick's tree-clad foothills. The trees reached right to the water-
line, as if the lake had drowned the rest of the valley, and the water
was so still that the undulating hillside was reflected in perfect
facsimile, the two halves forming a giant, green crocodile.

The minivan dropped the group near the "beach," a pebbly
stretch of shore that was always busy with swimmers and kids in
the summer, and which was also where you could rent paddle-
boards. Connie made sure everyone was kitted out with lifejackets,

boards and paddles, and then led them into the shallows, wading through the water and pushing the SUP in front of her.

"Will we be having a lesson, Connie?" asked Elaine, whose too-big lifejacket was right up round her ears. "I'm not sure I have a clue what I'm meant to be doing."

Connie looked out at the paddleboarders on the lake, taking in their wide-legged stance and position on the board. They made it look easy.

"I think it's fairly straightforward," she told Elaine, with more confidence than she felt.

"Yeah, how hard can it be?" said Jerry, taking a drag on his cigarette. Then he clambered onto his board, got into a wobbly crouch and stood up. There was an almighty splash and Jerry resurfaced, the dripping cigarette still clenched between his teeth.

"Pretty hard, as it turns out," he said.

"You can just kneel down if you prefer," called Andie, who was already paddling out ahead of them. "See?"

As the group made wobbly progress out onto the lake, Glen came powering past them on his board at such high speed that he almost left a wake. Connie got a glimpse of his clenched jaw, like the granite cliff of Maverick, and bulging eyes. On the back was Pikachu, the poor dog's legs braced to stop him from falling off.

Soon the group was steadily making their way around the reservoir, the only sound the gentle plop and splash of their paddles. Connie pointed out the beveled stump of a tree left by a beaver on the shoreline, and then a family of loons, their black-and-white feathers giving the look of tuxedos. As they passed, one of the birds took flight, tiptoeing across the surface of the water, wings beating furiously, before it managed to launch itself into the air. A large raptor circled overhead, a black hieroglyph on a blue page. It was perfectly peaceful—until an all-too-familiar noise shattered the calm.

"Sorry, that's me!" called Andie.

Jerry was open-mouthed. "You brought your *phone* out here?"

"It was just in case of—hello? Oh, oops!" A soft plop. "NO!" A bigger splash, as Andie jumped into the water. She surfaced, spluttering: "I dropped my cell in the water!"

"Praise be," muttered Jerry.

"I can't find it!" She ducked under the water, resurfacing moments later. "It must have sunk!"

Connie jumped in the water to help her look for it, but it had gone.

Treading water, Andie was on the verge of tears. "What if it was an emergency? If he can't hold of me, then..."

"I'm sure Kevin will call the inn, who can then contact me," said Connie.

"We have to get back right now." Andie pulled herself onto her board. "I need to speak to him, to find out what's wrong..."

Elaine had paddled over to join them. "Andie, Kevin will be able to cope without you just fine. He's a grown man, and you've raised two other children, so I'm sure he can just about remember which end is up."

"But what if he can't?" she wailed.

"Well then, he can just ask someone else. Or google it. Or perhaps sort it out on his own for once."

Sitting on her board, Andie ran her hair through her wet curls. "I guess so," she said, clearly unconvinced.

"We should probably be heading back now anyway," said Connie, checking her watch. "We just need to find Glen first."

Jerry scanned the water. "He's probably halfway to Maine by now."

Somehow, Connie managed to limp through the rest of the afternoon. She felt like a 100-year-old who had just run a marathon at the same time as going through a nasty divorce. *This time tomorrow it will all be over*, she reminded herself, as she laid out the menus for the evening's Taste of Vermont dinner with the help of Shae, the restaurant manager. They had decided to seat the press trip group out on the open-air terrace, so they could enjoy the view of Maverick against the star-filled night sky. The scent of roses hung in the evening air and strings of fairy lights crisscrossing above the long table provided a welcoming glow.

"Any word from Spencer?" asked Shae, arranging little jars with posies of red clover, Vermont's state flower, around the table.

"No, but Carole got an update from Mitch," said Connie.

It had been a frustratingly brief conversation: Connie had pumped her for details, but Carole seemed more concerned that Mitch hadn't been able to have a proper lunch.

Connie went on: "It sounds like Piper's very poorly, and they're still trying to work out what course of action would be in the best interest for her and the baby."

Shae shook her head. "I'm so worried about her."

"Me too."

They stood back and surveyed the table; even Connie had to admit it looked perfectly Instagram-worthy.

"How are you getting on with the journalists?" asked Shae. "Do you think the weekend's been a success so far?"

Connie grimaced. "Well, we've only managed to lose one person, which I suppose counts as a win."

When they'd got back to the inn after the SUP trip, Carole had met them in the lobby and gleefully informed them that Mimi was still AWOL. Glen took the news in silence, then stalked off upstairs, Pikachu clutched under his arm like a wet, fluffy man-purse. Brody hadn't messaged her again, but Connie had seen that Mimi had posted to Instagram that afternoon. It was a photo of the landscape, with Mount Maverick in the far background, and Mimi's pastel-manicured hand holding an ice cream cone in the foreground. She had captioned it "always in the mood for sprinkles" and among the litter of hashtags underneath was #whenbaeguessesyourflavorfirsttime #VTvacayvibes. Despite scrutinizing it for clues, Connie had no idea where the photo had been taken.

The post had already racked up hundreds of likes, and it was a small silver lining that Mimi was at least alive and had remembered to tag the Covered Bridge Inn in her post.

Connie thought about Shae's question: had the weekend been a success? She really had no idea. Elaine seemed to be enjoying herself, and she was pretty sure that Andie would be complimentary. Since losing her phone, she seemed to have rediscovered her mojo. When she had got back to the inn, Andie had asked have a slice of chocolate cake sent up to her room.

"I'm gonna have it in the bath, while reading a magazine," she said, eyes sparkling.

"And if Kevin calls?" asked Connie.

Andie grinned. "Tell him I'm lost somewhere up a mountain."

That only left Jerry, and his all-important syndicated review for hundreds of local newspapers. Connie found it hard to imagine it would be positive, but then Jerry wasn't exactly a positive sort of person. Hopefully, she thought, he would be won over by the dinner tonight, which was set to be the highlight of the weekend— and then Carole wouldn't have an excuse to fire her after all.

TWENTY-NINE

By 8 p.m. the restaurant was full, the bustling room soundtracked by the familiar burble of chatter, reassuring Connie everything was running smoothly and as it should be. She was hovering at the entrance to the restaurant, ready to escort the press group to their table, where she too would join them for dinner. As she waited, she ran an eye over the room like a director surveying the stage, reassured that tonight's performance was proceeding without a hitch.

"Connie!" She looked up to see Nell and Jackson strolling toward her, arm in arm.

"Hello, lovebirds! I'll show you to your table. You're out on the terrace tonight."

"Oh, how lovely," said Nell, her English accent undiminished after more than a year in Tansy Falls.

Once Connie had seated them, she caught Jackson's eye and he gave a slight nod. Moments later she saw him say something to Nell, then he got up and walked over to where Connie was stationed by the restaurant entrance. She drew him out of sight, behind a large potted plant.

He opened his hand to reveal a princess-cut solitaire diamond set on a platinum band. "Do you think Nell will like it?'

"Oh, Jackson, it's stunning!" Connie put it in her pocket. "I promise I'll look after it."

He shot her a nervous smile. "Well, I guess I'll see you on the other side."

"Good luck!" Connie softly called after him.

Moments later, Andie and Elaine arrived.

"Well, don't you two look spectacular?" said Connie, taking in Elaine's purple robe trimmed with marabou feathers and Andie's pale pink jumpsuit, her skin glowing and her hair swept on top of her head. "This way, dinner is al fresco tonight."

As they emerged out onto the starlit terrace, Connie was pleased to see both women in raptures over the table, with Elaine snapping photos on her phone.

"Can I get you something to drink? We have a winery right near Tansy Falls that makes a very interesting sparkling wine. We say it's like champagne's wilder little sister."

"Ooh, I like the sound of that," said Elaine. "Andie?"

"I have a rule never to say no to bubbles."

Just then, Jerry joined them. "Ladies." He nodded, taking a seat. "I'll have a glass of whatever the others are having, Connie, thank you."

As she went off to the bar to place their order, she passed Glen coming in the other way. He was wearing a buttoned-up shirt with tailored shorts that barely contained his bulging physique. The effect was faintly ridiculous, like the Incredible Hulk on his way to a wedding, and Connie felt a pang of sympathy for the poor guy. He was very much alone; Mimi still hadn't reappeared.

"How are you doing, Glen?"

"I've been listening to a TED Talk called 'Your Ego Is Not Your Amigo.'"

"And has it helped?"

He raised a meaty shoulder. "I guess."

"Well, that's great. One step at a time."

Having made sure the group all had drinks, Connie headed off to the kitchen to check on the starters. After the calm of the dining room, the kitchen felt like a subway station at rush hour. She and Rosa, the inn's head chef, had put a great deal of thought into the evening's menu, which was intended to showcase the best of Tansy Falls' produce. They were starting with locally foraged wild mushrooms on sourdough topped with lardons and a poached bantam egg, and Connie was standing out of the way, watching the team assemble the finished dish, when she suddenly remembered the ring.

She hurried over to where Rosa was tasting something from a bubbling pan. "Where shall I put this? It's for Jackson's proposal."

The head chef whistled. "That's some rock. Give it to Miguel, he'll be plating dessert."

By the time the group started on the main course, which was fried rabbit with sunchokes and crème fraiche, Glen had his huge arm draped over Jerry's shoulders. The pair of them had red and watery eyes, but Connie was pretty sure it was more to do with the three empty bottles in front of them, rather than Tansy Falls' pollen count.

Carole and Mitch had wanted to sit with the group, but Connie had persuaded them that they would be better able to keep an eye on the proceedings from their own table at the other end of terrace. She knew Carole wasn't convinced by the more contemporary direction Rosa was taking the food at the inn, and during the evening she occasionally saw her prodding suspiciously at her plate.

"Compliments to the chef, Connie, that was outstanding," said Elaine, pushing her knife and fork together with a contented sigh.

"Yeah, it was super good," agreed Glen. "The ideal ratio of protein, fat and carbohydrate."

"I'm glad you all enjoyed it. Now, we couldn't show off our local ingredients without including maple syrup, so for dessert we have a maple panna cotta with brioche crumbs and a pear coulis."

As the group murmured their approval, Connie spotted Shae

crossing the terrace toward the table where Jackson and Nell were sitting. She was carrying a dessert plate, and as she passed Connie she shot her a look that said: *all sorted.* Connie replied with a thumbs-up, relieved that it had gone to plan and excited about what was about to unfold.

But just as Shae reached Jackson and Nell's table, Connie heard a bubbly voice shriek, 'I'm back!" and she spun round to see Mimi weaving through the restaurant trailing a sheepishly grinning Brody Knott. Oh, this was not good. Did Brody have a death wish?

With a roar, Glen jumped up and threw back his chair, sending Andie's red wine flying all over her pale pink jumpsuit, then flew at Brody like a battering ram. The pair of them came crashing down, knocking Shae off her feet and sending the plate she had been carrying—and with it the diamond-topped meringue —high up into the air. Jackson leapt to his feet, while Brody and Glen rolled around on the floor, sending the other diners scrabbling for safety. After a moment Brody managed to get away from Glen, crawling through the fallen furniture until he emerged next to Jackson and Nell's table.

"Hey, Nell." He grinned as he clambered to his feet. He had tried to seduce her back when she first arrived in town, and clearly couldn't resist a second chance. "And Jackson, sorry about disturbing your—"

But then Glen was on him again and this time landed a punch squarely on his jaw, and Brody crumpled to the floor.

Connie had been frozen in horror but now worked her way across the room towards the chaos. "Glen, he's not worth it!" she shouted. "Your ego is not your amigo—remember?"

Muttering the sort of language that would make Carole faint, Brody staggered to his feet, squashed meringue all over his pants. So *that* was where Nell's dessert plate had got to, thought Connie, diving to the floor to find the ring. Meanwhile, Brody tried to land a punch on Glen, but despite the latter's vast bulk he was nimble, and he dodged the fist, then felled Brody with a blow to his stomach.

"Glenny, please—no!" shrieked Mimi, her hands clutching her cheeks.

Glen's red mist had fully descended, though, and he would have gone in to finish the job if Jerry hadn't put a steadying hand on his arm, giving Brody a chance to get up again.

Then Connie spotted something sparkling amid the mess of broken tableware and crushed meringue and pounced. "Jackson!" She held up the ring and he sprinted over to get it, and as the entire restaurant looked on, shell-shocked by what had just occurred, Jackson dropped to his knee in front of Nell.

"Penelope Swift, will you do me the honor of becoming my wife?"

Her hands flew to her mouth. "Yes! Oh yes, of course I will."

They fell into each other's arms and the entire restaurant erupted into cheers. Even Brody, who was leaning on a table nearby, with cream in his hair and a bloody nose, whooped and whistled.

"This is so great, man," he called to Jackson. "Congratu—"

As Glen's fist connected with his cheek Brody crumpled to the ground in a heap, this time out cold.

THIRTY

The buzz of a message arriving on her phone woke Connie the next morning. She opened her eyes a crack; judging by how dark the room was, it was sometime before dawn. *Go back to sleep*, she urged herself, but while her body was willing, her limbs as heavy as if anaesthetized, her brain was already wide awake, flicking between the day's agenda and the events of last night.

She had stayed at the inn until the early hours, working alongside the restaurant team to clear up the smashed plates and broken furniture. An apologetic Brody had stayed behind to help too, brushing off Connie's worries about a concussion, although the integrity of his facial symmetry was clearly proving a concern.

"What d'you think, Connie?" Brody turned his head from side to side in front of a mirror. "Does my nose look crooked to you?" He gingerly touched his battered face. "Ouch."

"Hard to tell, because it's so swollen," she said, walking past carrying a stack of chairs.

"I think it might be broken," said Brody morosely.

Nearby, Shae was picking up shards of glass. "No more than you deserve," she had muttered.

Spread-eagled on the mattress, in the exact position she'd collapsed a few hours earlier, Connie finally admitted defeat: the

USS *Sleep* had set sail without her. With a groan, she stuck out an arm and fumbled for her phone, bringing it to her face so she could read the message. She clicked on the alert—and immediately scrabbled up to sitting.

It was a photo of a baby wrapped in a hospital blanket.

Our miraculous son, Edison Hunter Gridley, arrived at 4:32 a.m. on Sunday, weighing 5lb 5oz. Mom and baby both doing beautifully.

Fingers trembling at her lips, Connie reread Spencer's message. "Thank the Lord," she murmured, blinking away tears that had appeared out of nowhere. As she looked at the photo, marveling at this perfect new human who gazed into the camera with Piper's eyes, another message popped up.

He's here, Connie!! A hellish forty-eight hours followed by an emergency caesarean, but Piper's out of danger and already recovering. Edison is perfect and we can't wait to introduce him to his Auntie Conn. Thank you from the bottom of our hearts for everything you've done this weekend. We're very lucky to have you.

Connie smiled at his words, but judging by her tirade last night Carole felt very differently to her grandson. And when it came to Connie's future job prospects, Grandma Gridley's opinion was unfortunately the only one that mattered.

The last event on the press trip itinerary that Sunday was meant to be Piper's baking masterclass. A professionally trained pastry chef, Piper had been intending to teach the group how to make a matcha green tea and pistachio cake, one of the inn's most popular daily specials. Instead, Carole was now leading the class—and she had always disapproved of Piper's "fussy, French" style of patisserie.

When Connie went to the kitchen, she found Jerry, Andie and

Elaine positioned around the large table in front of piles of ingredients, all wearing the branded Covered Bridge aprons that she had ordered as souvenirs for the group.

"You guys look so great. Let me take a photo!" said Connie, reaching for her phone.

"Make it quick," said Carole, "we're about to get started."

Connie did as she was told, then joined the others at the table. "No sign of Mimi or Glen?" she asked.

Andie shook her head. "I can understand why they haven't showed up."

"Mimi must be mortified," said Elaine.

"I didn't see them at breakfast either," added Jerry.

Carole clapped her hands, making them all jump. "Quiet, please, bakers! During today's lesson I expect you to maintain a neat and tidy area at all times. If you need help, please raise your hand. I will not tolerate excessive chitter-chatter."

"Uh, are we baking cakes or heading out on military maneuvers?" asked Jerry.

Carole ignored him. "Today we'll be making the Covered Bridge's world-famous banana muffins. Pay close attention to the recipe, as I will be giving points for taste, crumb quality and overall appearance."

"Ooh, are they the muffins we had at breakfast with the chia and cardamon?" asked Elaine. "They were absolutely delicious."

Carole's eyes bulged. "These are the *original* Covered Bridge banana muffins. People come to stay here solely for these muffins. Chia seeds have no business being anywhere near a *muffin!*"

She stared around the room with a Terminator glare, as if primed to laser anyone who contradicted her.

"Right, we'll start by mixing the dry ingredients. Firstly, we need one and a half cups of flour." She filled the measure in front of her, tapping and leveling with precision, while keeping an eye on the rest of the group. "The gentleman at the back—that is *not* how we measure flour. If you pack it in like that you'll end up with a dusty muffin."

"That sounds uncomfy," said Andie, making the others snigger.

Judging by the amount of spilled flour on Jerry's bench—not to mention the fact that he'd just picked up the baking soda when he was meant to be adding sugar—Connie could see he was struggling.

"Here, let me help you," she said.

"Thanks, Connie." His face relaxed in relief. "I'll be honest, I'm not much of a baker. My late wife, Susan, she used to make the most delicious cakes and cookies, so I was happy to leave her to it..." He drifted off for a moment, then shot Connie a quick smile. "Ah well. I guess it's high time I learned to make them myself."

"Yo, homies!"

Mimi had burst into the kitchen, her arms snaked around Glen, who looked like the cat who ate an entire aviary of canaries. Their hands were all over each other and they were as giggly as newlyweds; contrary to Elaine's assumption, Mimi looked about as far from mortified as it was possible to get. It was as if last night's drama had never even happened.

"Can we join in?" She bounced over to Elaine. "What are we making?"

"We're baking banana muffins, dear, and then Carole's going to grade us on our efforts."

"And if your muffins don't rise, you'll be court marshaled," added Andie.

"OMG, are these the vegan chia muffins we had at breakfast yesterday?" Mimi made a heart shape with her fingers in front of her chest. "Love!"

Carole looked as if she might just combust.

The minivan had been loaded up with luggage and the driver climbed in, signaling that it was time to leave for the airport. Feeling curiously emotional, Connie began her farewells to the press trip guests. She started with Elaine, who clasped both her hands in hers, her cheeks dimpling.

"Well, Connie, it's been an action-packed few days. I certainly won't be short of copy for the magazine."

Having no idea whether this was actually a positive thing, Connie just smiled. "Thank you so much for coming, Elaine, you've been a ray of sunshine. We've loved hosting you."

"Oh, I'm not sure Carole would agree. She gave me a very poor GPA for my muffins, although I thought they were delicious, 'overly coarse crumb grain' and all!" She kissed Connie's cheek. "Goodbye, my dear, take care."

Andie was almost unrecognizable from the hunched, haunted woman who had arrived two days ago, cellphone perma-clamped to her ear. Her skin was glowing and she was sauntering along as if on a beach, rather than a blazing-hot parking lot.

"Have you got all the information you need for your article?" Connie asked her.

"I think it's all in the press pack, but I'll email if not. Thanks for everything, Connie."

They hugged, and Andie turned to get on the bus.

"Don't forget to send us the dry-cleaning invoice for your jumpsuit!" Connie called after her.

Andie waved away her concern, even though it was probably ruined. In fact all of the journalists had been very sweet and understanding about last night's disaster, though Connie cringed when she thought about what they might write about it in their articles.

Jerry stuck out his hand. "See ya, Connie. I'll be filing the copy first thing tomorrow and will send it over to you next week so you can take a look."

"I do hope you've enjoyed your stay."

"It's been... well, eye-opening." He gave a snort of laughter. "At least I now know how it feels to appear in a daytime soap." Jerry turned his head. "Actually, where *are* Elizabeth Taylor and Richard Burton?"

Connie looked around the car park, but Glen and Mimi were nowhere to be seen.

"Back in a sec," she shouted to the driver.

After a panicked few minutes, she eventually located the love-birds in the walled garden. Mimi was performing a headstand among the flowerbeds, wearing a yellow sports bra and leggings that matched her yoga mat. Meanwhile Glen was acting as photographer, with Pikachu in one hand and his iPhone in the other.

"That looks sick, babe," he was saying. "How about you try a downward dog?"

Hovering by the hollyhocks, Connie cleared her throat. "Sorry to interrupt guys, but the minivan is leaving."

Mimi turned herself the right way up. "Boo." She pouted.

While she rolled up her mat, Glen came over to Connie.

"Thanks, man, it's been a blast," he said. "I'm afraid I'm not going to be able to post about it on Insta, though. The lack of a gym..."

"It's okay, Glen, I understand."

They walked back to the minivan together, Mimi threading her arm through Connie's.

"Thank you so much for everything, I've had the *best* time. I'm gonna tell all my followers how much I loved staying in Randy Falls."

"Thanks, Mimi. And it's *Tansy* Falls."

She slapped her forehead, giggling. "I'm such a goof! I'll get it right on my posts, cross my heart." She looked over to where Glen was stowing their bags onto the minivan, then brought her face close to Connie. "Will you message me Brody's number?"

"Oh! Um, yes—sure."

"You're a doll." Mimi took a last look around and blew a two-handed kiss into the air. "Bye, Pansy Falls, I'll be back!"

When Connie came back into the lobby, she found Carole and Mitch waiting for her.

"What a farce," said Carole, her arms folded across her ample bosom as if to stop it escaping. "I very much doubt we'll get any positive press out of it. In fact it's probably going to actively harm our reputation." She poked a finger at Connie. "This is on you," she fumed, then stalked off as best she could with her bad hip.

Watching her go, Connie's heart sank.

"You did your best, honey." Mitch patted her arm. "Can't win 'em all..."

THIRTY-ONE

At the end of her shift, Connie decided to leave her car at the inn and walk home. Her body was wilting with exhaustion, but her mind was like a computer with dozens of tabs left open. Now the press trip was out of the way, the rest of her problems rushed in. Her marriage was over, her career was possibly ruined, her son's once-bright future uncertain. Connie hoped that some fresh air and trees would help; it was a remedy that hadn't failed her before. Besides, Connie was in no rush to get home, because then she would have to face up to her feelings for James—and that was a knot she had no idea how to untie.

There was a part of her that yearned for him, in the same way you'd long for water when thirsty, or warmth when cold: a deep, physical need. This was the part of her that kept returning to the conversation they had on Maverick, savoring the memory of James's eyes on hers, and her ache of desire when he told her she was beautiful. There was another part, though, that wanted only to make things right with Nate, which had already forgiven him for San Francisco and just wanted him home again. Through this lens, there could be no Connie without Nate—or, at least, not a Connie that she herself recognized. If Nate wasn't by her side, she would have to start over and build herself into an entirely new woman. But could she do that? Did she even want to?

As Connie walked past the town hall her phone began to vibrate. She looked at the screen: Lana. They had last spoken a few days ago, when Connie had called to reschedule their weekend swim and ended up sobbing out the latest news about Ethan and Nate.

"Hey there, Mrs. Austen," Lana greeted her. "I'm phoning to make sure you haven't tumbled into a bottomless pit of despair."

Just the sound of her best friend's voice made Connie smile. "It's been a close-run thing, but I'm just about managing to stay away from the edge. I've made it through the press trip weekend, though it's not exactly been smooth sailing."

"Knowing you, I'm sure it's been a fabulous success."

"We'll see." She didn't have the strength to give her all the gory details right now; that was a story to share over a stiff drink.

"When's Ethan going to talk to the police?"

"Tomorrow afternoon."

"And your lousy, stinking toad of a husband is coming back on...?"

"Thursday. I've got a day off tomorrow, thank goodness."

"Do you want me to come over tonight? We could get takeout, maybe watch a movie."

"That would be lovely, but..." Connie chewed her lip. "I've got myself in a bit of a"—she grappled for the right word—"a situation. With James. The lodger."

"I see." A pause. "And is this a situation of a... romantic nature?"

"I suppose you could say that, yes. He told me last week that he's attracted to me. That he thinks I'm beautiful, and can't stop thinking about me."

"Wow. That's intense."

"It is. I'm flattered and freaked out in equal measures."

"How do you feel about him?"

It took so long for her to answer, Lana had to check she was still there.

"I do find him attractive," Connie admitted. "He's so charming, and I enjoy hanging out with him. He makes me laugh, he listens to me—I mean, *properly* listens—and I've got to admit that I really like the feeling of being desired after years of feeling like the invisible woman."

"Yeah, that must be powerful stuff."

"It is. And I'd be lying if I said I didn't want more of it. This sounds horribly shallow, but I guess I've missed being admired." She sighed. "The problem is that inside I still feel like I'm twenty-three, but the rest of the world just sees a tired, middle-aged woman who lost her allure around the time of Obama's first term."

"Don't sell yourself short, Conn. His second term, maybe."

"Ha! Thank you, sweetie. The point I'm trying to make is that James *doesn't* seem to see me that way." Connie sat down on a bench by the sidewalk. "Yet despite everything that's happened, and even though he seems to have lost all interest in me and our marriage, I still love Nate. I can't help it, Lana. I know it's a cliché to say that he completes me, but he really does. These past few months, it's like I've been walking around as half a person... But am I being naive? Perhaps my marriage is over, and I need to deal with that and move on with my life."

"Will James be at home this evening?"

"Yes. And he's told me he wants to talk. What do you think I should do?"

Connie was gazing blankly at the street in front of her when a motorbike parked next to the curb caught her attention. It was a vintage Harley-Davidson, but the reason she noticed it was that it looked exactly like her father's. In fact, she realized, checking the license plate, it *was* her father's. Connie got up from the bench, scanning the street, and spotted Kurt a couple of blocks down standing with a man in a suit. The pair of them were deep in conversation outside a brick building that used to be a physiotherapy clinic, but had been vacant for many months. Connie noticed a FOR SALE sign stuck outside.

"Sorry, Lana, can I call you back? I've just seen Kurt, and should probably say hello."

"Make sure you do. We need to finish this conversation."

"I will. Love you."

As she crossed the street, Kurt looked around and saw her. He froze mid-conversation, but quickly recovered his composure and waved, before turning back to the man who he talking to and shook hands, clearly wrapping up their conversation.

"Connie! This is a nice surprise."

"Hey, Dad. I was just walking home from work and spotted your Harley. Have you had business in town?"

"I have," he said. Behind him, Connie noticed the man he'd been talking to take down the FOR SALE sign. "I've been looking into some real estate opportunities."

"That sounds interesting. Can you share any details?"

Kurt rubbed his jaw. "Skye has been looking for premises from which to run her healing practice. I've got money sitting in the bank doing nothing, so I thought it would be sensible to invest it in a local business."

"Ah, so Skye's buying the old physio clinic?"

"*I'm* buying it," he clarified. "Then Skye can focus on her shamanism and won't need to work in the Thompsonville store to supplement her income. It's a waste that she's spending so much of her time stacking shelves when she has such an amazing gift."

Connie gaped at him. "You're buying this place—for Skye?"

"That's what I said."

"But—but when I asked you for financial help last year, you refused."

"I'm not Skye's father, Connie. This is completely different."

Let it go, a voice inside her urged. For once, though, Connie ignored it. "It *is* different, yes, because all I was asking for was a small, temporary loan to stop us going into debt after Nate got made redundant. Not a boatload of money to start a new business."

Kurt's expression hardened. "How I spend my money is none of your concern, Connie."

"Of course it isn't, but I don't understand why you wouldn't help me when I was in a really difficult position."

"As I've said to you before, I've always believed that it's important that you stand on your own two feet."

Her voice was getting higher. "Do you not remember *anything* about my childhood? I've been standing on my own two feet virtually since I could stand!"

"I can hear that you're upset with me, Connie, but—"

"You're darn right I'm upset with you!" She was shaking, the warning tremors of a long dormant volcano. Her instinct had always been to force the anger down, to keep any messy emotions inside, but not this time—not after the week she'd had. Capable Connie had spent her life playing nice, keeping the peace and never rocking the boat—and what good had that done her? Her husband was leaving her and she was about to lose her job. With a howl, the fury came exploding out of her. "Do you have any idea how tough it was for me when I was a child? I had to raise both myself and Everly while you and Mom got high in a field on your parents' dollar! I missed out on going to college because I needed to be home to make sandwiches after school and help with homework, because you and Mom were too selfish to parent your own children. And not once have you ever thanked me, or even acknowledged what I did!" She noticed a couple staring as they walked by, but Connie was beyond caring. "I never once asked for anything from you when I was growing up. I just got on with it, never complaining, taking care of the job that you and Mom should have been doing. And the *one time* I ask for your help, when Nate and I were so worried we thought we'd have to sell our home, you refused to even hear me out. Yet you're happily giving away hundreds of thousands of dollars to a woman you've known for—what? Three months?" She gave a hollow laugh. "And to think I defended Skye when Everly accused her of being a gold digger... So yeah, I'm upset with you. I'm upset and hurt and really, really angry. And d'you know what? I think that's a pretty reasonable reaction."

Kurt just stared at her. She'd never known him to be lost for words. "That is a lot to process."

"I think you need to spend a little less time processing, and a little more time appreciating what I've done for you over the years."

Connie turned on her heel and crossed the road, heading for the path that led alongside the river. She heard Kurt call after her, but didn't look around. As the force of her fury faded, she put up her hand to wipe away the tears and discovered that she wasn't crying. She had now reached the river and she stopped on the bank, watching the water bubbling over the rocky bed and leaves rustling on the branches overhead. At that moment, Connie suddenly became acutely aware of the touch of the air on her skin and the firmness of the ground beneath her feet. She felt like a reptile that had just sloughed off a layer of old skin. Her phone started to ring, but she ignored it. Pressing her lips together, she set off toward home.

James's car was parked in the driveway, but he wasn't in the house. Connie wasn't sure whether to be disappointed or relieved. Before calling Lana back, she got a glass and went to fill it with water at the fridge—which was where she found a note, stuck to the door with a magnet. She instantly recognized James's elegant handwriting.

"Meet me under the big tree by the lake. Dress casual. Arrive hungry."

THIRTY-TWO

The sun was setting, casting the hills along the horizon into purple shadow and flushing the sky the color of pale rosé wine. Connie opened the screen door and stepped out onto the deck; apart from the buzz of cicadas, the world was still, as if waiting to see what she would decide to do next. She could see James under the cotton-wood tree across the other side of the lake, stretched out in the grass with his arms cradled beneath his head, exactly like the first time she had laid eyes on him. Had that really only been last month? It seemed like yesterday, yet also years ago.

Connie took the stairs down from the deck one at a time, doubt dragging at her feet. If she turned around right now and went back into the house her life would be much simpler, that was for sure. Would it be better, though? She should have called Lana back and asked her opinion—this wasn't the sort of situation she should be walking into without some level-headed advice. Deep down, though, she knew the reason she hadn't was that there was a strong possibility that Lana would have told her not to meet with James. And she wasn't sure she wanted to follow that particular advice.

Stopping at the bottom of the steps, Connie turned and looked back at her home, its pale green walls glowing in the golden twilight. She remembered the long debate she'd had with Nate when they first moved in over what color to paint the outside walls: he'd wanted gray, but she'd persuaded him to go for the color of an underripe apple—"It is an old cider farmhouse after all." A pain gripped her chest at the memory of that first summer they'd spent here, the tough, physical work it had taken to make the place habitable, but also the laughter and lingering kisses. Man, they had been crazy about each other! Never in a million years would the Nate of twenty years ago have just assumed she would be happy for him to move across the country without her. Bracing against a wave of sadness, Connie turned toward the lake and James. She needed to face facts. Nate didn't love her anymore.

As she got closer to James, Connie noticed that he was lying next to a wicker picnic basket and ice bucket. She thought he might be asleep, but as she reached the cottonwood tree James opened his eyes and broke into a smile.

"She walks in beauty like the night," he said, rolling onto his side to look up at her.

"Sorry?"

"It's from a poem by Byron." James paused—then squinted at her. "Too corny?"

"A little. But I'll overlook it because I'm hungry."

"You won't be after this." He threw open the picnic basket. "This is what happens when a greedy man who's had no time for lunch is let loose in Tansy Falls Fine Cheeses."

As he unpacked the various cartons and packages, Connie's pupils dilated like she was in love or drunk, or both. There were lobster rolls, a green salad topped with wild blueberries and goat cheese, stuffed bell peppers, a whole chocolate cherry torte, a cheeseboard; he'd even brought a vase of wildflowers as a centerpiece. Connie couldn't help but compare the trouble he'd gone to with the disappointment of her and Nate's anniversary dinner, and hated herself for it.

Food had been way down her list of priorities this past week and Connie set about eating with the determination of a marathon runner going for their personal best. James seemed to sense that she needed some time to decompress from the weekend and they ate in silence, but she noticed that whenever he handed her something his fingers lingered on her skin a little longer than necessary and occasionally, out of the corner of her eye, she'd catch him looking at her. Any self-consciousness she might have felt, however, floated away with the champagne bubbles. It had been so long since she'd been spoiled and she was determined to enjoy it.

When they had eaten beyond the limits of comfort, James produced a sketchpad from the bottom of the basket.

"Can I draw you?"

She gave a snort of laughter. "What, like one of your French girls?"

"No, you can keep your clothes on." He raised an eyebrow. "This time, anyway."

Connie felt warmth flush through her body, lingering at her cheeks, and she shifted position, suddenly unsure what to do with her limbs.

"Just relax," urged James, picking up a pencil. "You don't need to pose. You're imprinted on my mind anyway."

It only took him five minutes, and once he had finished James handed her the sketchpad. He had written "my beautiful Connie" and put the date.

"That's incredible," she murmured, marveling at how just a few pencil strokes could create something that was as unmistakably her as if it had been a photo.

James dipped his head in acknowledgement and said: "Keep it." He reached for the champagne bottle and held it up with a question in his eyes.

"Yes, please," she said.

James moved closer to her to refill her glass and didn't move back once he'd done so. Connie was acutely aware of his proximity. She felt his presence as surely as if he had been touching her.

James took a big gulp of champagne and gave a sigh, leaning back on his elbows. After a moment, he turned to look at her.

"So, sweet Connie, are you going to tell me your answer?"

"I don't know what your question is," she replied, trying to keep her tone light.

"I have three. Do you want to hear them?"

Connie wasn't remotely ready for whatever was coming next, but she nodded.

"Okay." James sat up, resting his forearms on his knees. "My first question is, will you leave Nate? Not because of me—although I can't deny I'd be delighted if you did—but for yourself. For the sake of your happiness and all that potential that's currently being wasted on a relationship you've outgrown."

Connie's mouth was dry. "Wow," she managed. "That's direct."

"Better that way. No room for confusion. So?"

She swallowed, hearing the sound of her throat. "I'm thinking about it."

James pulled a face. "That's not an answer."

"It's the best I can give you right now."

He paused, thinking this over. "Well, perhaps my second question will help you make up your mind. Would you like to come to Spain with me?"

"Spain?"

"My family own a finca in the hills near Granada. I want to take you there. No strings, no pressure—we can even have separate bedrooms if you wish. You would have all the space you need to think about your answer to my first question." He gazed at her, his eyes heavy-lidded. "I can look after you, Connie. I want to ease those creases on that beautiful brow."

She thought about her and Nate's plans to go to Andalusia together, remembering her go-to fantasy of the pair of them sitting together on a low stone wall at sunset, glasses of sangria in hand, gazing at the view of the hills. She tried to replace the image of Nate with James.

"I do love Spain," she admitted.

"I'll take that as a yes." James put down his glass. "So, *mi amor*, my final question is this. *Puedo besarte?*"

"I—I'm not sure what that means," she said, although she was pretty sure she could guess.

"Let me show you then."

Moving slowly, James reached out and touched her cheek, then moved his fingers over her lips with a feather lightness. His touch caused a pulsing at her core. It felt so good—but it also triggered an alarm. *This is wrong. Get up and walk away.* Then Connie's mind spooled back over the weekend—the press trip a failure despite all her hard work, the argument she'd had with Kurt. *You've spent your life doing the right thing,* she told herself. *And where has that got you?*

"Beautiful Connie," murmured James, his face just inches from hers, his eyes burning with desire.

She held her breath as James moved toward her, his lips slightly parted. It was as if she was made of stone, rooted to the spot, powerless to escape even if she'd wanted to. As she sensed his breath on her cheek, her eyes drifted shut, and a moment later his lips brushed against hers, shooting electricity through her body, making her gasp. It was such an intense, long-forgotten sensation, like she was sinking into a deep bath, cocooned in warmth...

Suddenly, a banshee shriek from somewhere nearby jerked Connie back to reality at whiplash speed. It was Jocelyn the donkey, and it sounded as if she were just a few feet away. She pulled away from James, her hand flying to her mouth, and she swung her head wildly about, terrified that Frank was out here with Jocelyn and had seen her, but the light had faded and they were hidden by the lower branches of the cottonwood tree. Yet her relief at not being discovered instantly gave way to panic.

What on earth was she playing at? How could she do this to Nate?

"I'm sorry, I can't. Whatever might happen between us in future, right now I'm married."

James was watching her, as calm as she was agitated. "Did it *feel* wrong, Connie?"

"No. Yes!" She struggled to her feet. "I need to sort out what's happening with my marriage before—before any of this."

"I understand." He nodded slowly. "But let me say this. I can give you what you're looking for, Connie. I know exactly what that is. Nate might have been able to once upon a time, but he can't anymore. You've both changed, and the sooner you accept that, the happier you'll be."

"I've got to go," she said. "I'm tired, I need some sleep. I'm sorry."

He stood up, so they were facing each other, and took her hand, his fingers running over hers.

"This isn't over," he said softly. "I know that we belong together. And deep down, I think you know that too."

Connie woke at the sound of a car starting outside. Her bedroom was filled with sunlight, the drapes rippling gently. Judging by the purr of the engine, it was James leaving for the work. In a way she was relieved that she wouldn't have to face him this morning, to have to confront the push-pull of her emotions again, but the flame lit by their brief kiss last night still flickered inside her. The tires crunched in the dirt as his car pulled away, and as the rumble faded she turned onto her back and looked up at the ceiling.

Connie's whole body felt heavy. Sleep had eluded her for much of the night; she had felt physically sick with the guilt of what had happened with James, for cheating on Nate. At the same time, her worries about Ethan's interview with the police—*oh my, that was tomorrow!*—were amplified by the darkness, spinning out of control.

At this time on a Monday she would usually be at her desk at the Covered Bridge, but she had a rare day off today. The thought of spending it in bed, hiding from the world and her problems, was tempting, but she knew that the best thing for her would be to get up and get moving. She sat up, rubbing some life into her face. A hike would sort her out. She would walk up to Moonshine Hollow, have a swim and a think.

Connie dressed quickly, keen to get outside before the heat became oppressive. She poured herself a flask of coffee and was making a sandwich to eat on the trail when she heard a car coming down the driveway. She froze, listening as it approached. Was that James back again? It didn't sound like his car. She crossed over to the window and looked out, just in time to see a small red hatchback pull up outside.

Frowning, Connie went to find out who it was, and as she opened the screen door she saw a dark-haired woman emerge from the driver's seat. She was tiny and slender, but heavily pregnant. It took a moment for Connie to recognize Mia Callaghan, the young woman who was staying at the inn.

Mia hovered by the car, shielding her eyes to look toward Connie—and as their eyes met her hand flew to her mouth.

"Mia!" Connie waved and walked toward her, though wondering why on earth she was here. "This is a pleasant surprise."

Mia stood rooted to the spot, her eyes wide. "This... this is your house?" she stammered.

"Yes, it is," said Connie, with a kind smile. The poor girl looked as if she was in shock. "What are you doing here?"

Mia's hand fluttered to her stomach—and in that moment Connie knew. A chill raced through her, the smile vanishing from her face.

"Your baby's father," she said, her voice shaky. "He lives here."

Nate.

THIRTY-THREE

Connie stuck out a hand to the hood of Mia's car to support herself, a rushing sound in her ears. Memories slotted into place as if she was finishing a jigsaw at warp speed: Nate's unexplained disappearances, the time he lied about being with Tom Frost, his emotional distance. Then with a heave in her stomach, Connie remembered that Piper had told her Mia mentioned she was originally from San Francisco. No wonder Nate had been so keen to move to the West Coast without her.

She felt Mia's hand on her arm. "Are you okay?"

"Just give me a minute." She was still leaning on the car, forcing herself to breathe in and out. After a few moments, the nausea faded a little and she managed to straighten up.

"I'm afraid he's not here right now," said Connie. "If you were coming over to see him."

"I came to drop off a letter. To tell him I'm leaving, and that I won't be bothering him again."

Pain gripped Connie's heart. "I can give it to him."

Mia hesitated, and then reached into her bag. Connie noticed a tear fall down her cheek; she looked so young, and despite everything she felt a rush of sympathy. She had no idea Nate was capable of such heartlessness—toward both of them.

Mia held out an envelope and as Connie took it from her she noticed the name on the front of the envelope.

She looked up at Mia, her heart hammering. "*James* is the father of your baby?"

"Yes." She frowned at Connie's expression. "Your lodger?"

"I thought..." Connie squeezed her eyes shut, shaking her head as if trying to get her thoughts in order. "Mia, why don't you come in? I can make some tea and we can talk."

She hesitated, then nodded. "I'd like that, thank you."

A little while later they were sitting together at the kitchen table. Mia was hunched over her mug, which she was cradling in both hands. She must be in her mid-twenties, no older—far too young to be dealing with this kind of heartache.

"I've been here, to your house, a few times before," said Mia. "At night, mainly—James was keen to keep me a secret. Ashamed of me, no doubt. I called your phone number once too, but I put the phone down when there was a woman's voice at the other end. It must have been you. I'm so sorry, Connie. If I'd known this was your home..."

"Please don't apologize, none of this is not your fault. Are you and James"—she hesitated—"are you in a relationship?"

"Not anymore." Mia was staring at the mug, trying hard not to cry.

"I'm happy to listen—if you want to talk about what happened?"

Mia managed a small smile. "Thank you. It might help." She took a sip of her tea. "It all started a couple of years ago when I started working at the same interior design company as James. I was a junior associate and he was one of the partners. Almost at once, he took an interest in me, seeming to think I showed promise as a designer. I got the impression the other juniors were jealous at the attention he paid me, and I remember thinking that I must have genuine talent." She gave a snort of laughter. "Naively, I was flattered. And when James asked me out for lunch one day, to a restaurant I could never afford on my salary, I thought—*this is it*. My big break, the beginning of a glittering career. I was so proud of myself..." Mia wiped away a tear. "What an idiot."

She took a moment to compose herself, then began again. "As you can probably guess, it quickly became obvious that James wasn't interested in me for my design skills. I should have stopped it then, made it clear I wanted to keep our relationship professional, but I was not in a good place personally. My mom had died the year before, and I had only just moved to New York. I was lonely and grieving. So when this handsome, successful man started showering me with attention..." She tailed off. "I realize now that James is attracted to vulnerability. He can smell it, like a shark sensing blood in the water. I think he gets a kick from being this savior figure—hero to the weak, lonely and lost. I think it turns him on."

Connie flinched; this was all way too close to home.

"James told me he couldn't live without me, and he was the one person who could make me happy," said Mia. "It was overwhelming. I knew that he was married, but he insisted they were separated and in the process of divorcing, and I had no reason not to believe him. It wasn't true, as it turned out—although they're certainly divorcing now, after his wife found out about this." She gestured to her stomach. Although Mia was trying to look brave, Connie should see how scared she was. She couldn't begin to imagine how it must feel, to face the prospect of raising a child on your own when that had never been your intention.

"The baby wasn't planned, obviously," Mia went on. "When I told James I was pregnant, he became a completely different person. He stopped taking my calls, refused to speak to me at work. He wouldn't even look at me. He tried to get me fired, but I stood my ground. Firing a woman you'd just gotten pregnant would have been a pretty bad look." Here, she managed a grim smile. "So James's colleagues advised him to come and work up here until I'd had the baby."

Connie's heart was racing. The idea that James, the charming, handsome man she had been falling for, was in reality an unprincipled womanizer literally took her breath away.

"So why did you come up to Tansy Falls?" she asked.

"Don't judge me, but I thought I might be able to convince James to make a go of it with me. I know what he is, but he can also be so sweet and charming. One of the nights I visited him here I thought he might be changing his mind, that he would stand by me and the baby after all, but it all turned out to be more lies. We had this terrible argument. I'm surprised you didn't hear us."

With a start, Connie remembered the night she'd heard raised voices. "What was the argument about?"

"I had just spoken to one of my colleagues back in the office, who told me that it had been an open secret that James regularly cheated on his wife. Apparently he has this property in Spain, which was where he used to take his mistresses." She shook her head. "It seems his wife turned a blind eye to his cheating in the past, but the baby was the final straw."

Connie's head was reeling. "Did James know you were staying at the Covered Bridge?"

"He did. In fact, I was originally staying at a different hotel and he suggested I move to the Covered Bridge."

"That's strange. If he was desperate to keep you a secret, you'd think he'd want to keep you away from his landlady's place of work."

"But that's typical James! He's so arrogant that he thinks he'll never get caught—and if he does, he's confident he can sweet-talk his way out of any situation. You know, I think he gets a kick out of the danger. He certainly enjoys playing people off against each other."

"Well, it sounds as if you're far better off without him," said Connie savagely.

"I do know that. Yet somehow I can't keep away from him. When he turns the full beam of his attention on you, it makes you feel like the most adored person in the world. It's very seductive."

Don't I know it, thought Connie bitterly.

. . .

After Mia had left, promising to keep in touch, Connie went back and sat at the kitchen table on her own. She was ramrod straight in the chair, her hands knitted together on the table in front of her, her eyes fixed on the opposite wall. The only sound was the ticking of the clock, although to Connie it felt as if time were standing still. As perfectly still as her body was, though, her insides roiled with emotion and her mind felt like the cloverleaf interchange of a highway, thoughts zipping every which way at top speed.

There was shame, of course; embarrassment for falling for James Ortiz's lies; a ton of guilt at having betrayed Nate. Connie bit her lip so hard it hurt; she deserved the pain. How could she have been so naive? She could blame James or the rockiness of her marriage, but the fault was hers. She wasn't a vulnerable girl like Mia; she was a grown woman, with a wonderful life and family she'd put at risk for a few sweet lies.

Blazing through all these other emotions, though, was white-hot anger. Her body burned with it, her skin tingling and nerves sparking. She hadn't realized she was capable of such fury. Usually such a calm person, it was as if a lifetime's worth of slights and grievances had hit her all at once, and she was now itching for revenge.

In a sudden movement, Connie put her hands flat on the table and pushed back her chair. She crossed the room, wrenched the front door open and headed for the car, slamming the front door behind her with such a force that it vibrated through her body.

She had no real plan and no idea what she was going to say, but she knew this couldn't wait.

THIRTY-FOUR

When the developers of Maverick Lodge had first arrived in Tansy Falls, they embarked on a charm offensive targeting the local hotels, tourist attractions and relevant town officials. The CEO, a glamorous New Yorker named Liza DiSouza, had taken Piper and Spencer out for a fancy dinner, over which she made repeated reassurances that DiSouza Developments would work alongside the town's other stakeholders to preserve the unique character of Tansy Falls. Consequently, in the early days of the new resort being built Connie had been kept closely in the loop of what was going on, touring the site on several occasions. She'd been given a personalized hardhat and promises of spa membership and free dinners once the resort was open. Six months ago, however, now that all the necessary permissions and local permits had been rubber-stamped, DiSouza Developments had suddenly lost interest in the people they had seemed so keen to befriend. Not only that, but Liza DiSouza's promises of working with the community had been swept away by a wave of shady business deals and underhand offers to local businesses, including a particularly nasty episode involving Fiske's General Store, which had left the people of Tansy Falls feeling rather like they'd been ghosted by a once-devoted suitor.

As a result, it had been a long time since Connie had last visited Maverick Lodge, and when she got out of the car she was frozen to the spot by her first glimpse of the completed resort. It looked, she thought, like the mutant offspring of an alpine log cabin and the NASA space station, and rather than blending into the countryside as DiSouza Developments had promised, it looked as out of place as a tropical parrot in a chicken coop. Directly behind the resort stood Mount Maverick, and this morning dark clouds clustered moodily about its peak, as if it too was appalled by its brash new neighbor.

The old Connie might have tried of think of something nice to say about the resort—perhaps complimenting the bold look of the modern spa complex, which had the look of a Soviet nuclear bunker—but after the past couple of days, Connie was not in the mood for being polite.

"What a gigantic eyesore," she announced loudly to nobody in particular.

"You're not wrong there," muttered a man in a hardhat passing by.

Connie jumped, then called after him. "Excuse me?"

"Yeah?"

"I'm looking for James Ortiz. He works on the interior design team."

"No idea. Maybe check at head office?" He gestured vaguely toward the far end of the site, then set off again.

Connie looked over to where he had pointed, and then down at her sandals. The ground between her and the site office was so rutted and churned up that she would end up with seriously dirty feet or worse, and she certainly wasn't going to risk a twisted ankle for James Ortiz. Hands planted on hips, she scanned the area again, as if expecting him to appear from behind a bulldozer, then took out her phone and sent a message.

I'm up at the resort—by the spa building. Can you come and meet me?

A reply appeared almost instantly.

What a wonderful surprise! I'll be right there.

Connie gritted her teeth. She very much doubted he'd find it quite so wonderful once she'd finished with him.

Five minutes later, she spotted James emerging from the cavernous entrance to the main hotel building. For a split second her body responded instinctively to the sight of his square shoulders, swoop of dark hair and confident stride, but then her rational brain kicked in and her jaw tensed. Now, seeing him through the lens of Mia's revelations, James looked fake: a caricature of a charming man, too polished and contrived to be credible.

"Connie!"

He kissed her on both cheeks, his mouth lingering on her skin. Less than an hour ago this would have turn her to jelly; now, it took an effort not to shudder.

"Let's walk," he said, snaking an arm around her back. "To what do I owe this pleasure?"

"I've just had a visitor to the house. Mia Callaghan."

James didn't even hesitate. "Oh gosh, I'm so sorry you had to deal with that, Connie. I wanted to shield you from what was going on, but she just won't leave me alone."

He gave a theatrical sigh and paused, as if expecting sympathy. When Connie just stared at him, he went on.

"She's been stalking me for months. I'm afraid I'm going to have to get the police involved. I'm beginning to worry what she might be capable of. The woman's a deranged fantasist."

It was like he was an actor, delivering the lines of the script. If she'd had any doubts about Mia's story, his posturing put them to rest completely.

"She doesn't seem at all deranged," said Connie. "She seems like a young woman who's been taken advantage of and treated appallingly by an older work colleague."

"Wait—you don't *believe* her, do you? Whatever she told you, Connie, it's all lies."

"So you're not the father of her baby?"

He hesitated. "It was a moment of weakness that I've regretted ever since. Believe me, I punish myself for it every single day. It's no excuse, but when it happened my marriage was breaking down, I was hurting and lonely, and along came this young woman offering a shoulder to cry on just when I was at my most vulnerable. Mia Callaghan seduced me with the intention of getting pregnant and has been hassling me to support her and the baby ever since."

"That's odd, because according to Mia pretty much the opposite of that happened."

He gaped at her. "I hope you're not choosing to believe a complete stranger over me. Surely you know me better than that?"

"But that's just it, James. I don't think I know you at all."

He considered her for a moment, and when he spoke again his voice was like honey. "Connie, this is all just a silly misunderstanding. Forget about Mia Callaghan." He reached out to touch her face, and she pulled away. "You're just so beautiful. Come to Spain with me, *mi amor*. I want to show you my beautiful home, to lie with you beneath the olive trees..."

"Like you do with all your mistresses?"

James's eyes flashed. "Oh, for goodness' sake, this is ridiculous! After everything I've done for you."

It was fascinating really, thought Connie, watching him maneuver between cajoling, playing the victim and outright bullying in an attempt to get his way. It was a master class in coercion. The spell had been broken, though, and now Connie saw him for what he really was.

"I'd like you to move out."

"Are you serious? I can't believe you're actually going to let that crazy woman's lies destroy your last chance at happiness! You've disappointed me, Connie."

"In that case you won't mind clearing your things out of my house by the end of the day."

James opened his mouth as if to protest, but changed his mind. His face was tight with barely contained anger.

"Fine, I'll do that. You were never anything more than a distraction anyway—a way to pass the time while I was stuck out here in the back of beyond. We might be the same age, Connie, but I've got women young enough to be your daughter throwing themselves at me. Who on earth's going to be interested in *you*? Certainly not your husband, who's moving across the country to get away from you," he said with a sneer. "I feel sorry for you, really. It's pathetic."

Connie stood a little straighter. "No, I tell you what's pathetic. Being such a small, weak man that you have to get your kicks by manipulating women into liking you. Trying to fire a girl you got pregnant because you're too scared to be in the same room as her. Pretending to be a completely different person because the real you is rotten to the core." Connie made herself catch a breath, determined not to lose control. "My marriage might not be perfect, but at least I can hold my head up knowing that I'm a decent person and that I have people who love me. I very much doubt that you could say the same."

He snorted with derision. "You might want to look into HRT to help with those mood swings." Then he waved his hand, as if dismissing her. "I'll move my things out of your house tonight."

"Wonderful, thank you," she said, then turned and started walking away. "Try not to fall into the giant hogweed on your way out," she added under her breath.

It took all Connie's effort not to shrink and scuttle away, but she wouldn't give James the satisfaction of knowing he had hurt her. Considering the hurricane of emotion whipping up insides, it was amazing that she'd managed to come up with a coherent retort and deliver it without bursting into tears or screaming, and she allowed herself a little smile of triumph at this fact. Right now, all she had was her dignity, and she was darn sure she was going to leave with that intact. The tears would come, though, she could feel them gathering inside of her like looming storm clouds, ready to burst once she was alone.

THIRTY-FIVE

On the drive home Connie flew past stop signs and raced wildly around bends, her usual caution abandoned. She had all the windows open, as if she could blast away James's touch from her skin, and her hair whipped wildly around her face. All she wanted was to get home and hide away in her bedroom to have a good cry and then sleep for the rest of the day, but as she sped up the driveway toward her house, she spotted someone sitting on the front porch. Getting closer, she realized it was Skye.

"Darn it," she muttered, yanking at the parking brake. What on earth was she doing here? She got out of the car, brushing her windswept hair off her face. "I'm sorry, Skye, this isn't a good time," she called out, cursing the tremble in her voice.

Skye stood up as she climbed the steps to the deck. "Five minutes, Connie, that's all I'm asking. Kurt told me about your conversation and I wanted to explain what's going on."

"I appreciate you coming over, but I can't deal with this right now."

Skye's head tilted in concern. "What's wrong?"

"I just need some space, if you don't mind."

"Okay." She turned to go, but paused. "Are you sure you don't want to talk about it, Connie? My spirit guide—"

"Oh, for goodness' sake, will you please just leave me alone!"

Connie broke into shuddering sobs, beyond caring that Skye was watching her. It felt like her world was falling apart, but she could have coped with that and more if she still had Nate. At the thought of him, she sank to the floor, dropping her head in her hands. She missed him so much that it suddenly felt unbearable. She could see it so clearly now: James had was simply an easy distraction from the challenges of their marriage. She had enjoyed the boost to her flagging self-esteem he'd given her, but she didn't have a single doubt that her heart belonged to Nate. Was it too late though?

After a little while, Connie felt Skye's hand come to rest lightly on her back as she sat on the top step. She was surprised how comforting this felt, and they sat together in silence, side by side, until Connie's sobs started to ease.

Eventually, she sat up and Skye handed her a Kleenex, her eyes full of concern.

Connie wiped her eyes. "You want to know what's wrong? *Everything.* My marriage is a mess. My son might be thrown out of college. I've probably lost my job. And for the first time in my life, I don't have a clue how to fix any of it." She shook her head. "Capable Connie, my family used to call me. Well, not anymore."

"That sure sounds like a lot for one person to deal with," said Skye. "I'd really like to help you, if you'd let me?"

"I'm afraid you can't. This is my mess and I need to sort it out."

"I get the impression you've never been very good at accepting help."

"That's because I'm always the one doing the helping."

"I can see that."

Skye shot her a smile, and Connie realized she was glad that she was here. Then she remembered that Skye had been waiting for her when she arrived home. "What was it that you wanted to talk to me about?"

"It doesn't matter now."

"No, please, I'd like to know."

Skye looked down at her hands. "Kurt was quite upset after your conversation yesterday."

"I'm afraid I don't have much sympathy."

"I do understand. While I dearly love your father, I can see that he's not the easiest man. He's self-centered, and that must have been difficult when you were a child."

"That's true."

"But despite his flaws, he does love you very deeply. He told me what you'd said, about him refusing to lend you money when you needed it, and it struck a chord. For what it's worth, he feels terrible about it."

"Clearly not terrible enough to apologize, though."

"Give him time." Skye put a hand on her shoulder. "I really like you, Connie, and it's important to me that you understand the part your father is playing in my business."

"Really, it's okay..."

"Please, just hear me out. I never asked Kurt for money, but when I told him I'd found a premises for my healing practice, he told me he wanted to invest in the business. He was so excited about it—he really thought it had potential." They were sitting alongside each other, so Skye had to lean forward to look in Connie's eyes. "I intend to pay it all back, I promise you. I can imagine what you must think of me, but you have to believe me that I'm not with Kurt for his money."

She wasn't sure why, but Connie had no doubt Skye was telling the truth. "I believe you," she said.

"Thank you, I really appreciate that. And if I can give you a bit of advice, from one child of a less-than-perfect parent to another? Kurt does have his flaws, but it would help you if you could try to accept them and focus on the good in him, because until you let go of your expectations, he'll have the power to keep hurting you." She gave a small shrug. "But then what do I know? I'm just the wicked not-quite-stepmother."

They both laughed, and Connie realized that having Skye in the family wouldn't be quite such a terrible prospect after all.

"And now, perhaps I can do something for you. I'm leading a sister circle tonight and I'd love for you to join us."

Connie was already shaking her head. "Oh no. You're very kind, Skye, but I'm not interested."

"I thought you might say that, but I'm going to leave this with you in case you change your mind."

She placed a flyer on the step between them. Connie looked at it but made no move to pick it up. "Skye, I know you mean well, but my childhood was ruined by this kind of thing."

"I understand. And I'm certainly not suggesting that participating in the circle will solve all your problems, but it might give you a different perspective on them. It's a full moon tonight, so the power of the circle will be particularly strong. Will you at least think about it?"

Connie didn't want to offend her, so said that she would.

"Thank you." Skye stood up. "I hope to see you later then, but I'll understand if not."

THIRTY-SIX

Connie slammed her car door, the sound echoing like a gunshot in the silent darkness. She was standing alone in the dirt parking lot at the foot of the trail that led up to the Smugglers Leap falls, a tiny speck of civilization in the midst of the wilderness. She had been here dozens of times over the years—the waterfall had been a favorite place to picnic when Ethan was a child—but never at night, and under the eerie glow of the full moon the place looked entirely unfamiliar, a silver-and-black landscape of mysterious shadows and watchful eyes. Strange dark shapes loomed above her and there was a sharp, feral scent in the air, and she had to fight the urge to get back in the car and lock all the doors. She gazed up at the moon, which seemed astonishingly bright and close to the earth, and felt a shiver of fear.

Connie's attitude to Skye's sister circle hadn't changed—she still thought it was self-indulgent mumbo-jumbo—but she had decided to come for the simple reason that it would get her out of the house for when James came back to get his things. Faced with the prospect of another confrontation with him, a little moon-worshipping didn't seem so terrible after all. She supposed she could have gone to see Lana, who had messaged her several times since yesterday asking why she hadn't called back, but she knew her friend would want to know all about what had happened with James, and she didn't feel up to an interrogation—even a loving one.

It didn't take long for Connie's eyes to adjust as she set off along the trail; she had brought a flashlight, but the moon provided more than enough light to guide the way. To start with she jumped at every noise—and there were plenty of those out here in the wilderness, both familiar, such as the whirr of a nighthawk, but also otherworldly yelps and croaks—but she quickly realized that the thought of being alone in the woods at night was far more terrifying than the reality, and soon, far from appearing threatening, the dark woods had transformed into a magical place, a sanctuary from the rush and stress of daytime life.

Suddenly, a little way up ahead, she saw a rustling in the undergrowth by the trail and before she had a chance to react a dark shape emerged from the bushes. Connie gasped, the breath frozen in her chest. It was a bear cub, no bigger than a dog, its thick coat turned silver under the moonlight. They stared at each other, the moments ticking by, and then from the place the cub had appeared there was more movement and its mother appeared by its side.

Black bears were shy creatures, Connie knew, and not usually aggressive, but she was alone out here at night in the mother's territory. Adrenaline flooded her system, ordering her to run, but before she could find her feet the bears ambled away into the darkness on the other side of the trail.

Connie let out a long exhale and broke into a shaky smile. That was a moment she would remember for some time.

She had been following the trail for about twenty minutes when she glimpsed a light through the trees a way off the path. She headed toward it, glad of the long pants she was wearing as she plunged through the undergrowth. She'd had no idea what to wear tonight; her only reference point had been her mom's floral headdresses and Skye's flowing skirts, neither of which were items she had in her closet. In the end she'd decided on beige hiking pants and a T-shirt. *Practical as ever*, a little voice inside her said, with a fondness that reminded her of her mom.

Connie was now approaching a clearing in which shadowy figures were milling around, lit by a circle of candles. Her footsteps slowed as she reached the edge of the trees and she hung back in the shadows, feeling like the new kid at school.

She reckoned there were about twenty women ahead of her in the clearing. A few were wearing flower garlands and floaty dresses, but Connie was relieved to see that most were in practical gear like her own. It was an eclectic group—one girl looked to be in her teens, while another appeared old enough to be her great-great-grandma—and they were chatting and laughing as if catching up over drinks in a bar. Connie had been expecting some chanting at the very least, and the familiar sound of social chatter gave her the confidence she needed to step into the clearing.

"Connie!" Skye spotted her and rushed over. She was wearing a metallic dress that shimmered in the candlelight as if it was made of water. "I'm so glad you're here."

"Thank you for asking me." She glanced warily around. "Is it okay if I just, well, sit and watch?"

"Of course, there's no pressure to take part. Come with me, I'll introduce you..."

Connie was welcomed with smiles and hugs, and offered cakes and cups of herbal tea. She hadn't been sure exactly what to expect, but it felt weirdly normal, like a school PTA meeting. Nobody asked who she was or why she had come; there just seemed to be an acceptance that everyone in the clearing was meant to be there. Connie had started to relax when, as if by some unseen signal, the women fell silent. They moved to form a large circle and Connie followed suit, clearing the twigs and rocks away from the ground before she sat. Once everyone was seated, Connie noticed that there was a grid of crystals laid out around a cluster of candles in the center of the circle and it triggered a memory of her mother, cross-legged in front of a chunk of quartz, absorbed in some lengthy ritual while the young

Connie watched from the doorway, yearning for her to come and play.

She shifted uneasily, bringing her focus back to what was happening in the present. Skye was walking around the circle waving a smoldering bunch of herbs over each participant and when it came to her turn the smoke made Connie cough. "Sorry," she muttered, her stomach gripping with embarrassment. This was *exactly* why she hadn't wanted to come tonight. Well, she couldn't get up and leave now, it would be rude. She would just sit it out and think about something else instead, such as how she was going to handle Carole Gridley at work tomorrow...

"Welcome to our sister circle to celebrate this new moon," said Skye, raising her hands to the sky. "We gather to connect with the feminine wisdom of our wombspace, and with Mother Nature. The circle is a supportive place for self-reflection and rest, where we can be seen and heard without judgement."

Connie smothered a blatantly judgmental eye-roll.

"New moons represent new beginnings. They are a time to plant seeds and set intentions, but also an opportunity to take ownership for what we wish to manifest and to commit to the actions, thoughts and behaviors necessary to get us there." She ran her eyes around the circle. "I would now like to invite you to introduce yourself with your name and one word to describe your current emotional state. Silence is fine. I'll go first." She paused. "Skye. Curious."

Sitting next to her was the older woman who had offered Connie the tea. "Mary," she said, with a radiant smile. "Content."

Then: "Lateysha. Disenchanted."

And so it went on, each woman seemingly fluent in the language of hippie-ese and entirely comfortable with spilling her feelings to a group of strangers. As it got closer to her turn, Connie could feel herself tensing up. She wouldn't say anything, she decided. Silence was fine; after all, the alternative was "Connie. Cynical." But when the group's eyes came to rest on her, she was surprised to find herself opening her mouth to speak.

"Connie. Um..." She hesitated. "Scared."

Her eyes flicked to Skye, who gave her the ghost of a nod, and Connie felt the tightness in her chest ease a little. She had bared her soul to the group and nothing terrible had happened; nobody had laughed at her.

"Thank you all for sharing," said Skye. "I would now like to invite you to join me in a gratitude meditation."

Around her, the women closed their eyes and Connie did the same, trying to ignore her prickle of discomfort at the word "meditation."

When Skye spoke again, her voice was soft and hypnotic. "Take a deep breath, feeling the air fill and expand your lungs..."

Connie became aware of something sharp digging into her thigh. She fidgeted, trying to get comfortable. Perhaps she should have brought a cushion.

"Focus on your heart-space. Imagine it is filled with a brilliant white light..."

I wonder if I locked the car, thought Connie. *Did I leave any valuables in there?*

"Now, I want you to visualize one person that you are grateful for. I want you to imagine they are sitting in front of you right now."

Connie had that moment been deliberating whether to have eggs or oatmeal for breakfast tomorrow, but at this an image of Nate popped into her mind. He was smiling at her, his eyes crinkling with happiness, his messy hair flopping over his brow: it was the old, carefree Nate, from before their recent troubles. Connie was hit by a wave of emotion that knocked the breath from her. Gosh, she missed him so much...

"I want the gratitude you feel toward this person to flood over you and fill you like that brilliant white light. Now—what you would say to this person if they were in front of you, right now?"

I'm sorry. I want to make things right again. I love you so much. The words appeared without her even needing to think about. She had a flashback to their conversation last week, when Nate had told her about San Francisco, remembering his exact words and the pain in his eyes as he said them: "I've been falling to pieces and you haven't even noticed."

The memory hit Connie like a runaway train. Was that really true? She remembered times when Nate had wanted to talk to her and how she'd reacted: by shutting him out and refusing to listen, because—well, why had she? Because, she supposed, she was scared of what he might say. Because she had assumed that *she* was the injured party, too busy coping with their financial struggles to think that Nate might be finding this hard. And because she had assumed Nate would cope with the redundancy in the way she always dealt with adversity: by filing away any messy feelings in a box labeled DANGER—KEEP OUT and soldiering on. It occurred to her now, though, thinking back over the past few months, that perhaps this strategy hadn't been working out so well for her after all. And all this time Nate had been trying to deal with not only the loss of his job, but of his identity, and she'd ignored him, unwilling to engage with his fears in the same way she shut down her own emotions when they got too difficult.

Tears started to trickle down her cheek. How could she have been so stupid? It seemed as blindingly obvious to her now as if someone were standing in front of her using flip charts and graphs to explain what had happened. Their marriage wasn't in trouble because Nate didn't love her anymore—quite the opposite, in fact. It was in trouble because he thought *she* didn't love *him*.

Connie blinked away the tears, her mind reeling. She felt sick at all the missed opportunities to help Nate, but if she was partly to blame for their problems, perhaps she had the power to fix them too. Had she left it too late, though?

When Skye told them to open their eyes, the clearing seemed as bright as if it were midday. Connie noticed Skye was looking at her, her expression concerned. "Thank you," she mouthed, and Skye replied with a dip of her head, her hand on her heart.

The rest of the night was a blur. There was chanting, true, and also drumming and dancing, and Connie had joined in with all of it without a hint of self-consciousness. Perhaps Mary had spiked the herbal tea, but all Connie's inhibitions had vanished and she felt freer than she could ever remember. At one point an image of James popped into her head and to her surprise she started to laugh. A woman who was dancing nearby caught hold of her hands and twirled her round, and they had spun together in the moonlight, staring up at the stars.

THIRTY-SEVEN

Connie opened her eyes. She lay still for a moment, waiting to be hit by the crushing weight of doom that had been her usual wake-up call these past few weeks. Curiously, though, it didn't arrive.

Judging by the light peeking through the drapes it was still early; she sat up and looked at the clock: 5:30 a.m. She hadn't got home from Skye's sister circle until after midnight, so she had only slept a handful of hours, yet she felt as well-rested as if she'd enjoyed a weekend at a spa. In fact, she couldn't wait to get out of bed. Confused, she reminded herself that today was Tuesday, the day that Ethan was being interviewed by the police and Carole was possibly firing her, but even this didn't dent her mood. *You've got this*, a little voice whispered—and she believed it. Whatever happened with Ethan, she would support him. If Carole fired her, she would find another job. It was as if her mind had downloaded a software upgrade overnight and she had a whole new, glitch-free operating system. More likely though, it was down to the fact that after last night's revelations she felt like she had a chance of fixing things with Nate. Life had always been easier with him by her side —as a team, they were invincible. She wondered whether she should phone him, to tell him how much she loved him and that she was sorry, but it would be better to have that conversation in person. Only two more days and he would be home!

Half an hour later Connie pulled up in the inn's parking lot, greeting one of the gardeners who was watering the flowerbeds, and an early rising guest swimming lengths in the pool. Boomer was lying on the couch in the lobby and he raised his head when she came in, but it was a half-hearted attempt at a greeting, and he instantly dropped back to sleep.

She had been planning to go straight to her office to catch up on her emails, but as she crossed the lobby she heard a strange mewling sound coming from the corridor that led to the kitchen. Connie stopped to listen, frowning—then her heart leapt as she realized what the noise was. Her eyes lighting up, she hurried to the kitchen and there was Spencer, clad in a robe and slippers, cradling a squawking, blanket-wrapped bundle in his arms.

"You're home!" cried Connie, rushing over to give him a hug.

"We got back last night. Piper's still asleep, but this one had other ideas." His face softened as he gazed down at his son. "Connie, I'd like to introduce you to Edison Hunter Gridley."

She peeked over the edge of the blanket; Edison's little red face was scrunched up and angry and completely adorable.

"May I?" she asked, holding out her arms.

Spencer looked relieved. "That would be great, if you don't mind." He transferred Edison to her arms with excessive new-dad caution. "I couldn't work out how to make coffee and hold him at the same time. Would you like some?"

Connie shook her head, her gaze fixed on Edison. "Hey, sweetie," she murmured, gently jigging on the spot. "I'm so happy to finally meet you. You gave us all a bit of a worry, you know..."

The wails quieted and soon stopped altogether, then Edison opened his huge blue eyes and gazed up at Connie and she beamed at him, bringing him closer so her cheek brushed the top of his downy head.

"Well, Auntie Connie clearly has the magic touch," smiled

Spencer, gratefully cradling his coffee. "You'll have to show me how you do it. I'm still wondering when we're gonna to get the manual."

"Oh, I promise, it will soon become second nature—although having said that, I don't think any parent ever feels like they know exactly what they're doing. Not even by the time their children are grown up." She paused, thinking about Ethan. "You just muddle through as best you can, and as long as you love them—well, that's good enough."

After she had helped Spencer and Edison back upstairs and looked in on Piper, who sleepily blew her a kiss, Connie went back down to her office and got started on her inbox. Now the madness of the press weekend was out of the way, it was a relief to get back to her usual routine. It felt good to be sitting at her desk, working through the issues that had arisen while she was herding stray journalists around Tansy Falls. It helped take her mind off Ethan's meeting with the police. She had messaged him earlier to send him her love, and to wish him well with the interview, and had received one word—"thanks"—in reply. As much as she was desperate to speak to him, to find out how he was feeling, she knew her son, and she knew he wouldn't appreciate her fussing over him right now. She would just have to wait until he got in touch with her.

She hadn't been at her desk long when the door opened and Carole bustled in. She was wearing a T-shirt that read BORN TO SPARKLE and her usual lemon-sucking scowl. Connie hoped she looked more pleased to see her than she felt.

"Morning, Carole! You must be thrilled with your new great-grandson, he's gorgeous."

She grunted. "He's a cutie, but what kind of a name is Edison? I hoped Spencer might give him Mitch's daddy's first name."

Connie tried to remember what this was. "You mean Gridley?"

"Yes. It's a strong name."

"Absolutely, but perhaps Piper and Spencer thought Gridley Gridley was a little bit, well, *too* strong?"

Carole batted away the suggestion, then pulled up a chair and lowered herself into it with an *oof*.

"Now, Connie, you and I need to talk about this darn press trip."

Connie closed the ledger she was working on, her heart sinking. "Of course."

"As you well know, Mitch and I were opposed to the idea from the start."

"I know, and I'm sorry that—"

Carole held up a hand. "I'm not done. As I was saying, Mitch and I were not keen. Not. Keen. At. All. The idea of giving some ragtag bunch of journalists and Facebookers an all-expenses-paid weekend at the inn—well, suffice to say I suspected it would end in tears, and I was right. Not only tears, but a fistfight in my dining room! The only reason we allowed it to go ahead was because you seemed so sure it would bring about lots of complimentary newspaper articles about the inn."

Connie cringed, imagining Carole's response to Mimi's yoga and green juice Instagram posts. It seemed unlikely she would be hashtag grateful.

"However." Carole brushed a speck of fluff from her leg. "Despite the many, *many* disasters, it appears that at least one of the journalists seemed to enjoy their time at the Covered Bridge."

She pushed a piece of paper across the desk. Connie glanced down: the headline was FALLING INN LOVE and the byline was Jerry Whitlock. There was a fluttering in her chest as she picked it up and started to read.

"Nestled in the Vermont hills is the picture-perfect Covered Bridge Inn, where service comes with not only a smile, but with a heartfelt warmth that makes you feel like you've come home."

Connie's eyes widened. *Jerry* had written this? She read on, searching for the part where he wrote about the punch-up in the restaurant, or Carole's baking bootcamp, but it continued in the same gushing vein. He'd even mentioned her by name, describing her as "the inn's superlative manager."

The final paragraph read: "The Covered Bridge offers guests the best of all worlds: a charming old-world New England inn that serves blueberry pie just like Grandma used to make (if Grandma had been a professional pastry chef) combined with the exacting standards of the very best five-star hotels. Be sure to book your stay at this little piece of paradise in Tansy Falls before the secret gets out."

Connie looked up, astonished. The other journalist's pieces were yet to be published, but if Jerry liked it—a man who, by Connie's reckoning, smiled only twice the entire weekend—then the pressure was very much off.

"Apparently it's going to run in hundreds of local papers nationwide." Even Carole couldn't keep a cheery look off her face at this prospect. "So I just wanted to say—well done, Connie. We may not always see eye to eye, but you did a good job."

"Thank you, Carole, that means a lot."

She got up to leave, but as she reached the door she hesitated. "So you'll organize another press trip next year?"

Connie's mouth dropped open.

"Wonderful," simpered Carole, and closed the door behind her.

It wasn't until Connie was driving home later that afternoon that her cellphone started to ring with the distinctive tune that told her it was Ethan. She swerved over to the side of the road and answered it.

"Ethan?"

The line was silent, but she thought she heard a sob.

"Honey?" Connie's voice was frantic. "What's happened?"

After a few agonizing moments she heard: "Can you hear me, Mom? I think this is a bad line."

"Yes! I can hear you now. How did it go?"

"It was all—" The line broke up again, and Connie let out a

howl of frustration. She looked at the screen; she only had one bar of coverage.

"Ethan? Are you there?"

"—made an arrest."

"Honey, this line is terrible, can you say that again?"

This time his voice was clear. "It was fine, Mom. It's all fine. The police just wanted a witness statement from me. They've arrested an older kid for the assault."

Connie closed her eyes, letting out a huge breath. "Oh, thank goodness."

"I spoke to my faculty advisor too, and he told me the college won't be taking any action about the underage drinking. Oh, and I heard from Kayla! She's gone home to St. Louis for a while, but she's coming back next semester. She's being so strong—it's incredible." He paused. "Thank you so much, Mom, for everything. I'm really sorry to have given you such a scare."

"Oh, Ethan, I'm just glad it's all worked out."

Then Connie heard someone say something in the background of the call.

"I gotta go, Mom. Ben and I are going to play soccer. Will you let Dad know I called? Love you."

"Love you too, honey. See you soon."

Connie drove the rest of the way with a new lightness inside of her. Ethan had made a silly mistake that could have cost him dearly, but the last few days had punished him way beyond anything he deserved. She imagined him now out on the soccer field with his friends, as carefree as he should be at his age, and the smile remained on her face the whole way home.

It wasn't until Connie was approaching the front door that she realized something was wrong. It was a small thing, but she noticed it instantly: the kitchen blinds were all closed. A crease appeared between her brows. She was sure she had opened them that morning. It was a regular part of her morning routine, as clockwork as cleaning her teeth. Nothing else seemed amiss, though; perhaps she had just forgotten after all.

Nevertheless, she felt a flicker of trepidation as she put her key in the lock. Opening it as warily as if she might discover a burglar on the other side, she peered into the kitchen—and at the sight of what was inside, the keys fell from her hand to the floor. Connie stared around the room, open-mouthed. Dozens of tealight candles had been dotted over the surfaces, and in their soft light she saw that the walls had been covered with photos.

She stepped inside the room, moving as if in a trance. It was exactly like the scene of Nate's marriage proposal, only this time there were so many more photos—hundreds of them— each capturing a moment of happiness from their shared history, and this time some with Ethan too. She paused by a photo of the three of them at Smugglers Leap falls. She remembered it so well: It had been such a blazing-hot summer that there had been wildfires in the foothills of Maverick. She and Nate were sitting on a boulder near the foot of the falls, her head resting lovingly on his shoulder, while Ethan—who must have been in middle school—did a thumbs-up from the swimming hole, his hair slicked wet like an otter. They all looked so happy; Connie now had no doubt they could be again. It was so overwhelming that it took Connie a moment to register that Nate must be here, in the house. Excitement surged inside her.

"Nate?"

She hurried through to the living room to find more candles and more photos, together with a sign. ARE YOU READY FOR OUR NEXT BIG ADVENTURE?

With trembling hands, she tore open the envelope to find a note. "The journey starts in the bedroom."

Connie laughed out loud and raced upstairs. She threw open their bedroom door and there was Nate, sitting on the bed, dressed in a tuxedo.

"Oh, honey, I don't know what to say!" she cried.

When he looked up, though, his expression sent a chill through her.

She froze. His eyes were red, as if he'd been crying. "Nate? Whatever's the matter?"

Then she noticed he was clutching a piece of paper, and her heart dropped to the pit of her stomach as she saw that it was the portrait James had drawn of her.

THIRTY-EIGHT

"It's a good likeness," said Nate. "And he's right, you are beautiful."

Connie was rooted to the spot, her entire body numb.

"All this"—he gestured at the rose petals scattered around the bed—"was because I was going to ask if you wanted to renew our marriage vows. Looks like I'm too late."

"Nate, I..." Connie tried to swallow, but a lump was blocking her throat.

"I knew there was something off with that guy, I just *knew* it..." He lifted his chin. "So I guess you're in love with him then?"

"No!" It came out like a cry of anguish. She rushed over and knelt at his feet, her hands gripping his leg as if it were a life raft in a storm.

"I wouldn't blame you if you were. I've not exactly been much of a husband of late."

"It's not what it looks like, I promise you. Please, will you just let me explain what happened?"

He made a hopeless gesture—part shrug, part nod—but it was enough for Connie. She took a seat next to him on the bed and began to tell Nate the story of what had happened between her and James. She included every detail: the dawn meetings in the kitchen, the posy left on her windscreen, all the sweet things he'd said to her. She confessed her worries that she was fading into the background—that she was no longer attractive—and how this had played into James's hands. She even told Nate about the flirtation with Theo Welles on her birthday. She had never been so open with him in her life, but she thought that if she confessed every tiny detail, Nate might be more likely to understand why she'd been such a fool.

He remained silent the entire time she was speaking, his expression giving nothing away. Perhaps he thought she was lying? She paused every now and then to wait for a reaction, but he would just nod, as if telling her to go on.

In time, though, the words finally dried up.

"That's it," she said. "That's the whole sorry story."

Nate took a long inhale and then slowly let it out. He stared up at the ceiling.

Just say something, please. The wait was agonizing.

Finally, Nate turned to look at her. "All of this—everything—is my fault."

"Did you not hear anything I just told you?"

"It's my fault," he repeated firmly. "I could have fixed all of our problems months ago just by telling you—I mean, *really* telling you —how I feel about you. So that's what I'm going to do now." He took her hands in his. "You are the best thing in my life, Connie Austen. You become more beautiful to me every day. Every time I look at you, I feel lucky that you're mine. Without you..." His voice cracked with emotion. "Without you I would be like a body without a soul. No purpose, no feelings, no dreams—just existing. That's how I've felt these past few months."

"Nate, I'm so sorry—"

"Please, just let me finish. Since I lost my job, I've felt so unworthy of you, but I haven't known how to tell you that, or how to fix it. And then this opportunity in San Francisco came up, and I thought that if I moved away for a few months, it might be like pressing the reset button on our relationship, a way to make things right again." He gave a flat chuckle. "What a dumb idea that turned out to be. I couldn't even manage a week away from you without feeling like I'd had a limb cut off. And all this time, what I *really* needed to do was take you in my arms and tell you just how deeply, intensely and totally I love you."

He gathered her in his arms and held her against him with the same fierceness that was now burning inside her.

"I love you, Connie," he said, his face buried in her hair. "It's only you. It always will be."

They stayed like that for a moment, clutching each other as desperately as if they had only now realized what they'd very nearly lost.

"Is it too late for us, Conn? Can we fix this?"

"Oh, honey, we already have," she said softly.

Nate pulled away to look at her, breaking into a smile that lit Connie up from within, and they just sat like that for a moment, gazing at each other, overwhelmed by the intensity of their feelings. Then in a fluid move, Nate got down on one knee by the bed and produced a little box from his jacket pocket.

Connie's hands flew to her mouth.

With a grin, Nate eased the lid open. Inside was a gold band set with three tiny diamonds: one for her, one for Nate and one for Ethan.

"Connie Austen, will you do me the honor of becoming my wife all over again?"

She bent down and they kissed with a passion that shook her to the core.

"I will," said Connie, her eyes sparkling with happiness. "Always and forever, Nate Austen, I'm yours."

A LETTER FROM CATE

Dear reader,

Thank you so much for choosing to read *A Secret at Tansy Falls*. If you enjoyed the book and want to keep up to date with my latest releases, just sign up at the following link. Your email address will never be shared and you can unsubscribe at any time.

www.bookouture.com/cate-woods

I wrote this book in London during the long months of lockdown and, though writing can often be challenging, it was a real treat to be able to escape to the lush hills of Vermont in between the homeschooling, walks round the block and trying to think of something different to do with chicken joints. This is my second visit to Tansy Falls now and the characters are starting to feel like old friends. I reveled in the prospect of visiting Piper and Boomer at the Covered Bridge Inn, or heading to Fiske's General Store for a cup of Darlene's extra-strong "jet fuel"—and I hope you got as much joy out of joining Connie and Lana at the Moonshine Hollow swimming hole as I did.

I'll be making a final trip to Tansy Falls for the third book in the series, but in the meantime if you enjoyed reading this latest installment, I would be very grateful if you could write a review. I would love to hear what you think, and it makes such a difference in helping new readers discover my books.

If you have any questions or comments, please do get in touch with me via Facebook or Twitter as I love hearing from readers.

All best wishes,

Cate

facebook.com/catewoodswriter

twitter.com/catewoodswriter

instagram.com/catewoodswriter

ACKNOWLEDGEMENTS

Like raising a child it takes a village to publish a book, and I've been lucky enough to have the support of a number of brilliant people during the creation of this one. My heartfelt thanks in particular go to Lydia Vassar-Smith, Kathryn Taussig and the entire team at Bookouture; my agent, Rowan Lawton; the Liggett family (for the love, food and accommodation during The Week of Writing Panic); and to my squad—Oliver, Daisy and Bear.

Printed in Great Britain
by Amazon